Twilight Destiny

Books by Amanda Ashley

"Born of the Night" in Stroke of Midnight
"Midnight Pleasures" in Darkfest
"Music of the Night" in Mammoth Book of Vampire Romance
A Darker Dream
A Fire in the Blood
A Whisper of Eternity
After Sundown
As Twilight Falls
Beauty's Beast
Beneath a Midnight Moon
Bound by Blood
Bound by Night
Dark of the Moon
Dead Perfect
Dead Sexy
Deeper Than the Night
Desire After Dark
Desire the Night
Donovan's Woman
Embrace the Night
Everlasting Collection
Everlasting Desire
Everlasting Embrace
Everlasting Kiss
His Dark Embrace
Immortal Sins

In the Dark of the Night
Jessie's Girl
Maiden's Song
Masquerade
Midnight and Moonlight
Midnight Embrace
Midnight Enchantment
Night's Kiss
Night's Master
Night's Mistress
Night's Pleasure
Night's Promise
Night's Surrender
Night's Touch
Quinn's Lady
Quinn's Revenge
Sandy's Angel
Seasons of the Night
Shades of Gray
Sunlight Moonlight
Surrender the Dawn
The Captive
The Music of the Night
Twilight Desires
Twilight Destiny
Twilight Dreams

Books by Madeline Baker

A Whisper in the Wind
Apache Flame
Apache Runaway
Beneath a Midnight Moon
Callie's Cowboy
Chase the Lightning
Chase The Wind
Cheyenne Surrender
Comanche Flame
Dakota Dreams
Dude Ranch Bride
Every Inch a Cowboy
Feather in the Wind
First Love, Wild Love
Forbidden Fires
Hawk's Woman
Kade
Lacey's Way
Lakota Love Song
Lakota Renegade
Love Forevermore
Love in the Wind
Midnight Fire
Prairie Heat
Reckless Desire
Reckless Destiny

Reckless Embrace
Reckless Embrace
Reckless Heart
Reckless Love
Renegade Heart
Shadows Through Time
Spirit's Song
The Angel and the Outlaw
The Reckless Series
The Spirit Path
Under a Prairie Moon
Under Apache Skies
Unforgettable
Warrior's Lady
West Texas Bride
Wolf Shadow

Twilight Destiny

Amanda Ashley

Twilight Destiny

This edition published 2023

Cover by Cynthia Lucas

ISBN: 978-1-68068-326-4

This book is published on behalf of the author by the Ethan Ellenberg Literary Agency.

You can reach the author at:
Email: darkwritr@aol.com
Websites: www.amandaashley.net and www.madelinebaker.net

Dedication

For Annie Hill Grabiak
and
Carol Ramsey
Who both sent me suggestions
for one more story
and
For all those
who love Rylan Saintcrow
as much as I do

Contents

Chapter One

Hands shoved deep in the pockets of his jeans, Rylan Saintcrow strolled through the business district of Morgan Creek. All the stores and shops were closed at this time of the night. The only place still open was the hotel. He knew a moment of satisfaction as he passed by. Rooms and campsites were booked a solid year in advance. No one looking at the town now would ever guess it had once been a haven for a coven of vampires. Sometimes he could scarcely believe it himself. There was a hell of a lot of history here, all of it bad, he thought with a grin, until Kadie Andrews—now Kadie Saintcrow—stumbled into Morgan Creek. From that fateful night on, things had never been the same.

His head snapped up as a car drove across the bridge that separated the town from the highway. He muttered an oath when he recognized the young woman behind the wheel. Rosa Ravenwood. He'd had dealings with her brother, Micah, and the Ravenwood family in the past. What the devil was she doing here?

She slammed on the brakes when he stepped in front of the car.

Rosa switched off the engine and rolled down the window. "What are you trying to do?" she exclaimed. "Get yourself killed? Oh, it's you."

"What are you doing here?" Saintcrow growled. "Why aren't you in Italy with Kadie and the rest of your family?"

"That's not a very nice way to greet a guest."

"No one ever accused me of being nice."

"Well, I can certainly see why," she retorted.

He blew out a sigh. "What are you doing here?"

"I have a favor to ask and it isn't something to discuss over the phone."

"Yeah? Must be a hell of a favor." Sliding into the passenger seat, Saintcrow closed the door. "You can tell me about it when we get to my place." He gave her directions, then stretched his legs out in front of him. With Kadie away from home, the big old house was too quiet. It might be nice to have a little company for a day or two.

Rosa recognized the big, white house her brother-in-law, Ethan, had built for her youngest sister, Sofia, as they passed it by. Sofie had sent her numerous photos during and after construction.

Rosa frowned, thinking it would have been nice to stay there while Sofia and Ethan were on vacation, but she hadn't been able to think of a single logical reason why she would visit Morgan Creek when Sofie wasn't there. And she could hardly tell her sister why she'd come here.

Her brother, Micah, had lived in Morgan Creek for a while, but about a year ago, he had moved back to Arizona to be close to their parents. Micah had always been her favorite brother. He and his wife, Holly, had bought a house not far from her apartment and she was glad to have him back in town again.

Saintcrow's house was nearby. Large and square, it was made of weathered gray stone. There were turrets at the four corners, which gave the place the look of an old English castle. Thick iron bars covered the front door and the windows.

Rosa parked her rented Kia in the driveway. She was reaching for the handle when Saintcrow appeared at her door and opened it for her. Surprised by his show of manners, she followed him through the heavy wooden door into a spacious living room that was beautifully decorated with expensive furniture and tables. Several paintings adorned the walls. Fancy draperies covered the windows.

When Saintcrow gestured for her to sit down, she perched on the edge of a leather couch, hands tightly folded in her lap. She had been around Saintcrow a few times before, but she was suddenly aware of the fact that they were alone in the house, and that he was a vampire. And friend of the family or not, she was prey. The thought should have frightened her. Instead, it filled her with an odd sense of excitement. It was easy to see why Kadie had fallen in love with him. He was one of the most handsome men she had ever seen, broad-shouldered and lean-hipped, with inky-black hair that brushed the collar of his gray shirt, and eyes that were black and unfathomable. A thin, white scar ran from the outer corner of his left eye, down his cheek, and disappeared under his shirt collar. His preternatural power danced lightly over her skin.

He stood with his back to the fireplace, watching her through narrowed eyes. "It's for damn sure that neither Micah or Sofia knew you were coming here."

Rosa shrugged. That was for darn sure. If her brother had gotten wind of the real reason she hadn't gone to Italy with the rest of the family, he would have locked her up and thrown away the key! No doubt her sister, Sofia, felt the same way.

"So, what brings you to Morgan Creek?" Saintcrow asked for the third time.

"I want to meet a vampire."

"Don't you think you've already met more than your share?" he remarked dryly.

"I want to meet one who isn't family. Or a friend of the family."

He wasn't surprised. Ethan had told him Rosa had asked a lot of questions about vampire life, the kind of questions that had led him to believe she was toying with the idea of becoming one. "I'm not running a dating service."

"I know, but... maybe you could tell me where to find one. Or two."

With a shake of his head, Saintcrow dropped into the overstuffed chair across from her. "I'm guessing neither Sofia or anyone else in the family knows what you're up to."

"Of course not. They think I went to Florida with a couple of girlfriends."

"Why this sudden urge to meet a vampire?"

"I'm just curious."

"Uh-huh."

She shrugged. "Sofia's one. Micah's one. Holly's one."

"And you're feeling left out?"

She made a face at him. But it was true. In a way, she did feel left out. But it was more than that. The last time she had talked to Sofia, Rosa had mentioned she was thinking she might like to be a vampire, too. To her surprise, Sofie had tried her best to talk her out of it.

Rosa wasn't sure why. Sofia and her husband, Ethan, Micah and Holly, Rylan Saintcrow and Kadie, were all vampires and seemed happy to be so. Her brother's objection was that she was too young, blah, blah, blah. How could she be too young when she was older than Sofie? Besides, she was intrigued by all the cool powers vampires possessed—they could think themselves wherever they wanted to go, read minds, they never got sick, never grew old. Not only that, they could light a fire with just a thought, run faster than The Flash, dissolve into mist. So many cool things that she couldn't do. Why did they want her to wait? She was old enough to know her own mind and make her own decisions.

Of course, she knew there was a downside. She would have to give up all the foods she loved and exist on blood. Say goodbye to the sun. Hunt for prey like some kind of wild animal. The blood thing gave her pause, but Sofia didn't seem to mind it, and neither did any of the others.

Whether her family liked it or not, she was determined to meet a vampire, preferably one who would give her the Dark Gift if she decided she really wanted it.

"Why is everyone trying to talk me out of it?" she asked. "Why is it right for them and wrong for me?"

"You might want to enjoy being human for a few more years, that's all. Most of us were turned against our will," he replied, his voice quiet and thoughtful. "Some accepted it to save their lives. I don't know anyone who went looking for it."

"What about Sofia? She asked Ethan to turn her."

Saintcrow nodded. "True enough. But Lilith turned Micah against his will. The vampire who made me turned me and left me. I never saw her again, never even knew her name. As for Ethan, he was dying when I brought him across. You're a healthy, young woman. There's no reason why you shouldn't wait a few years. You can't change your mind, you know. Once it's done, it's forever."

"I don't suppose you'd turn me?"

He shook his head. "And bring your whole family down on me? No way, darlin'." He frowned at her. "How old are you, anyway?"

"What difference does it make?"

"None, I guess." Sofia was the youngest girl in the Ravenwood family and she was over twenty-one now, so Rosa had to be a couple of years older than that, certainly old enough to make up her own mind, no matter what anyone else thought.

"You won't tell Micah or Sofie that I'm here, will you?"

"No." Saintcrow scrubbed his hand over his jaw. He had never known anyone so determined to give up their humanity. And if he couldn't talk her out of it, well, it was better for her to go trolling with him than go out on her own. And he would be there to keep her out of trouble.

Besides, with Kadie out of town, he didn't have anything better to do.

"I know a place or two where you might find what you're looking for," he said. "Come on, I'll show you where to bed down. We'll go vampire hunting tomorrow night."

Vampire hunting. Saintcrow grinned inwardly, amused by the thought of one vampire hunting another, not for revenge, but matchmaking.

Chapter Two

Rosa woke slowly. She experienced a moment of panic when she opened her eyes and found herself in a strange bed in a strange room. And then she remembered. She was in Saintcrow's house in Morgan Creek, and he had agreed to help her find a vampire. She hoped it wouldn't take long. She only had two weeks off and then she had to go back to work. Her rent was due at the end of the month, and she couldn't afford to get fired. Not now, when jobs were scarce.

Bounding out of bed, she threw open the windows and gazed outside. It was a beautiful, clear day. Blue sky, a slight breeze, and endless possibilities. Saintcrow was an old vampire. She knew he could be awake during the day if he wished, but if he rested until the sun went down, she had a whole day with nothing to do.

Rosa frowned when her stomach growled. "I don't suppose there's any food in the house," she muttered as she grabbed her robe and padded downstairs to the kitchen. As she'd suspected, the cupboards were bare, as was the refrigerator. The appliances looked relatively new and she guessed Saintcrow had bought them for Kadie before he turned her.

She found a note on the counter, written in a bold, masculine scrawl.

Rosa, I've advised all the businesses in town that you're my guest. Buy anything you want and charge it to me. RS

Rosa grinned as she read it a second time. The man was full of surprises. When her stomach growled again, she hurried upstairs to shower and dress.

⚜ ⚜ ⚜

On the way into town, Rosa cruised along a residential street lined with well-kept homes. She recognized the pale yellow house at the top of the hill from photos Sofia had sent. Her sister had told her it was known as Blair House and that it had once been the lair of the Morgan Creek vampires. Like Saintcrow's house, this one also had iron bars on the doors and windows. Ethan had remodeled the place and he and Sofia had lived there for several months while their new home was being built. The thought of living in a house where vampires had lived sent a shiver down her spine. Which was odd, she mused, since she was thinking of becoming one.

Sofia was deeply in love with Ethan and Rosa knew her sister had never been happier in her whole life than she was now. And even though envy was one of the Seven Deadly Sins, Rosa was green with jealousy, not just because Sofia was married, but because she had a husband who was not only strikingly handsome, but a vampire.

Morgan Creek was nothing like she had expected and certainly didn't look like a town that had once been inhabited by a coven of bloodthirsty vampires. The hotel was modern, a dozen specialty shops lined both sides of Main Street. Ordinary people strolled along the sidewalks, talking and laughing as if they were in any small city in America instead of a town once filled with vampires who had imprisoned humans to feed on.

And Saintcrow had been the man in charge.

And Kadie had once been his prisoner.

But that was all in the past.

Rosa parked her rental in a lot at the end of the block, locked the doors and strolled down the street. The exteriors of all the buildings, like the tavern and the hotel, reflected a kind of 1920's charm. Curious, Rosa stepped into the hotel lobby and looked around. The walls were papered with a cabbage rose pattern that complemented the sofas and chairs scattered around the room. A large crystal chandelier sparkled from the ceiling. A young man smiled at her from behind the curved registration desk. An arched doorway to the left led to a combination bar and restaurant.

Outside again, she ambled down the sidewalk. She passed a grocery store whose exterior looked like something out of an old movie, but when she peered through one of the windows, she saw that the interior was contemporary. Moving on, she saw a couple of department stores, a barber shop and a beauty salon, a drug store, and two family restaurants. There was a gas station at the end of the block.

Stepping into the nearest restaurant, Rosa found a vacant table and sat down, suddenly self-conscious because she was the only single woman in the place. Several of the other tables were occupied by young couples. A few of them were obviously on their honeymoon, judging by the way they gazed adoringly into each other's eyes. There were a few older couples, and one or two single men. The majority of the diners were young families, likely on vacation.

After studying the menu for several minutes, Rosa decided on a blueberry waffle, bacon, and a glass of orange juice. When she became a vampire, she wouldn't have to decide what to have for breakfast, she mused, or for any other meal. Putting the thought aside, she glanced out the window, wondering again what time Saintcrow woke up.

After breakfast, she signed Saintcrow's name to the check and left the restaurant. Deciding to go exploring, she got into her car and drove to the other side of town where she saw a movie theater and a large library. Making a right turn, she passed a swimming pool set in the middle of a beautiful park surrounded by tall trees. In the distance, she saw a campground populated with RVs and tents.

Rolling down the window, Rosa drove up and down the streets with no particular destination in mind. After forty minutes or so, she headed back to Saintcrow's. Somewhere along the way, she took a wrong turn and found herself in front of a decrepit cemetery.

Stepping out of the car, she opened the rickety wooden gate and picked her way toward the nearest grave. It was marked by a wooden cross and nothing more. Glancing around, she saw row after row of weathered wooden crosses, a few with names scratched into the wood, but most carried no names and no dates. She shook her head. Whoever heard of laying people to rest without including at least their name?

She was about to leave the cemetery when she noticed a marble cross in the midst of all the wooden ones. Curious, she walked toward it. The wording on the marker read,

Shirley Elizabeth Hague
Gone But Never Forgotten

Shirley must have been someone special, Rosa mused, to have warranted such a lovely monument. But even this marker lacked any information save her name. There were no dates of birth or death. Just her name and a simple sentiment.

Rosa shivered as a chill slithered down her spine. She didn't believe in ghosts, but she had the sudden, disconcerting sensation that there was one nearby.

Muttering, "There are no such things as disembodied spirits," she ran out of the graveyard, scrambled into her car, and drove away as fast as the road allowed.

Luck was with her and she pulled up in front of Saintcrow's house a short time later. She cut the ignition, dashed inside, and closed and locked the door. Better to be in the company of a vampire she knew than a ghost she didn't.

⚜ ⚜ ⚜

That evening, Saintcrow took her out to dinner in the hotel dining room. Rosa had finished eating before she found the nerve to ask the question that had niggled in the back of her mind all afternoon. "Is the graveyard haunted?"

Saintcrow stared at her. "What?"

"I saw the cemetery today. Is it haunted?"

He shrugged. "Kadie thinks so. Why?"

"Who was Shirley?"

"A woman who lived here some years back." Apparently Micah hadn't gotten around to telling his little sister about his love affair with an older woman, he thought.

"Why is she the only one with a nice marker?"

"I guess because she's the only one buried there that anyone cared about."

"Oh." She shivered, thinking of all the people who had died in this town. People who had meant nothing more to the vampires than a ready blood supply.

"Are you through asking questions? I thought you wanted to meet a vampire."

"I do."

"Let's go, then."

Rosa dropped her napkin on the table, grabbed her handbag and followed Saintcrow out of the restaurant. Although he hadn't paid for the meal, he had left the waitress a generous tip.

He opened the car door for her, held it until she was settled in the seat before rounding the Viper and sliding behind the wheel. The furnishings in his house were expensive. So was his car, she mused, as she ran her hand over the soft, black leather seat. It was obvious the town was doing well if he could afford such luxuries. The car came to life with a low growl.

"Where are we going?" she asked as he drove across the bridge and turned right onto the road.

"A nightclub."

"But…"

"It's a vampire bar."

"Oh."

He didn't seem inclined to talk, so Rosa stared out the window, but there was nothing to see, just miles and miles of open land and a highway that seemed to go on forever. She slid a glance at Saintcrow. His profile was sharp and clean, his clothes top of the line. Had he always been so self-assured?

Eventually, he made a left turn onto a paved road that led to a large parking lot. A single-story building sat in the middle, surrounded by perhaps a dozen cars.

Rosa felt a quiver of unease when Saintcrow parked the Viper and she saw the name of the nightclub spelled out in bright, crimson neon letters—*The Bloody Rose.* She almost told him she'd changed her mind until she saw the expression on his face. He was watching her, an amused gleam in his dark eyes, and she knew he was just waiting for her to chicken out.

"Ready?" she asked.

"I am if you are."

"Let's go," she said, with far more enthusiasm than she felt. She was out of the car before he could open her door. Striding toward the entrance, she reminded herself that she had come to Morgan Creek to meet vampires, and this was the first step.

Saintcrow held the door open for her, and followed her inside.

Rosa came to an abrupt halt. The room was dimly lit, the walls dark gray, the floor black and gray tile. Black leather booths. Tables covered with black cloths. Black chairs. There were no other colors to break the monotony save for a bright neon rose that spanned the entire length of the wall behind the bar. Three men attired in gray shirts and black ties served drinks. Even the music coming from the sound system was dark.

Taking her arm, Saintcrow led her toward the bar, indicated she should take a seat on one of the padded stools.

"Couldn't you have found a place not quite so…so gloomy?" Rosa whispered.

Saintcrow shrugged.

Rosa glanced around the room. Couples sat at a few of the tables. A handful of single men sat at the bar. "Is everyone in here a vampire but me?"

Saintcrow's gaze darted around the room. "Pretty much. What'll you have?" he asked as one of the bartenders paused in front of them.

"A Sea Breeze, light on the vodka."

The bartender looked at Saintcrow. "What can I get you tonight?"

"The usual."

"What's the usual?" Rosa asked when the bartender left to mix their drinks.

"Red wine with a little extra kick."

"What does that mean?"

"It's the house special," he said. "Red wine laced with blood."

"I don't believe you."

"Want a taste?" he asked as the bartender set their drinks in front of them.

Rosa looked at the contents of his glass. The liquid was blood-red, but was it really blood, she wondered, or was he just trying to freak her out? And then she grunted softly. Why wouldn't it be blood? He was a vampire in a vampire bar. She couldn't help wondering where they got the 'extra kick' from. And shied away from the obvious answer.

She sipped her drink, knew a moment of relief when she tasted mainly cranberry juice, grapefruit juice, and a hint of vodka.

"Hey, Saintcrow, who's the cute chick?"

Rosa glanced over her shoulder at the man who had come up behind them. He wore faded jeans, cowboy boots, and a black sweatshirt with the words *Vampires Do it in The Dark* printed across the front. A thick, gold band embossed with what looked like Celtic runes peeked out from under his left shirt sleeve. His size, his very presence, were intimidating.

"Jake, this is Rosa. She's a friend of mine. Rosa, this is Jake Kincaid."

She nodded, unable to speak or even think while he was looking at her, his gaze moving over her as if he was a hungry wolf and she was the fatted calf.

She shivered when he repeated her name, his voice like liquid velvet as it caressed her.

"Mind if I join you?" Kincaid asked. He was talking to Saintcrow, but he was looking at her.

She couldn't help noticing that the stranger was incredibly handsome. He was a big man, well over six feet, broad-shouldered, with dusky skin. His hair, long and thick, was the color of rich, dark chocolate, as were his eyes. She usually preferred men who were clean-shaven, but she rather liked his sexy mustache and the five o'clock shadow along his jawline.

"Be my guest," Saintcrow said. He jerked his head toward a booth in the back. "I see an old friend of mine."

Rosa stared at him, suddenly alarmed. "You're going?"

"Not far." Saintcrow winked at her. "Holler if you need me."

Kincaid took the stool next to hers as Saintcrow sauntered toward the back of the club.

"Rosa," Kincaid murmured. "Pretty name for a pretty flower."

His voice, deep and strangely compelling, sent a shiver down her spine. "Thank you."

"Have you known Saintcrow long?"

"He's married to a friend of my sister's."

"I see." He frowned. "What are *you* doing in here?"

She blinked at him. She could hardly tell him the truth. It was too embarrassing. She felt like Alice lost in an alternative Wonderland. Why had she wanted to come here? She was way out of her league. And more scared than she wanted to admit. Being a vampire suddenly didn't seem as appealing as it had been when she set out for Morgan Creek.

His smile was warm and understanding. "Did Saintcrow dare you to come here?"

"No." Her gaze slid away from his. "I have a brother and a sister and a cousin who are vampires, and … "

"And you thought you'd like to be one, too?"

She looked up at him. "How did you know? Did Saintcrow tell you?"

"No." He took a deep breath, his gaze moving to the hollow of her throat and lingering there.

The look in his dark eyes sent another shiver down her spine. "It doesn't matter. Anyway. I've changed my mind."

"Not on my account, I hope."

With a shake of her head, Rosa looked around for Saintcrow. Where was he? She wanted to get out of here, now. The look in Jake Kincaid's eyes terrified her on some instinctive level. She breathed a sigh of relief when Saintcrow came striding toward them.

Something unspoken passed between the two vampires. Whatever it was made the short hairs along Rosa's arms stand at attention.

A moment later, Jake Kincaid rose abruptly and headed for the door.

"Ready to go home, Rosie?" Saintcrow asked.

Rosa stared at him, suddenly certain that Saintcrow had brought her here to scare her off, and that he had known perfectly well that meeting Jake Kincaid would frighten the living daylights out of her. Had, in fact, been counting on it.

And she had fallen for it.

Saintcrow grinned inwardly. Smart girl, he mused, pleased that she'd had the innate ability to recognize when she was in danger. And with good cause. Kincaid was an old vampire, powerful not just physically but with the strength that came with having survived so many centuries.

Rosa had sensed it, whether she realized it or not. It was a talent that might one day save her life.

Chapter Three

When Rosa woke in the morning, her first thought was of the vampire she had met the night before. Jake Kincaid. He wasn't as scary as Saintcrow, but damn, he was a close second. Thinking about it now, she was even more certain that Saintcrow had arranged the meeting knowing that Kincaid would intimidate her and scare her off. It embarrassed her to think she had fallen for such an obvious ruse. But it had been hard to think clearly surrounded by all that testosterone.

Rising, she pulled on a pair of jeans and a red sweater, brushed her hair and her teeth, stepped into a pair of sneakers and drove to the hotel restaurant.

She couldn't stop thinking about Jake Kincaid as she tucked into her breakfast. Was he really as scary as he had seemed, or had it just been an act? Not that it mattered. She would probably never see him again. She told herself she was relieved as she left the dining room.

At loose ends, she stood on the sidewalk a moment, then drove to the movie theater to see what was playing. It was a four-plex. Three of the auditoriums were showing new releases, the fourth was playing *The Lost Boys*, which was an old vampire movie. She recalled watching it on Netflix with Sofie late one night.

Rosa grinned as she pulled into the parking lot. Saintcrow had a twisted sense of humor, she thought, as she bought a ticket to the vampire flick. As she took her seat, she wondered if she would still think Jason Patric was hot.

The movie had been playing for about fifteen minutes when a man took the empty seat next to hers. Rosa knew a moment of irritation as she slid a sideways glance at him. There were plenty of other empty seats he could have chosen.

She let out a startled gasp when she recognized Jake Kincaid. "You!" she hissed. "What are you doing here?"

"I like vampire movies," he whispered. "Although I'm not crazy about the way this one ends."

She could hardly blame him for that, she thought, since all the vampires were destroyed in graphic and hideous ways.

Unable to think of a response, Rosa focused on the screen, but the actors might as well have been speaking Chinese because she couldn't concentrate on the dialog or anything else. She was far too aware of the incredibly handsome man beside her. What was he doing here when the sun was out and it was hours until dark? Micah had told her only very old vampires like Saintcrow could endure the heat and light of the sun. Which meant Kincaid must be one of the ancient ones.

Her heart skipped a beat when his shoulder brushed hers, and again when she felt his gaze on her face. Never in her whole life had she been so aware of another person.

She stood and headed for the aisle as soon as the credits rolled.

She didn't have to look over her shoulder to know that he was right behind her.

Outside the theater, she whirled around to confront him. "Why are you following me?"

He shrugged. "I'd like to know you better."

She arched one brow. "Oh?"

"You got a problem with that?"

"Did Saintcrow put you up to this?"

"No, ma'am. Coming here was all my idea."

"But he asked you to be at the nightclub last night, didn't he? To scare me away?"

His smile was devastating. "That he did."

She hadn't expected him to admit it.

"Mind if I walk you to your car?"

"I guess not," she murmured after a moment.

He fell into step beside her, a tall man who exuded raw masculinity. She had forgotten how big he was. It was like walking next to a mountain. He was wearing jeans and cowboy boots again, and a jean jacket over a black tee shirt. Try as she might, she couldn't think of a single thing to say.

He stood beside her while she unlocked the car door. "I'd like to see you again," he said.

She looked up at him. Lordy, he was gorgeous, his deep brown eyes almost as hypnotic as his voice.

"Rosa?"

"I... I don't know."

"Would you mind if I called you?"

She nibbled on her lower lip while she made up her mind. "I guess it would be all right." Wondering if she was doing the right thing, she gave him her cell number.

"It was nice to see you again, lovely lady. I hope we can get together before you leave town."

Rosa nodded, her whole body tingling at his nearness. His voice was deep and dark and hypnotic, like his eyes.

She blew out a breath when he turned and walked away, and then vanished from her sight.

She stared after him, the word *vampire* playing and replaying in her mind.

⚜ ⚜ ⚜

Saintcrow's eyes narrowed when he saw Rosa that night. What the hell? She'd been with Kincaid. "So," he drawled softly. "How was your day?"

"Okay," she said with a shrug. "I went to the movies. I thought it was kind of funny that you were showing an old vampire flick."

"Is that right?"

"Just seemed odd to me."

He grunted softly. "Are you ready to go to dinner?"

"I'm not hungry. I had a sandwich a little while ago."

He nodded. "Maybe you'd like to go vampire hunting again?"

"At *The Bloody Rose?*"

"I was thinking of another place."

She shrugged. "Might as well. It's why I came here, after all."

Saintcrow grinned inwardly, amused by her forced nonchalance.

⚜ ⚜ ⚜

Rosa groaned when she followed Saintcrow into the nightclub. It was every bit as dark and dreary as *The Bloody Rose.* "Are all vamp nightclubs so depressing? What have you people got against cheerful colors and music that doesn't sound like a funeral dirge?"

Saintcrow laughed as he held her chair for her. "What do you want, bright lights and salsa music?"

"It would be a nice change."

"Maybe so," he said, taking the seat across from hers. "But vampires are nocturnal creatures, you know. We prefer the dark. It's easier to seduce your prey when the lights are low and the music is soft and sensual."

Rosa shivered as his gaze met hers, felt a sudden unaccountable, irresistible sexual attraction to him. She stood when he did, went willingly into his arms when he led her onto the dance floor.

Saintcrow mesmerized her with a glance, then bent his head to her neck, took a few sips of her life's blood, and blocked the memory from her mind. She was sweet, he mused, though not near so sweet as his Kadie. But that wasn't why he had tasted Rosa. Taking her blood formed a link of sorts between them. Should she ever get into trouble, and that seemed likely if she continued to see Kincaid, it would allow him to find her.

When the music ended, he led her back to their table. "Rosa?"

"Hmm?"

Holding her gaze with his, he unblocked the memory of his bite.

She blinked at him and then, wide-eyed, lifted a hand to her neck. "You bit me!" she whispered, her voice laced with horror.

Saintcrow nodded.

"And you did something else, too. What was it?"

"A little vampire glamour to make you want me."

Rosa stared at him. "I don't believe you." And yet, she *had* felt an unwanted rush of desire for him.

"It's true. Vampires can mesmerize you and make you do whatever they want. You need to remember that. They can seduce you, drink from you, and wipe it all from your mind."

"Is that what you did to Kadie? Make her fall in love with you?"

"No. I didn't want a robot. She hated me for a long time, with good cause, and I let her."

"And if she'd never fallen in love with you? What would you have done then?"

"I honestly don't know. She was attracted to me even when she hated me." Saintcrow lifted a hand to stay the question he read in her eyes. "I didn't exert any influence on her, the way I did you. Although all vampires have a certain inherent allure. That's something else you might want to remember."

Rosa sat back in her chair, troubled by what Saintcrow had told her. Maybe looking for a vampire wasn't such a good idea. Maybe Sofia and Holly had just been lucky that the vampires they had fallen in love with had basically been good, decent men who hadn't been inclined to take advantage of them. She might not be so lucky.

⚜ ⚜ ⚜

Late that night, long after Rosa had turned in, Saintcrow wandered the town's dark streets, his mind filled with thoughts of the past. And Kadie. Always Kadie. She had turned both the town and his life upside down. But for her, Morgan Creek would still be a haven for vampires, a prison without bars for the mortals who innocently wandered into town and found themselves trapped inside, preyed upon by the coven. In his defense, he had seen to it that the men and women had been treated well. The vampires hadn't been allowed to mistreat them or kill them. He had built them comfortable homes to live in, provided food to eat, movies, a library, a tavern. He hadn't felt guilty about keeping them or preying on them. He was a vampire, after all. He had been guilt-free until Kadie got under his skin. To please her, he had returned the men and women to their homes and sent the vampires away. He would have done anything to please her. Anything. Except let her go.

He had seen far worse cruelty in his time, Saintcrow mused, as he neared home. He had been turned during the Crusades. Fatally wounded in battle, with the stink of fear and death all around him, he had dragged himself away from the field of battle, determined to die alone. A vampire had found him there. She had given him a drink of water, sang him a song. Cradling his head in her lap, she had talked to him for what seemed a long time, though he had no clear recollection of what she'd said. He had felt himself slipping away into oblivion when she asked him if he wanted to die. He had thought it a foolish question under the circumstances, but by then, he had been past answering. He didn't remember much of anything that happened after that. She had buried her fangs in this throat and he had felt himself drifting away on a crimson tide. He'd known he was dying, but it had no longer seemed important. All he had wanted to do was surrender to the darkness that beckoned him, but she hadn't been finished with him yet. She had forced his mouth open and made him drink what he'd later realized was her blood.

He had never seen her again. Never knew her name, or why she had chosen to turn him instead of taking his life.

With a shake of his head, Saintcrow materialized inside his lair. Kadie had not only turned his life upside down, she had turned his cheerless lair into a home. Kadie. Damn, but he missed her. The house seemed lifeless without her. And then he grinned, thinking it was no longer lifeless as he listened to the slow, steady beat of Rosa's heart.

He had a wanna-be vampire under his roof. Now, what was he going to do about it?

One thing for sure, he needed to talk to Jake Kincaid and find out what he was up to, and there was no time like the present.

Chapter Four

Kincaid strolled along a deserted street in Cheyenne, his thoughts on the pretty little mortal staying with Saintcrow. Rosa. She had wanted to meet a vampire and Saintcrow had arranged for the two of them to get together.

Kincaid snorted. Saintcrow had wanted him to scare the girl off, but once he met her, that had been the farthest thing from his mind. She was lovely, a little feisty, and untouched, a rarity in this day and age. He hadn't known virgins still existed, which only proved how long it had been since he'd been intimate with a decent woman.

He found his prey waiting for a taxi. He mesmerized the woman with a glance, took what he needed, and sealed the twin punctures in her throat before sending her on her way. Blood. He never tired of it, never got enough. But Saintcrow didn't condone needless killing in his territory, another testament to the power of a decent woman, he thought with a wry grin. He had known Rylan Saintcrow a hell of a long time. The master vampire had never been squeamish about taking a life until Kadie arrived on the scene. But Saintcrow was still a master vampire and one to be reckoned with if one wanted to continue his existence. And while Kincaid had considered ending his centuries-long existence from time to time, it was no longer an option.

Not until he got to know Saintcrow's pretty little protégé better.

He was about to return to his lair when the master vampire fell into step beside him. Kincaid tensed as the other vampire's power rolled over him.

"You were with Rosa today," Saintcrow said. It wasn't a question, but an accusation. "What the hell were you thinking?"

"You wanted me to scare her off, didn't you?"

"Uh-huh. But that's not what you were doing."

There was no point in lying, not to Saintcrow. "I like her."

"Leave her alone."

"What if I don't want to?" Kincaid flinched as the master vampire's ancient power lashed out at him. It felt like knives slicing into his flesh. It took all the strength he possessed to stand against it. "She gave me her phone number." He spoke through gritted teeth. "Are you going to destroy me if I call her?"

Saintcrow withdrew his power. "We've been friends a long time," he said, his voice like ice over steel. "But if you lay a hand on her, I'll take your head. If you make her one of us, I'll take your head. Do we understand each other?"

Kincaid nodded curtly.

"I see you're still wearing that talisman the witch gave you."

Kincaid ran his thumb over the wide gold band. "Damn right."

"I guess it's still working."

"So far."

"Remember what I said about Rosa."

As if he could forget, Kincaid thought, and blew out an enormous sigh of relief when Saintcrow vanished from his sight. He stood there a moment, thinking he was lucky to still be alive. Saintcrow's power wasn't a whole hell of a lot stronger than his own, but it was powerful enough to make him wary and respectful.

As he returned to his lair, there wasn't a doubt in Kincaid's mind that the master vampire would carry out his threats without a qualm.

Chapter Five

Rosa sat on the sofa, staring at a daytime soap opera, her mind elsewhere. Saintcrow was a truly scary creature and if what he had told her the other night was true, mortals were helpless to resist his kind. How could you withstand someone who could read your thoughts and force you to do their bidding against your will? Someone who could drain you of every drop of blood? Or turn you into a nightwalker at their whim? It occurred to her that even though she knew several vampires, she really didn't know much about the dark side of their lives.

She thought of her brother, Micah. She couldn't imagine him doing any of the things Saintcrow had mentioned. But then, how well did she really know him, now that he was a vampire? And what about her cousin, Holly? Was she capable of the same kind of power? Would Micah one day be as strong and invincible as Saintcrow? Would it change him from the loving brother she knew into some kind of monster? And what about Ethan and Sofia? Were they changing even now, becoming more like blood-thirsty vampires and less human?

She jumped a foot when Saintcrow suddenly appeared beside her on the sofa.

"You're going to give yourself nightmares if you keep thinking like that."

"Can you blame me? I've heard stories about you. Will Micah and Sofia turn into ... into ... "

"Into me?"

Her gaze slid away from his and she nodded.

He rested his arm along the back of the sofa. "Becoming a vampire doesn't usually change who a person is. Decent people don't turn into ravening monsters who go around killing indiscriminately. People who like to cause pain and destruction generally get worse when they realize no one can stop them. There are exceptions, of course. Being a vampire is a major life change, there's no doubt about that. But you don't turn into a monster unless you want to."

"I know you're a Master Vampire, but what does that mean, exactly? Why isn't Jake one, too? He's almost as old as you are."

"I'm considered a Master Vampire because I've claimed a certain territory for my own and I've fought to keep it."

"So, if another vampire came along and defeated you, then he'd become a master, too?"

"Right."

Rosa nodded as she considered that. "Do you ever get tired of living? I mean, what do you do when you've seen everything, been everywhere, done everything? Don't you ever get bored?"

"Most of the old ones go to ground every now and then."

"Go to ground? What does that mean?"

"Old vampires sometimes bury themselves deep in the earth."

Rosa shuddered.

"It's revitalizing," Saintcrow said. "I've done it myself from time to time."

"For how long?"

"Sometimes a decade or two, sometimes longer. Waking up in a new century makes life exciting again. New trends in fashion. New modes of transportation. New inventions. Sometimes whole new countries."

"Sounds…horrible. Like being buried alive." She couldn't think of anything more terrifying.

He shrugged. And then his gaze met hers. "Why didn't you tell me you were with Kincaid yesterday?"

She stared at him, eyes wide. "How did you know?"

"Darlin', I know everyone you were with yesterday, everything you did."

Rosa hugged herself, thinking that was probably the most disturbing thing he'd said yet.

Saintcrow stretched his legs out in front of him. "Kincaid is an old vampire. Almost as old as I am, although the vampire who turned me was much stronger."

"Does that matter?"

He nodded. "The stronger your sire, the stronger you will be. My sire was ancient when she turned me."

Rosa digested that for a moment. "So, if I wanted to be turned, I should find a powerful vampire?"

"Exactly. Ethan is stronger than Micah because I was stronger than Lilith. And also because I did a blood exchange with Ethan several years ago. I did something similar with Micah a while back, so he can be awake during the day."

Rosa frowned. If she decided to be a vampire, would Saintcrow do that blood exchange thing with her, too, so she wouldn't have to sleep the days away? "You mentioned Lilith before. Who is she?"

"One of the vampires who lived in Morgan Creek. She was a nasty piece of work. No one liked her."

"Why did she stay? Why did you let her stay?"

"When I came to Morgan Creek, life was a lot more dangerous for vampires than it is now. There were hunters everywhere, and the government was offering big bounties on our kind. I found this place when it had been abandoned and decided to stay. Now and then, some mortal would wander in. Others of my kind heard about a vampire hideout in Wyoming and made their way here. I allowed them to stay with two conditions—they were not to hurt or kill the humans we kept here. To do so meant death. There were no second chances. The other condition was, once they came here, they couldn't leave."

"Why not?"

"Vampires gossip just like anyone else. I didn't want to take a chance that the wrong people might hear about this place. It was a perfect set-up," he said, somewhat sadly. "Until Kadie crossed the bridge."

"How did you keep everyone inside the town?"

"I put wards on the bridge and around the mountains. The wards allowed people to come into the area, but prevented both humans and vampires from leaving."

"What are wards, exactly?"

"It's like vampire witchcraft."

Rosa shook her head. It was all so fascinating. The more she learned, the more intrigued she became. Imagine being such a powerful creature, living for centuries, immune to age and disease? In spite of her earlier trepidation, she found herself thinking being a vampire didn't really sound so bad after all.

Saintcrow chuckled as he read her thoughts. She was so young, so innocent. Sure, being a vampire had some perks. And he wouldn't be human again if he could. But there was a sweetness to life that was denied vampires. The knowledge that human life was brief made it more meaningful, more precious. The ability to father a child was forever lost to vampires. For centuries, he'd told himself he didn't care, that it didn't matter, but deep down inside, where he rarely looked, was an emptiness that could never be filled. His only regrets in life were that not only had he lost the ability to father a child, but he had denied Kadie the opportunity to have a baby of her own.

"Saintcrow?"

"What?"

"Where did you go?"

He frowned at her then grunted softly. "You don't want to know. Come on, let's get out of here."

⚜ ⚜ ⚜

He took her to a nightclub, but it was as different from the last two as day from night. The lighting was subdued but not dark, the men and women just ordinary people who laughed and danced and indulged in steak and lobster, shrimp and chicken.

Rosa ordered prime rib, rare, a baked potato, broccoli, and a green salad.

Saintcrow ordered a bottle of red wine that cost more than she spent on food in a month.

"What are we doing here?" she asked when the waitress left to turn in their order.

"I thought you'd like a change of pace."

"I'm not going to meet any vampires in here," she said, glancing around.

"So, you're still looking for someone to turn you?"

She hesitated a moment, then said, "I don't know. I'm still thinking about it. You said it's best to be turned by an old vampire."

Saintcrow nodded, afraid he knew what was coming.

She took a deep breath, then said, "Jake Kincaid is old."

"Don't even think about it."

"Why not? You said I need someone old. And you won't do it."

"Damn right, I won't."

"I thought he was your friend."

"Friendship has nothing to do with it. If he turns you, I'll have his head."

"What?" Rosa clapped a hand over her mouth as the people at the next table turned to stare at her. "What do you mean?" she whispered.

"Just what I said. And he knows it."

Rosa stared at Saintcrow as if seeing him for the first time. Did he mean it?

"Don't doubt it for a minute."

The most frightening thing was, she didn't doubt it at all.

⚜ ⚜ ⚜

Rosa tossed and turned for hours before finally falling asleep, only to dream that Kincaid turned her and when Saintcrow found out, he carried out his threat. She saw the whole ghastly thing in living color and woke bathed in a cold sweat.

Sitting up, she clutched her pillow to her chest. What was she worrying about? She had only seen Jake Kincaid twice. He had never called. It was obvious that Saintcrow had warned him away. She couldn't help thinking that Kincaid had been smart to listen. Saintcrow appeared to be a far more formidable enemy than she had supposed. Apparently Kincaid knew it, too.

Unable to get back to sleep, Rosa shuffled into the bathroom and showered, pulled on a pair of sweats and a long-sleeved tee shirt, and made her way downstairs.

Tired of eating out all the time, she had gone shopping for a few things the other afternoon—bread, eggs, bacon, milk, orange juice—mostly stuff for breakfast.

She had just finished eating and was loading the dishwasher when her cell phone rang. She frowned at the unfamiliar number, followed by a flutter of excitement. What if it was Kincaid?

She let the phone ring several times before answering. "Hello?"

"Hey."

She closed her eyes at the sound of his voice. Low and intimate, it wrapped around her like a warm blanket on a chilly day.

"Rosa? You there?"

"Yes. I... I'm just surprised to hear from you." Was he crazy? Why was he calling her when Saintcrow had threatened to take his head?

Kincaid grunted softly. "Been talking to Saintcrow, have you?"

"Yes."

"Any chance I can take you out tonight?"

"Do you think that's wise? He said..."

"I know what he said. I'm not planning to hurt you or drink from you, or turn you into a nightwalker. I'm just looking to spend a little time with a lovely lady."

Her cheeks warmed at the compliment. "What did you have in mind?"

"I hadn't thought that far ahead," he admitted. "We can decide when I get there."

She should say no, she thought. She didn't want to put his life in danger.

"Rosa?"

"All right."

"Where should I pick you up?"

Good question, she thought. Then, with an inward shrug, she said, "I'll meet you outside the Italian restaurant on Main Street at seven."

"Great. See you then."

She had second thoughts as soon as the call ended. What would Saintcrow say when he found out? What would he do?

With a whole day stretching out in front of her, Rosa put her hair up in a ponytail and spent the late morning and afternoon cleaning the house. Not that it was all that dirty. Saintcrow was surprisingly tidy and while she tended to be a little sloppy about picking up after herself at home, she was a guest here and on her best behavior.

She hummed as she dusted everything, mopped the kitchen floor, scrubbed the sink, and put the clean dishes away. She changed the sheets on her bed and tossed the dirty ones in the washer. While adding soap to the machine, she found herself wondering what Saintcrow's lair looked like. With Kadie away, did he make the bed every day when he got up? Did he sleep in a bed, or a coffin? Was he doing his own laundry? If so, he must be doing it while she was out, or after she went to bed. He didn't leave any dirty dishes in the sink, she thought, with a grin.

When she finished in the house, she went for a long walk. She saw a few of the tourists, who smiled and nodded as she passed by. What would they think, she wondered, if they knew the town was owned by a vampire?

She was returning to Saintcrow's when it occurred to her that she hadn't seen him all day, which was odd. He usually spent part of it with her.

At 5:30, she went up to her room to get ready, thinking she would have plenty of time to eat before Kincaid showed up. She showered and dressed, grabbed her phone, her keys, and her handbag, and drove into town.

The sidewalks were crowded with people. Street lamps came on as the sun slipped behind the mountains. The lights in the park were also on and she saw a couple of families picnicking on the grass. There was a line in front of the movie theater. The tavern was crowded, as were the stores that sold souvenirs. It was amazing, she thought, all these people laughing and talking, never knowing that Morgan Creek had once housed a coven of vampires, or that a vampire owned the town and most, if not all, of the businesses in it.

After parking her car, Rosa walked to the restaurant. She felt a little self-conscious as the hostess showed her to a table for two. She ordered a ham-and-pineapple pizza and a glass of iced tea, and wished she had eaten at the house. She was the only one there without a friend or family.

She had no sooner finished eating than Saintcrow slid into the chair across from hers.

"How's it going?" he asked.

"Fine. Where have you been all day?"

He shrugged. "I went to see Kadie."

Rosa stared at him. "You went to Italy?"

"Yeah."

He had been to Italy and back in a day, a trip that took almost twelve hours one way by plane. It was beyond belief. And then she frowned. "You didn't tell my family I'm here, did you?"

"Of course not."

Her relief was palpable.

"Just like you didn't tell me you have a date with Kincaid."

"How can you possibly know that?"

"He's waiting outside."

"Oh."

"Are you sure you know what you're doing?"

"What do you mean?"

Saintcrow shrugged. "Like I told you, he's an old vampire. Set in his ways. He's never settled down or shown any sign of wanting to do so."

"I'm not looking for a husband," Rosa said. "Just someone who might turn me, if I decide that's what I want."

"Still trying to make up your mind?"

"Well, like you said, once it's done, it's done, so I want to be sure. And the only way to do that is spend time with vampires, and see how they… ah, really live."

"You've got a brother and a sister who can tell you everything you need to know."

"But they can't be neutral. They've both made it crystal clear they're against it. And so have you."

"If you're determined to do it, you need to let Micah turn you. Or Ethan. They both have my blood in them, which will give you an edge over most fledglings."

Rosa nodded. He was right. If the one who turned her would be her sire, it should be someone she could trust 110 percent. "So, you didn't come here to tell me not to go out with Kincaid?"

"I would, if I thought you'd listen."

"Do you think he means me any harm?"

"Not if he values his head."

Rosa grinned at him. In spite of Saintcrow's apparent indifference, she was sure he cared about what happened to her, at least a little.

"Come on," he said, covering her check with a fifty dollar bill. "I'll walk you out."

⚜ ⚜ ⚜

Rosa felt the tension in the air as the two vampires nodded at each other. As had happened once before, she felt like there was a silent conversation going on between them.

"I'll see you at home, Rosa," Saintcrow said, and disappeared into the shadows.

She felt a rush of excitement when Jake smiled at her.

"I've waited all day to see you," he said as he opened the passenger door of the midnight blue Mustang convertible parked at the curb.

"Really? I thought... never mind," she said as she settled into the seat.

Kincaid laughed softly. "You thought I was dead to the world?" he remarked as he closed the door.

She felt her cheeks bloom with embarrassment as she watched him walk around the front of the car and slide into the driver's seat.

"Like Saintcrow, I can be awake during the day if I wish."

"Because you're an old vampire, right?"

He glanced over his shoulder as he pulled away from the curb. "I take it he's been teaching you about our kind?"

Rosa nodded.

"I've never known anyone who *wanted* to join the ranks of the undead."

Undead? Rosa shuddered as the image of a living corpse filled her mind. "Is that how you see yourself? Undead?"

"Not really. But that's how most people think of us." When he stopped at a red light, he reached for her hand. "Do I feel undead to you?"

His hand was large and cool and the mere touch of it sent frissons of heat racing up her arm, spreading warmth to every part of her being, until it settled deep inside her.

He grinned as he stepped on the gas. Damn! He didn't know what had just sparked between them but it had never happened to him before.

They were silent during the rest of the drive to the nightclub.

Kincaid parked the car, got out, and opened her door for her. He hesitated a moment before he reached for her hand to help her out of the Mustang. His gaze met hers as that same spark passed between them again.

Rosa stared up at him as warmth spiraled through her. "What are you doing?"

"Nothing."

"Nothing?"

He shook his head.

"You're not exerting your innate vampire allure to seduce me?"

Kincaid regarded her for a moment then threw back his head and laughed. She was delightfully outspoken. "Is that what you think?"

She glared at him. "Saintcrow told me vampires possess some kind of preternatural sex appeal."

"He did, huh? Well, I'll try to turn it down a notch."

"So I was right. You *were* trying to seduce me."

"I was kidding, Rosa. I wasn't *trying* to do anything."

But he could if he wanted to, she thought, suddenly frightened by the possibility. Tugging her hand from his, she said, "Well, see that you don't."

"Hey," he said with a grin, "I can't help it if you find me irresistible."

"Irresistible?" She stared at him, her cheeks bright pink with embarrassment because he was right. "I think you're totally resistible," she lied.

"I guess our date is off," he said quietly. "Come on, I'll take you back to your car."

The trip back to the restaurant parking lot was strained and silent.

He pulled up next to her rental, parked, got out, and opened the door of the Mustang for her.

Her hand trembled as she unlocked the Kia.

"I'm sorry if I offended you earlier," he said, his voice cold and flat.

His apology caught her completely off guard.

She felt a rush of regret when he turned away. Maybe she *was* over-reacting just a little. "Kincaid, wait!"

He paused a moment then turned to look at her, his expression impassive.

"I'm sorry. Please don't go."

"Are you sure?" he asked, a hint of mischief in his eyes. "You never know when my vampire allure might go into high gear."

Stifling a smile, she said, with mock seriousness, "Maybe you can warn me."

Closing the distance between them, he gazed into her eyes. "I'm warning you now."

"Oh?" It was suddenly hard to breathe.

"I'm going to kiss you."

"Oh."

With a nod, he lowered his head and claimed her lips with his, right there in the parking lot where anyone passing by could see them. It was a chaste kiss, just the brush of his lips on hers, and yet she felt it in every nerve and fiber of her body.

When he lifted his head, she stared up at him. Lordy, if that was how he kissed when he wasn't exerting any vampire allure, what must it be like when he did?

"Rosa?"

"Hmm?"

"What would you like to do this evening?"

She was tempted to ask him to kiss her again, but she suddenly realized they weren't alone. Several people were staring at them. "I don't care," she said, glancing around. "Let's just go."

"It's a nice night for a walk," he said, taking her hand in his.

"It is," she agreed, thinking she would have agreed to anything he wanted.

They strolled in silence until they reached the park where they sat on a wrought-iron bench beneath a tree.

"Tell me about yourself," Rosa said, studying the large, brown hand that engulfed hers. "What were you before you were a vampire?"

"I was a slave in Rome."

"A slave! That's terrible."

"You have no idea." Forced to work from dawn to dark seven days a week, the constant threat of the lash, cruel overseers, never enough to eat. "My mother was Greek. She was captured by the Romans when she was a young girl and forced into slavery. I have no idea who my father was. I didn't care much for being someone else's property, so one night I killed my master and ran away.

"They caught me, of course, whipped me until I was unconscious, and left me for dead. I didn't die, though. I wandered around aimlessly for a couple of years, always afraid they'd find me again.

"One night I tried to rob a man to get enough money to buy something to eat." He laughed a harsh, bitter, laugh. "Turned out he was a vampire. A very old one. He took me to his lair, locked me in a cage, and fed on me. I'm not sure how long he kept me locked up. I lost track of time after a while."

He paused at the look of horror on her face. "Should I go on?"

At her nod, he said, "It wasn't all bad. Drakos had been a scholar before he was turned and he taught me how to read and write and cipher. When he traveled to foreign lands, he took me with him. I learned to speak a couple of different languages along the way.

"He was a wealthy man, vain about his appearance. He dressed well, and he bought me a whole new wardrobe so that when he took me out in public, my appearance wouldn't shame him. We were on our way home from the opera one night when he was attacked and seriously injured. We barely made it back to his lair. He lost a lot of blood on the way home. He locked me up and then materialized inside my cage and drank from me. Drank until I was on the brink of death. He didn't let me die, though. He turned me, instead. And I hated him for it. He said he was sorry when he was himself again, that he hadn't meant to do it, but I didn't give a damn. I didn't want an apology, I wanted my life back. I would have killed him if I could. He taught me what it meant to be a vampire, how to survive. Eventually, he realized I was never going to forgive him, and he let me go. I never saw him again."

"What happened to your mother?"

"She died a few years before I ran away."

Rosa sat there, stunned by what he'd told her. And then she frowned. "Jake Kincaid doesn't sound like a Greek name."

"No. My mother named me Alexandru. I've changed it over the years. I used Kincaid during my cowboy period and it stuck with me."

That explained the jeans and boots he favored, and then she grinned, thinking she felt sorry for any horse that had had to carry him. "Where did you meet Saintcrow?"

"In Mexico. We both had our eye on a pretty little *senorita* at the time." Kincaid smiled with the memory. "He was a little older and stronger, but I wouldn't back down. While we were fighting over her, figurately speaking, her father married her off to some wealthy landowner. We've been friends ever since."

A charming story, Rosa thought. It made them both seem more human, somehow.

⚜ ⚜ ⚜

Saintcrow was waiting for her when she returned to his house. He quirked one brow when he saw her. "Just can't stay away from him, can you?"

Rosa dropped her handbag on a side table, kicked off her shoes, and settled into a corner of the sofa. "I like him." She looked up at Saintcrow. "Seems you like him, too."

"What makes you think that?"

"He told me how you met."

"Uh-huh."

She shrugged. "Since you didn't kill him, you must like him."

With a shake of his head, Saintcrow sat at the other end of the sofa, his long legs stretched out in front of him. "I don't kill everyone I meet," he said dryly.

"I'm beginning to wonder if you're as formidable as everyone says."

"Is that right?" He unleashed a hint of his preternatural power.

Rosa tensed as it slid over her, remembering all too clearly the last time he had done so. It had been much stronger then and she had no desire to experience it ever again. "All right, I take it back! You're the most dangerous man on the planet."

"And don't you forget it. As for the woman in Mexico, there were too many pretty females in the world to fight over one," he said with a shrug.

"Unless that one is Kadie?"

"Exactly. Are you going to keep seeing Kincaid?"

Rosa worried her lower lip between her teeth. "I don't know. I've been doing a lot of thinking. Maybe you're right and I should wait a while before I make any long-lasting, life-changing decisions."

"Honey, I'm always right."

"Of course," she said dryly. "The thing is, I don't want to stop seeing him, either."

"Well, that's a decision you'll have to make on your own."

"I know. Do you think he'll hurt me?"

"He might break your heart," Saintcrow said, "but he won't turn you against your will, or harm you in any way. Partly because way down deep, he's a pretty decent guy, and partly because he knows I'll destroy him if he hurts you physically."

Rosa nodded. "Good to know," she said, rising. "I'm going up to bed."

Saintcrow watched her climb the stairs, wondering which would win out—Rosa's growing affection for Kincaid, or her good sense.

Chapter Six

Rosa went to lunch at the restaurant in town the next afternoon. The place was crowded and she counted herself lucky to get the last table. She felt a little silly, sitting alone at a table for four, but what the heck, that's all they had, and she was hungry.

She had just turned in her order when a man neatly dressed in a pair of gray slacks and a sports coat approached her.

"Sorry to bother you," he said, "but would you mind sharing your table with me? I'll buy your lunch."

Rosa hesitated a moment, but figured she was safe enough in a room full of people. "Please do," she said. "And I can pay for my own lunch, thank you, anyway."

He smiled as he pulled out a chair and sat down. "As you wish, Miss…"

"Ravenwood."

"Pleased to meet you. I'm Paul Rhinehart."

"What brings you to Morgan Creek?"

"Curiosity. I'm a reporter."

"Oh?" He was of medium height, with light brown hair and eyes, and an easy manner, as if he was comfortable in his own skin. She thought he was probably in his late thirties or early forties.

He looked up when a waitress approached the table. "I'd like a roast beef sandwich, fries, and coffee," he said in answer to her query.

The waitress nodded, then smiled at Rosa. "Your order will be up shortly," she said. "We've been really busy today and we're a little short-handed."

"No problem," Rosa assured her with a smile.

"You'll probably think I'm crazy," Paul said, when the waitress left to turn in his order, "but I heard this place used to be run by vampires."

Rosa stared at him for a moment, then forced a laugh. "Vampires? Seriously?"

"You don't believe in them?"

"I don't think any sane person does."

He grunted softly. "I guess I can't blame you for thinking that way, but I know they're real. A friend of mine had a nasty encounter with one just a couple of weeks ago."

"Really?"

Paul nodded, his expression grim. "He was attacked while coming home from a party late one night. Darn near died from the amount of blood he lost. The vampire would probably have killed him if a cop hadn't come along."

"That's terrible."

"Yeah. Anyway, I don't expect to find any of them here now, but..." He shrugged one shoulder. "Curiosity got the best of me."

Rosa followed his gaze as he looked out the window. It was a beautiful day, warm and clear. The kind of day that made you think of roses and sunshine, not vampires.

"How long are you staying here?" he asked.

"A couple of weeks. I'm visiting a friend."

"Oh?" His brows shot up. "You know someone who lives here?"

Darn! Did she dare admit that? She didn't have to mention any names. "Yes, he, ah, owns the hotel."

"I don't suppose he's a vampire?"

Rosa laughed. "I never asked him, but I don't think so."

"I was going to wander through the town this afternoon," he said. "I don't suppose you'd like to give me a tour?"

Why not? she thought, as the waitress brought both of their orders. She had nothing better to do.

⚜ ⚜ ⚜

Paul Rhinehart turned out to be an entertaining companion, easy to talk to. They strolled through the business district, wandered through the park, stopped for ice cream at an outdoor vendor.

"That house on the hill," Paul remarked, looking up at Blair House. "Does anyone live there?"

"Not that I know of."

"Is it open to tourists?"

"I don't think so."

"Looks like an interesting place."

Rosa shrugged. "It's just an old house."

"What about those other two places?" he asked.

"I think the man who owns the hotel lives in one of them, and the other one belongs to the town manager."

"Who owns the town?"

Rosa shrugged again. "The state of Wyoming?"

"I can probably find out," Paul remarked as they headed back toward the business district. "I've got nothing to do this evening. Any chance you'd like to go to a movie?"

Rosa bit down on her lower lip. She had hoped to see Kincaid, although they hadn't made any plans. Maybe it would be a good idea to date a regular guy, for comparison. "I guess so."

"How about this? We can meet back at the restaurant for an early dinner and then hit the movies."

She thought it over, then said, "All right." After all, if she got into trouble, Saintcrow was only a phone call away.

⚜ ⚜ ⚜

Saintcrow rose with the setting sun. Opening his preternatural senses, he tracked Rosa's whereabouts to the restaurant in town. Letting his mind brush hers, he discovered she wasn't alone. And she wasn't with Kincaid. Curious, he dressed and willed himself into town.

⚜ ⚜ ⚜

Rosa looked up, unable to hide her surprise when Saintcrow strolled toward their table.

"What are you doing here?"

"I own the place, remember?" Saintcrow replied, his voice and his gaze icy as he regarded the man who was glaring at him. "I come here often." He inclined his head in the stranger's direction. "Aren't you going to introduce me to your friend, Miss Ravenwood?"

"Mr. Saintcrow, this is Paul Rhinehart. He's a reporter. Paul, this is Mr. Saintcrow."

Reporter, hell, Saintcrow thought as he shook the man's hand. He was a hunter. And a well-known one, at that.

"Order anything you like, you two," Saintcrow said. "It's on the house."

"Thank you," Rosa said curtly.

Sketching an old-fashioned bow, Saintcrow took his leave.

"He owns the hotel?" Paul asked, his gaze following Saintcrow.

"That's what he said."

"How do you happen to know him?"

Rosa bit down on her lower lip, wishing she had refused his invitation to dinner. "He's a friend of a friend of mine."

Paul nodded, his expression pensive.

Dinner was a strained affair and when it was over, Rosa pleaded a headache, thanked Paul Rhinehart for a lovely day, and made her escape as quickly as she could.

As she'd expected, Saintcrow was waiting for her at home. He sat on the sofa, his arms spread along the back, his legs stretched out in front of him, his expression impassive.

"Did you have a nice evening?" he asked.

Rosa swallowed hard. "Until you showed up."

"Indeed. And what did you tell Mr. Rhinehart about Morgan Creek?"

"Don't you know?" she snapped, then bit down on her lower lip as his power rolled through the room.

"Of course I know!"

"Then why ask me?" He was angry, she thought, but, darn it, so was she. What game was he playing, when all he had to do was read her mind?

"The man might be passing himself off as a reporter, but he's lying. Paul Rhinehart was once a world-renown vampire hunter, although he doesn't seem to be as active as he used to be."

Dumbfounded, Rosa stared at Saintcrow. A hunter? Paul hardly seemed big enough, strong enough, or tough enough to physically take on a vampire, even a fledgling.

Going against a nightwalker as old as Saintcrow would be suicide.

"The man has taken more heads than any hunter in the country."

"I don't believe you. He's a wimp."

Saintcrow snorted. "In this case, size doesn't matter. He knows what he's doing. I've heard that in recent months he's been working hand-in-hand with a powerful necromancer."

Rosa frowned. A necromancer? She wasn't even sure what that was, but it sounded scary as hell.

"It's someone who can reanimate dead bodies," Saintcrow remarked. "Someone who can communicate with spirits. Someone who practices black magic and has the power to control the dead. And the Undead."

Rosa went cold all over. Some people believed vampires were Undead. A necromancer and a hunter working together would be a lethal combination. If a necromancer could communicate with a vampire at rest, could he also render him helpless? Speak to his mind? Command him to walk out into the sunlight and destroy himself? Or do whatever else the necromancer desired?

Saintcrow nodded. "Rhinehart's witch is capable of doing all of those things."

"I don't know what to say." 'I'm sorry' hardly seem adequate.

Saintcrow blew out a sigh that seemed to come from the depths of his soul. "It's not your fault. You had no way of knowing who he is. I'm just glad Kadie and the others are out of the country."

"I can't stay locked up in this house day and night," Rosa said, frowning. "What should I do if I run into him again?"

"Try to act natural. Don't go into town alone at night. Pretend you don't know what I am. Don't go anywhere alone with him. And if you feel threatened, send me a mental SOS."

"He seemed so nice," Rosa said. "So harmless."

"Looks are often deceiving."

"Tell me about it." She tilted her head to the side. "Except in your case. No one would ever think you were harmless. Or weak. Or defenseless."

"It's a gift," he said, with a grin. "I'll see you tomorrow. Try to stay out of trouble until then."

Rosa made a face at him, but it was too late. He was already gone.

Chapter Seven

"What the hell's going on?" Kincaid asked, coming up beside Saintcrow. "I could feel your annoyance in the next town. Kind of ruined my appetite for the pretty little blonde in my arms."

"Sorry."

"So?"

"Our wanna-be vampire ran into Paul Rhinehart this afternoon."

"Rhinehart! No shit! What's he doing here?"

"What the hell do you think?"

"Right. Stupid question." Kincaid frowned. "Rosa was with him today?"

"Yeah. I guess he asked her a lot of questions about the town. Who owns it. Stuff like that."

"Well, damn."

"She seemed to think she needed to date a 'normal' guy, which you definitely aren't."

Kincaid shot him a dirty look. "What are you going to do about Rhinehart?"

"I haven't decided."

"Is she going to see him again?"

"Only by accident. Like she said, she can't stay inside indefinitely."

"Yeah. But I can make sure she has better things to do than spend her time with a hunter."

"I had a feeling you'd say that," Saintcrow said with a grin.

"I care for her," Kincaid said quietly.

"Tell me something I don't know."

Kincaid barked a laugh. "*Is* there anything you don't know?"

"Time will tell. Come on. Let's go find a couple of pretty women to take the edge off our thirst."

⚜ ⚜ ⚜

Rosa had just stepped out of the bathtub when her cell phone rang. Wrapping a towel around her middle, she scooped up the phone, felt a trickle of excitement when she saw Kincaid's name. She let it ring again so he wouldn't think she had just been sitting around waiting for his call. Taking a deep breath, she said, "Hello?"

"Hey, lovely lady. How's it going?"

"Very well, thank you."

"You mad at me?"

"Why would I be mad?"

"You tell me."

"I'm not mad."

"What are you doing?"

"If you must know, I'm getting ready for bed."

"Oh. I was hoping I could take you out for a nightcap."

"It's a little late for drinks."

"Yeah, I guess it is."

"I'd love some hot chocolate, though," she said, a smile in her voice. "The kind they serve in town is really good."

"Pick you up in ten minutes?"

She glanced at the puddle spreading at her feet. "Better make it fifteen."

Butterflies of excitement fluttered in the pit of her stomach as she quickly pulled on clean underwear, a pair of jeans, a warm sweater, and a pair of boots. She ran a comb through her hair, brushed her teeth, and skipped down the stairs.

The doorbell rang two minutes later.

Kincaid whistled softly when he saw her. "Hi, gorgeous."

"Hi, yourself." He looked positively yummy in a pair of faded black jeans and a pale blue, long-sleeved tee shirt that clearly outlined his muscular arms and broad shoulders. It was all she could do to keep from throwing herself into his arms, she was that happy to see him.

"Are you ready?"

She nodded, felt a rush of heat when his fingers entwined with hers. "Let's go."

He transported the two of them to a place swathed in shadows behind the restaurant. Hand in hand, they walked around to the front and stepped inside. This late, there were only a few people inside. Rosa thought they were mostly married couples stopping for coffee on the way home from a late movie.

They found a table for two in the back.

"How was your day?" Kincaid asked.

Rosa stared at him, her gaze narrowed. Was he fishing for information about Rhinehart? How much did he know? "How was yours?" she countered.

"Quiet as the grave. Seriously, I missed you."

"Did you?"

He nodded, his gaze searching hers.

"Saintcrow told you about the hunter, didn't he?"

"Yeah. You've got to be more careful, girl. If that hunter finds out about your family, you could be in real trouble."

Rosa grimaced as memories of Leticia Braga flashed through her mind. But for Saintcrow's intervention, the vindictive vampire might have killed her and her whole family.

"Rhinehart is as dangerous as hell," Kincaid said quietly. "You've got to stay away from him."

"I know. I will."

When the waitress arrived at their table, Rosa ordered a large cup of hot chocolate with extra whipped crème. Jake asked for a cup of black coffee she knew he wouldn't drink.

"Do you think Rhinehart is here for Saintcrow?" Rosa asked when they were alone again.

Kincaid shrugged. "Probably."

"Maybe he's here for you."

"It's possible, I guess."

"You don't seem very worried."

He shrugged. "I can take care of myself." His gaze caressed her. "And you, too, if you'll let me."

The heated look in his eyes, the deep timbre of his voice, made her insides melt like ice cream on a hot day. He was gorgeous, with those velvety brown eyes and that sexy, come-hither smile. Warmth spread through her when he took her hand in his. "It would be so easy to fall in love with you," he murmured.

Rosa stared at him. She knew he wanted her, but love? Seriously? They had only known each other a few days. "Is that a line? If so, it's a trifle soon, don't you think?" She tugged her hand free when the waitress arrived with their drinks.

Kincaid waited for the server to leave before he said, "It's true, nonetheless."

"I'm sure you've loved a lot of women," she said, her gaze focused on her cup.

"A few."

She looked up at him, her expression skeptical. "A few?"

"Okay, a lot. But loving and being in love are two different things."

"You loved the girl in Mexico."

He didn't deny it. "That was centuries ago." He tucked his forefinger under her chin and tilted her head up. "I'm over it."

Rosa stared at him, and then she laughed. Why was she upset by something that had happened centuries before she'd even been born? Besides, there was nothing serious going on between them. He probably told every woman he met that they'd be easy to love.

The thought that he might make such declarations indiscriminately bothered her a heck of a lot more than it should have. She couldn't deny that she was attracted to him. What woman wouldn't be? He was outrageously sexy, with those beautiful dark eyes and sexy voice, not to mention his amazing physique. But she didn't want to be just another conquest in a long line of women he'd loved and left.

Nevertheless, she went willingly into his arms for a good night kiss when he took her home an hour later. And dreamed of him all night long.

Chapter Eight

Paul Rhinehart moved stealthily through the night, his footsteps carrying him toward the two houses he had seen earlier in the day. The white one appeared to be uninhabited at the moment. Rosa had said the one with the turrets belonged to the owner of the hotel and the restaurant. He suspected Saintcrow owned the whole damn town.

Saintcrow. He couldn't control the shiver of apprehension that slithered down his spine as he contemplated trying to take the master vampire's head. Saintcrow was a force to be reckoned with. No one knew just how old he was, but Saintcrow was a legend among vampires and hunters alike. Some said the bloodsucker couldn't be destroyed. And while Paul hated to believe it, he feared it might be true.

Paul paused mid-stride. What the hell was he doing here, alone? Was attempting to destroy Saintcrow for Luca worth risking his life for? And what if he failed? What if all he did was piss off the master vampire?

Rhinehart shivered again. He didn't know why Luca wanted Saintcrow's destruction. But the necromancer scared the hell out of him. He should have arranged for Luca to meet him here. Instead, he had come charging in alone like some neophyte hunter still wet behind the ears.

Rhinehart squared his shoulders and straightened his spine. What the hell was he afraid of? He had destroyed more vampires than any other hunter in the country, maybe in the whole damn world! So, Saintcrow had a big reputation. Well, hell, so did he. Vampires trembled at the mention of his name.

Saintcrow hadn't, he thought. The bloodsucker had looked at him with outright disdain. "Pride goeth before destruction, and a haughty spirit before a fall," Rhinehart muttered.

A good reminder for the vampire.

And for himself.

He circled the house, getting the lay of the land, searching for any weakness in the vampire's wards, and finding none.

But he'd find a weakness, he mused as he headed back to town. He always did.

And in this case, he was certain it was the Ravenwood girl, Rosa.

Chapter Nine

Saintcrow ran his fingers along Kadie's silken thigh. The musky scent of their lovemaking hung heavy in the air. It still amazed him that she was his, that the love she held for him was stronger than the hatred and fear she had once felt.

"Rylan, what's troubling you?"

"Nothing now."

She rolled onto her side, her gaze searching his. "Something's bothering you. No secrets between us, remember?"

His fingers sifted through the wealth of her hair. "You can't tell any of the Ravenwoods what I'm about to tell you."

"I won't. I promise."

"Rosa's in Morgan Creek."

"Rosa! What on earth is she doing there? I thought she went to Florida."

"She wanted me to introduce her to some vampires."

Kadie frowned at him. "What on earth for? I mean, she has four vampires in the family."

"I know. But they won't give her the Dark Gift."

"She wants to be a vampire? Seriously?"

He nodded. "I took her to a couple of goth clubs and introduced her to a friend of mine. He was supposed to scare her away."

"But?"

"He likes her." He huffed a sigh. "She likes him."

"Oh, Rylan. Micah will kill you."

"He'll try. But that's not the worst of it."

She propped herself up on one elbow. "There's more?"

"There's a hunter in town."

Kadie stared at him. "A hunter? After all this time?"

"Yeah. And not just any hunter. It's Rhinehart."

"You've never mentioned him before, at least not to me."

"He's the best out there." Seeing the fear in her eyes, he trailed his fingertips down her cheek. "Not to worry, love."

"Right." Sitting up, she threw back the covers. "I'm coming home with you."

"Oh, no, you're not."

"Rylan ..."

He covered her mouth with his hand. "I need you to stay here and make sure Micah and Sofia don't come home early. Rosa's only going to be in town another week or so."

She shook off his hand. "I should ..."

He silenced her the best way he knew how. Tugging her back down on the mattress, he claimed her lips with his in a long, slow kiss that left her breathless and then he made love to her until the sun came up.

When she sank into the Dark Sleep, he pulled the covers over her, dressed, and returned to Morgan Creek.

The sooner he was rid of Paul Rhinehart, the sooner Kadie could come back home.

CHAPTER TEN

The next morning, Rosa decided to have breakfast at home. She told herself she was tired of eating out, but the truth was, after talking to Saintcrow last night, she was leery of going out alone. She hated to admit it, but Paul Rhinehart scared her. She had thought he was just a harmless reporter. Knowing he was a hunter changed everything. They were just as capable of meting out death and destruction as the vampires they hunted. What if Rhinehart kidnapped her in hopes of trapping Saintcrow? She had no paranormal powers, no supernatural strength, no way on earth to defend herself.

Pushing her fears to the back of her mind, she scrambled a couple of eggs, dropped two slices of bread into the toaster, and poured a tall glass of orange juice.

When everything was ready, she sat at the kitchen table, scanning the latest headlines on her phone while she ate. As always, the news was mostly bad—the endless debate over climate change, high taxes, inflation, ad nauseum. Somehow, none of it seemed important when there was a notorious hunter in town, and she liked a certain sexy vampire way too much.

Pushing her plate aside, she gazed out the window. She had been so certain she wanted to become a vampire when she came here, but now… Now she wasn't so sure. Yes, they were capable of doing fantastic things that no human could do, but most humans went their whole life without being hunted. Yes, vampires lived a very, very long time, but did she really want to exist only after dark? Of course, Saintcrow and Kincaid could be awake during the day, and so could Micah and Ethan, thanks to some kind of blood exchange with Saintcrow. But new vampires had to live a long time to be able to abide the sun's light. As for living hundreds of years… Saintcrow had told her vampires buried themselves in the earth when they grew weary of existing. He had been alive since the Crusades, something she couldn't imagine. What had he done all those centuries before he came to Morgan Creek? Before he met Kadie?

She carried her dishes to the sink, rinsed them off, and loaded them into the dishwasher.

Now what? Where was Jake Kincaid when she needed him? She wouldn't be worried about going into town or a movie if he went with her.

Going upstairs, she took a quick shower, pulled on a pair of jeans and a short-sleeved lavender sweater, combed her hair and brushed her teeth, then sat on the edge of the bed.

What *was* she going to do all day?

She drummed her fingers on the mattress, smiled when her phone rang and she saw Kincaid's name. "Hi!"

"Are you busy?"

"I wish."

He chuckled. "Want some company?"

"Desperately."

"I'm at the front door."

"I'll be right there!" Happiness added wings to her feet and she flew down the stairs, her heart skipping a beat when she opened the door and saw him standing there looking as sexy as sin. "Come on in."

He followed her into the living room. There was no sign of Saintcrow.

Sitting on the sofa, Rosa patted the cushion beside her, felt a thrill of excitement when his thigh brushed hers. He was so big, so blatantly male, everything female within her yearned toward him.

"What would you like to do today?" Kincaid asked. He knew what he wanted to do. Every instinct he possessed urged him to take her in his arms and make her his, taste her kisses, explore every delectable, feminine inch of her. Savor the warm nectar of her blood . . . damn!

"Can we talk for a while?"

Talk? That was the last thing on his mind. Reining in his desire, he said, "Sure. What about?"

"Do you like being a vampire?"

He hesitated before answering. Saintcrow wanted him to talk Rosa out of seeking the Dark Gift. But that was a decision only she could make. And she needed to know the good with the bad, fact from fiction.

"Jake?"

"There's no easy answer to that question," he said, after a moment's thought. "I hated it at first. Hated everything about it. Hated it so much that one morning I didn't seek shelter from the sun." The pain of that foolish decision had been almost beyond bearing. "I never tried that stunt again. After a while . . ." He shrugged. "Gradually, I embraced what I'd become." He didn't tell her how many lives he had ruined along the way.

"And now?"

"It's what I am. Who I am. I can't change it. I'm not sure I would if I could."

"So, if someone offered you a cure, you wouldn't take it?"

"I would have jumped at the chance when I was first turned, but not anymore."

She mulled that over for a moment before asking, "Do you sleep in a coffin?" She'd never found the nerve to ask Micah or Sofia about that.

"No."

"Does Saintcrow?"

"I don't know, but I doubt it. Not many of us do that anymore."

Well, that was a relief. "What's the best part of being what you are?"

"The power, the strength. There's nothing like it in all the world. It's like being Iron Man and Superman and Thor all rolled into one."

"Every boy's dream," Rosa muttered. "To be a super hero. "And then she smiled at him. "I love Thor." Maybe that was why she was so attracted to Jake. He looked like Odin's son only with dark hair.

"Yeah? Glad to hear it."

"What's the worst part?"

"Watching people you care for wither and die. After a while, you stop caring because it hurts too much."

"You must have had a family before," she said quietly. "I never thought about that."

Kincaid shrugged. "They've been gone a long time."

"Were you married back then?"

"No. Slaves weren't allowed to marry." But he'd had two half-brothers who hadn't survived childhood. And a mother who had died far too young.

Rosa bit down on her lower lip. How could she have forgotten that he had been a slave? He'd had a rough life, she thought. Slavery, then a thief, then imprisoned by a vampire who fed on him for years before turning him into a vampire and finally letting him go.

Kincaid watched the gamut of emotions chase themselves across her face. Pity was the main one, mixed with surprise that he hadn't turned into some kind of raving lunatic bent on revenge and destruction. It had been a close call. He'd had a few bad years when it seemed like he had nothing to live for, but his existence had been pretty good since then. And it was looking a hell of a lot better since the night Saintcrow introduced him to Rosa.

Rosa felt a sudden warmth spread through her when Jake's gaze met hers. Ever so slowly, he leaned toward her, his hand curling around her nape to draw her closer. Anticipation danced in the pit of her stomach as he bent his head to hers and kissed her, lightly at first, then with growing intensity. The warmth turned to a flame when he drew her body against his and deepened the kiss. She clutched his shoulders, wanting to be closer, and as his tongue dueled with hers, the flame turning into a conflagration that threatened to consume her. She moaned softly as he caressed her, awakening sensations she had never known before.

Kincaid released her abruptly, leaving her momentarily confused, until Saintcrow cleared his throat.

"Maybe you two should book a room at the hotel," the master vampire said dryly.

Rosa's cheeks burned with embarrassment.

Kincaid shrugged. "Been standing there long?"

"Long enough," Saintcrow replied, amusement evident in his tone.

Rosa refused to meet his gaze. Another few minutes and he might have caught them doing a lot more than kissing, she thought, and felt her cheeks grow even hotter.

"Did you come in here for a reason?" Kincaid asked.

"Excuse me, but this *is* my house, or did you forget that?"

Kincaid grinned at him. "I guess I did. Can you blame me?"

Saintcrow glanced at Rosa, who was staring at the floor as if the Berber carpet was the most fascinating thing in the room. "I'll leave you to it," he said, good-naturedly.

Rosa breathed a sigh of relief when she sensed Saintcrow had left the house.

"Hey," Kincaid said, tilting her head up. "There's nothing to be ashamed of."

"I'm not ashamed. Just embarrassed. I mean . . . I don't know what I mean."

He laughed softly. "It was a close call, wasn't it?"

"Too close. I hardly know you."

"I know how to remedy that."

She glared at him.

"Maybe we should take a walk or something?" he suggested.

"Good idea."

Standing, he took her hands in his and lifted her to her feet and into his arms. She leaned into him, feeling warm and safe. What was there about him? It had to be more than just his inherent vampire allure. Saintcrow had it, too, and he was sexy as all get out, but she wasn't drawn to him the way she was to Jake. Not even close.

He kissed the top of her head. "We'd better go, lovely lady," he said, his voice husky, "or we'll never get out of here."

They walked to town and went to a double feature. They held hands and shared a few kisses. And then a few kisses more. As bad as horny teenagers, she thought with a grin as they left the theater. Sometimes she even felt like a teen with her first crush, unable to think of anything else but the boy who made her heart skip a beat. Next, she'd be drawing hearts with his name in the middle.

Kincaid grinned at her. "I can hear your stomach growling," he said. "Where would you like to have dinner?"

Rosa shrugged. "The hotel in town, I guess." It was the only one that served a wide variety of choices. Of the other two restaurants, one was Italian and the other served mainly fried chicken and burgers.

"We don't have to stay here, you know." Slipping his arm around her waist, he said, "Hang on."

And the next thing she knew, they were in downtown Cheyenne.

"What are you in the mood for?" Kincaid asked.

"Prime rib sounds good."

He took her to T-Joe's Steakhouse and Saloon where she had the best prime rib she'd ever tasted. Kincaid nursed a glass of red wine while she ate.

"I'm stuffed," Rosa said, pushing her plate away. "I may never be hungry again."

Kincaid grunted. "Wish I could say that."

"Do you have to... you know... every night?"

"I can skip two or three days, if I have to, but it's damn painful if I wait too long." His gaze moved to the hollow of her throat and lingered there. He didn't know why he needed to feed so often. Most old vampires could go for a week or more without any discomfort. But he wasn't one of them. For some reason, abstaining affected his temper and his control. The results were never pretty.

"Are you hungry now? Or is thirsty?"

"A thirst like you can't imagine."

"Do you like it? The blood?"

"It's like an addiction."

"Did you... do that... tonight?"

"Not yet." He looked at her, a faint smile playing over his lips. "Do you want to come with me?"

Rosa stared at him. "Go with you? You mean... while you... you hunt?"

"Hey, if you're thinking about becoming one of us, you might as well check it out and see how it's done. It's a big part of our existence, after all. What do you say?"

"I don't know."

"Chicken?"

"No!" To be honest, she *was* a little curious. More than a little, actually. And as he'd said, it was a big part of being a nightwalker. "All right. You convinced me. Let's go."

After he paid the check, Kincaid transported her to another part of town, where the streets were dark and mostly deserted, and the only signs of life were the dim lights in the window of a seedy bar.

"What now?" she asked.

"We wait for someone to come out. If I was alone, I'd go inside."

Rosa glanced around the dark parking lot. What was she doing here with a vampire? Did she really want to watch Kincaid feed on some helpless mortal? It seemed so... intimate. And what if he killed his prey? How could she be part of that and still live with herself?

She started when he laid a hand on her shoulder. "Relax. I'm not going to kill anybody."

There were times, she thought, when she was glad he could read her mind. She frowned. Had he read her thoughts earlier today? she wondered. Was that why he'd called? Because she had been wishing he would?

They didn't have to wait long. A middle-aged couple staggered out the saloon door, laughing as they stumbled their way across the gravel parking lot.

Kincaid fell into step behind them, silent as a shadow.

Rosa trailed after him.

When the couple reached their car, they both stopped suddenly and just stood there, unmoving.

Rosa watched as Kincaid pulled the woman into his arms. She didn't struggle, didn't cry out, just stood there immobile while he bit her. He fed for only a moment or two. When he finished, he ran his tongue over the woman's neck, and the couple climbed into the car like nothing had happened.

Rosa stood beside Jake and watched them drive away. "What did you do?" she asked. "Why didn't she resist? Why did he just stand there and do nothing?"

"I spoke to their minds."

"Like hypnotism?"

"In a way. When I finished, I wiped the memory of what happened from their minds and sent them merrily on their way, none the wiser."

It was nothing like in the horror movies, Rosa thought. There hadn't been a struggle. There hadn't been blood spurting everywhere. He hadn't ripped out their throats. Still, it had been kind of repulsive, watching him, knowing what he was doing.

"You ready to go home?" he asked.

Looking pensive, she nodded.

As he transported them back to Morgan Creek, Kincaid couldn't help but wonder if he'd made a mistake, if she would look at him differently now.

"Thanks for tonight," Rosa said when they reached the front porch of Saintcrow's house.

She opened the door, then stood there with her back to him. "Did you read my mind this morning? Is that why you called me?"

"Yes. And no."

She turned to face him. "Which is it?"

"I was thinking about you, wondering what you were doing, when I sensed you were thinking about me. So…" He shrugged. "Can I ask you something now?"

She nodded.

"Did I make a mistake, taking you hunting with me? Are you going to think of me as some kind of a monster now?"

"No. I admit, it was kind of gross to watch. And kind of fascinating. I've always wondered what it's like for Micah and Sofie. And now I know."

"So, we're still good?"

She smiled at him as she went up on her tiptoes and kissed him lightly. "Better than good."

His gaze searched hers and then he wrapped his arms around her, drawing her body tightly against his, letting her feel the evidence of his desire as his mouth covered hers in a long, searing kiss that stole the strength from her legs and left her insides weak and trembling.

"Rosa." He groaned her name as he ravaged her mouth. "Let me."

She froze. Let him what? Make love to her? She wasn't ready for that, not yet.

When his tongue trailed fire along the length of her neck, she knew exactly what he wanted.

"Just a taste," he whispered, his voice almost a growl.

If she refused, would he mesmerize her the way he had his prey and take what he wanted anyway?

Abruptly, he put her away from him. "I'm sorry," he rasped. "Forgive me."

Weak with relief, she murmured, "There's nothing to forgive."

Taking her hand in his, he kissed her palm. "Good night, lovely lady."

It sounded like goodbye, but before she could say anything, he was striding away. A moment later, he disappeared into the darkness.

Chapter Eleven

Rhinehart paced the necromancer's chamber. "I thought you were going to conjure a spell to protect me from Saintcrow. What's taking so long?"

"You and I have underestimated the vampire's power," Luca snapped. "He is ancient. I have never known a vampire with such strength."

"Are you saying any spell you concoct to protect me won't work?"

"When we made our deal, I had no idea you were afraid to face him alone." The necromancer stared at him, eyes narrowed to mere slits. "Have you, perhaps, lost your nerve?"

"No, but he has a young woman with him. I'm afraid he might force the Dark Gift on her."

"Indeed? And what is that to me? We had a deal, hunter. Do not break it."

"There's another vampire with Saintcrow," Rhinehart said, hoping to change the subject. "They spend a lot of time together."

"Interesting. Is this other vampire of concern?"

"He's almost as powerful as Saintcrow."

"I know of only one other vampire who compares to him." Luca remarked, and then frowned as he turned to stare at Rhinehart. "What is the name of this other vampire?"

"Kincaid. Do you know him?"

"Indeed. He killed someone important to me long ago," Luca said, his pale eyes glittering with malice.

Rhinehart lifted one brow. It had to be a woman, he thought. Kincaid had foolishly taken the life of a woman the necromancer cared for.

Luca's power shook the furniture in the room and shattered the windows. "Kincaid is here," he murmured. "Here, in Wyoming?" He stared into the distance. "Last I knew, he was somewhere in the east."

Rhinehart took a wary step back. He had the distinct impression the necromancer had forgotten he was in the room, that he was, in fact, speaking to someone who wasn't there. A moment later, he was sure of it.

"So close, Katya," Luca murmured. "So close and I did not know."

Rhinehart clenched his hands at his sides as the whole house vibrated with his fury. Why hadn't Luca known the vampire was nearby? Surely, if the necromancer wanted Kincaid, he had the magical ability to find him. Why did he need help?

Luca's head snapped up. "Bring me Kincaid's head!"

"But... what about Saintcrow... ?"

"He can wait."

With a nod, Rhinehart backed out of the room. Damn! What had he gotten himself into? Not for the first time, he regretted that he had ever contacted Luca. It had been years ago, when he was a young hunter searching for enlightenment about destroying vampires. Going to Luca for help was surely the biggest mistakes he had ever made.

He took the stairs two at a time and fled the house.

Chapter Twelve

Considering how they had parted the night before, Rosa was surprised when Kincaid called her late the next morning.

"Hey, lovely lady, what are you doing today?"

"I don't have any plans, but I'm open to suggestions."

"Pack a lunch. I'll pick you up in an hour."

"Where are we going?"

"It'll ruin the surprise. One hour."

"I'll be ready!"

Filled with excitement, she settled for toast, cereal, and orange juice for breakfast. Not knowing what Jake had in mind, she took a quick shower, then pulled on a pair of jeans and a gauzy peasant blouse, tied her hair back in a ponytail. She found a large tote bag in a closet and tossed in her comb and brush, a skirt and sweater, a light jacket in case it got cold, and a pair of heels.

Grabbing her phone and her handbag, she headed to the kitchen where she packed a tuna fish sandwich in a plastic container and tossed it into her tote, along with an apple, and a bag of chips.

Knowing it was unnecessary, she wrote a short note for Saintcrow, telling him she had gone off to spend the day with Kincaid, and then went out on the front porch to wait.

Five minutes later, Kincaid materialized on the porch beside her. "Ready?"

When she nodded, he slipped his arm around her waist, and the next thing Rosa knew, they were in a swath of green grass and ferns. Sunlight sparkled on a lake in the middle of the meadow. Mountains rose on three sides. Tall trees sighed in the warm breeze. The air was fragrant with the scent of wildflowers. "Where are we?"

"Some lake in New York. I don't remember the name."

"It's beautiful." She did a slow turn, thinking it looked like something out a fairy tale. She wouldn't have been surprised to see a castle rise up in the distance, or fairies dancing on the water.

"I'll be back in a minute."

He was gone before she could ask where he was going. He returned almost immediately with a blanket draped over one shoulder, a bottle of wine in one hand, and a pair of crystal goblets in the other.

Rosa smiled as he set the bottle and glasses aside and spread the blanket on a flat stretch of ground. He dropped down on the blanket and patted the place beside him.

"Do you come here often?" she asked.

He shook his head. "I found this place years ago. I haven't been back since then." He glanced at the lake. "What do you say we go for a swim?"

"I don't have a suit."

"You don't need one. There's no one else here."

She lifted one brow. "You're here." She hadn't been skinny-dipping since she was five.

"You can wear your bra and panties," he said, with a shrug. "They cover about as much as today's bathing suits."

Rosa had to laugh. He was right about that. In fact, her underwear covered a lot more than most bikinis. "Turn around."

Rising, he turned his back to her.

After a moment, she tugged her blouse over her head, kicked off her sandals, then stood and peeled off her jeans. Unable to help herself, she glanced over her shoulder, blushed to the roots of her hair when she met Kincaid's grin.

He shrugged. "I'd say I'm sorry for peeking, but you seem to be just as guilty as I am."

She didn't say anything, just turned and plunged into the lake. The water was cool but not too cold. She heard a splash as Jake followed her.

They swam and splashed each other for an hour or so, then returned to the blanket on the shore. She tried not to stare at him, but it was impossible. He wore a pair of black bikini briefs that left little to the imagination. His body was beautifully sculpted, hard-muscled, without an ounce of fat. He should have been a model, she thought, one of those sexy hunks who modeled swim trunks, or did ads for expensive men's cologne while wearing a tux and a come-hither smile.

Kincaid grinned inwardly, pleased that she found him attractive. They made a good couple, he thought. She was softly rounded in all the right places, her legs long and shapely, her skin unblemished. And she was beautiful, with her black hair, dark eyes, and golden skin.

He rolled onto his stomach as his desire for her made itself known. "Why don't you pour us some wine?" he suggested, hoping to take his mind off the growing ache in his groin.

"All right." Suddenly uncomfortable clad in nothing but her underwear, she reached into her bag for her jacket and slipped it on before picking up the bottle. "You forgot a corkscrew."

"Give it to me." Propped on one elbow, he pulled the cork with his teeth and filled the glasses.

"What shall we drink to?" she asked.

His gaze ran over her, hotter than the sun shining down on them. "Getting to know each other better?"

"How much better?" she teased. As if she didn't know.

"I'll leave that up to you."

Thinking to change the subject, she pointed at his left wrist. "Every time I see you, you're wearing that gold band." Had a woman from his past given it to him? Someone he had cared for and didn't want to forget? "Does it have some special meaning?"

"You could say that."

"Is it a secret?"

"No. I got it from a black witch."

"What do those symbols mean?"

"I'm not sure. All I know is, it works."

"What is it supposed to do?"

"It shields my whereabouts from another witch, a necromancer. One who wants my head."

"A necromancer?" she asked, frowning. "Is it the same one working with Rhinehart?"

"Yeah."

"What did you do to him, that he wants you dead?"

"I killed someone he loved. He's had people looking for me on and off for over a century and a half."

Rosa stared at him. "So, he's after you *and* Saintcrow?" She shook her head, thinking the man must be awfully brave, or a darn fool, to go after two such powerful vampires.

Sitting up, Kincaid put his glass aside, took hers from her hand and placed it beside his before drawing her into his arms. "Forget about Luca."

Rosa's breath caught in her throat as his lips lightly brushed hers. When she didn't resist, he deepened the kiss. Falling back on the blanket, he tucked her body intimately against his. His bare skin, though cool against hers, ignited a flame deep inside her. They might as well as have been naked, she thought, for his trunks and her jacket were scant coverings at best. His desire pressed against her belly, a blatant indication of his arousal. It excited and frightened her at the same time. She had brothers. She'd accidentally seen them naked when they'd been boys. But Jake wasn't a boy.

In the distant part of her mind that was still rational, she gasped, "Someone might come."

"Not to worry. I've shielded our presence from the rest of the world."

Oh, lordy, did he mean to ravish her here, in broad daylight?

His lips moved against the side of her neck as he read her thoughts. "Would you mind?"

"Yes. No." She pressed herself against him, desperate to be closer, to be a part of him, and yet afraid at the same time. She knew he would never deliberately hurt her, yet she couldn't deny that he had the power to compel her to do anything he desired. Not knowing how she really felt or what she really wanted, she decided on the truth. "I don't know."

It took every ounce of his self-control to release her. To sit up. To put a little space between them. "I don't want to take you by force," he said, his voice thick. "Or when you're not sure." Rising, he reached for her hands.

"You're angry with me."

"No." He pulled her to her feet, and released her. "Only with myself." It had taken centuries to learn to control his thirst and his desire. Before that happened, he'd done a lot of things he regretted, some he was ashamed of. He had gorged himself on blood with no thought for his prey, ravished many a lovely maid. Until Rosa, he had been confident of his control, but, damn, he wanted her more than any other woman he'd ever known. And he wanted all of her.

The tension between them was palpable as they dressed. A muscle twitched in his jaw as he wrapped his arms around her.

Rossa closed her eyes as his unique masculine scent washed over her, followed by a rush of preternatural power.

A moment later, they were on the porch at Saintcrow's house.

"Jake? Will I see you again?"

His beautiful chocolate brown eyes caressed her face. "Do you think that's wise?"

"I don't know," she replied. "But I'd like to."

"I'll call you." He turned to leave, then turned back and pulled her into his arms for a long, lingering kiss that left her weak and yearning for so much more. "Sometime tomorrow," he murmured.

Rosa blinked, and he was gone. She pressed her fingertips to lips still bruised and tingling from his kisses. "Tomorrow," she murmured.

She was playing with wildfire, Rosa thought as she opened the door and went inside. She only hoped she was strong enough to survive the flames.

Chapter Thirteen

Kincaid willed himself to the next town. He knew he was about to tempt Saintcrow's wrath, but he just didn't give a damn. All he knew was that he needed a distraction, and there was no better distraction than the thrill of the hunt, or the high that came from draining his prey.

He stalked the deserted streets the way a lion stalked the jungle, every sense alert as he searched for that one unwary creature. He didn't want female prey tonight. He wanted a man—a strong man who would fight tooth and nail for his life.

He knew a rush of adrenaline when he saw the Marine. The man was as big as a tank, solid muscle. His scarred face and hands spoke of many battles fought and won.

Kincaid set his shoulders and strode toward him, purposely bumping the guy as he passed by.

The Marine was a little drunk. "Hey, buddy, why don't ya watch where you're goin'?" he growled.

"I was watching."

The Marine's eyes narrowed. "If you're spoilin' for a fight, friend, you found it."

Kincaid grinned at him. "Bring it on."

It was late, the streets deserted. Not wanting the battle to end too soon, Kincaid held back. He welcomed the man's blows, relished the pain. The Marine had the strength and stamina of a Brahma bull. He seemed immune to the punishment Kincaid dished out, until Kincaid's lust for blood kicked in and he fought in earnest.

Wrapping his arm around the Marine's neck from behind, Kincaid held him immobile. He knew the exact moment when his prey realized the tide had turned, and that the stranger he'd been grappling with had been playing with him the whole time.

The Marine froze when he felt the sharp prick of Kincaid's fangs in the side of his throat. "What the hell are you doing?"

Leaning close to the man's ear, he whispered, "I'm about to have dinner."

The Marine had guts. Kincaid had to give him that. He didn't beg or whine for mercy, just stood there, hands clenched, his whole body on edge as he waited for a chance to escape.

But there wasn't one.

The Marine cursed a blue streak as Kincaid sank his fangs into his throat and drank long and deep.

The man's courage in the face of imminent death gave Kincaid pause. A quick brush of the Marine's mind told Kincaid that his prey had a wife and five kids at home. He had served several tours of duty in foreign lands, been wounded numerous times. Kincaid swore under his breath. Hell, the guy was a decorated war hero. He should be thanking him for his years of service instead of making a meal out of him.

Huffing a sigh, Kincaid loosened his hold on the man's neck, ran his tongue over the punctures to heal the wounds. "I'm sorry," he muttered as he took a step back. "I was having a bad night."

The Marine laughed. "Not as bad as mine, vampire."

"Turn around."

The Marine hesitated before facing Kincaid. "Change your mind?"

"Looks like it. Come on, I'll buy you a drink."

⚜ ⚜ ⚜

Saintcrow paused in the act of feeding. Dammit, was he going to have to destroy Kincaid? The vampire was seconds away from taking a life. What the hell had gotten him into such a state of mind? A foolish question, he mused. Who else but a woman possessed the ability to screw up a man's mind until he couldn't think straight?

Wiping his memory from his prey's mind, Saintcrow was halfway to Kincaid's location when he felt the vampire back off.

Curious, he shielded his presence and continued on his way. He arrived in time to see Kincaid and a burly Marine striding down the street, as chummy as two old friends. What the hell?

With a shake of his head, Saintcrow willed himself back to Morgan Creek.

⚜ ⚜ ⚜

Knowing he was playing a dangerous game, Rhinehart checked into the hotel in Morgan Creek. As long as the girl was in town, there was a good chance Kincaid would show up. Of course, Saintcrow was there, too. He didn't know who posed the bigger risk to his continued good health—Rylan Saintcrow, Kincaid, or Luca. All three had the power to kill him in long and infinitely painful and inventive ways.

How the hell had he gotten mixed up in this mess? All he'd wanted to do was take Saintcrow's head, deliver it to Luca, and retire to Maui with his family.

How long could he make excuses for failing to destroy Saintcrow? And now the witch wanted Kincaid's head, too. He couldn't put Luca off forever. And there was no way to hide from him.

Or was there? Why couldn't Luca find Kincaid? The man was a powerful necromancer with all kinds of supernatural powers and Dark Magic at his command. He had seen the man do things—terrible things that still haunted his dreams. Miraculous things. But if Luca couldn't find Kincaid…

Rhinehart felt a slim ray of hope. Kincaid must have some kind of powerful, magic based talisman that hid his whereabouts from the necromancer. That was the only logical explanation. Maybe there was a chance a similar talisman or spell would work for him, as well.

But where to find the witch who had concocted it?

Was searching for a witch a chance worth taking?

And what would be the necromancer's reaction if he found out what he was doing?

It was something to think about.

Chapter Fourteen

Kadie sighed as she followed Micah and Holly into the hotel elevator. Italy was a beautiful place and she had seen some amazing sights—Venice and Pompeii, the Leaning Tower of Pisa, Palermo and Rome. Beautiful cities filled with amazing architecture and cathedrals, the Colosseum, Trevi Fountain, the Sistine Chapel. Sofia's family was delightful as they made allowances for the vampires in the group. But she missed Saintcrow. True, he had come to visit her on several occasions, but it wasn't the same. She even missed Morgan Creek.

Later that evening, when everyone had returned to the hotel after dinner, Kadie informed them she was going home. She had made her decision last night and packed her bags. Italy was beautiful, she loved the people. But it wasn't home.

"But we're leaving for Scotland tomorrow," Lena Ravenwood said.

"I know, but I miss Rylan." Kadie took Lena's hands in hers. "I've had a wonderful time, but I've been away from my husband far too long."

Lena nodded sympathetically. "I understand."

Kadie bid farewell to Mr. Ravenwood and the rest of Sofia's family.

"Call Rosa for me, will you?" Sofia asked. "I haven't heard from her in a while."

"Yeah," Micah said. "She's been avoiding my calls, too. Makes me wonder what mischief she's up to."

"Probably flirting with all the good-looking guys in Florida," Kadie said, hoping the other vampires couldn't tell she was lying. She wasn't sure why Micah and Sofia were so against their sister becoming a vampire, but it was none of her business.

"Yeah, that sounds like Rosie," Micah agreed.

"You all enjoy the rest of your vacation," Kadie said. "I'll see you when you get home."

There were hugs all around and last goodbyes, as well as another reminder from Micah to check in on Rosa.

Stepping out onto the hotel balcony, Kadie picked up her suitcases, closed her eyes and focused on Rylan and her desire to be with him.

When the world stopped spinning, she was in their lair. Dropping her suitcases on the floor, she quickly undressed, then slid under the covers and rested her head on her husband's shoulder.

⚜ ⚜ ⚜

Saintcrow came awake instantly when his nostrils filled with Kadie's scent. Rolling over, he pulled her into his arms. "Kadie." He whispered her name, then frowned. "Is everything okay? I wasn't expecting you home for another month."

"I missed you." She ran her hands over his broad chest and shoulders, down his muscular arms, to settle on his belly. "Every single inch."

He growled low in his throat as he flipped her onto her back and rose over her, his eyes hot. "Yeah?" he muttered, a wicked gleam in his eye. "Well, every single inch missed you, too."

"Show me, Rylan." She threaded her fingers through his hair and pulled his head down. "Show me how much."

He had missed her too much for foreplay. That could come next time. For now, he buried himself deep within her. No matter how many times they made love, it was never enough. She was his whole life, as he was hers. And she gave as good as she got.

⚜ ⚜ ⚜

Saintcrow woke smiling when he roused late the next morning. So, it hadn't been a dream. Kadie had come home. For a time, he simply lay there beside her, admiring the smoothness of her skin, the silky feel of her hair, her luscious curves, the way her lashes lay like dark fans on her cheeks, the faint smile on her face that told him she had been well-loved the night before.

He eased out of bed, knowing she would likely rest until sunset.

He showered and dressed before going upstairs. An indrawn breath told him Rosa was in the kitchen. There was a cake in the oven. Busy little homemaker, he mused, as he materialized in the doorway.

She smiled at him over her shoulder. "Good morning."

He nodded. "And to you."

"Too bad you can't eat," she remarked as the timer on the stove went off.

He grunted. "What's the occasion?"

"None," she said, as she removed the cake from the oven. "I just felt like baking."

"You gonna eat that whole thing by yourself?"

"Not until I frost it. Who eats cake without frosting?"

Saintcrow shrugged. He had never tasted cake and had long ago forgotten the taste of anything else he'd ever eaten.

"I'm not going to eat it all," she said. "A girl has to watch her weight. I thought I'd keep a slice or two and take what's left down to the hotel restaurant."

"I'm sure they'll appreciate it."

"I'll have to let it cool a while before I frost it."

"What are your plans for today?" He pulled a chair from the table, turned it around, and straddled the seat.

Taking the chair across from his, she said, "I don't really have any."

"Kadie came home last night."

"Oh? Is something wrong?" Rosa asked, and then frowned. "She didn't say anything to Micah or Sofia about me being here, did she?"

"No. But she did mention that both Sofia and Micah asked her to check up on you."

"Of course they did."

"So, have you made up your mind?" he asked with a grin. "To be or not to be?"

"Not entirely. But even if I decide to ask Micah to turn me, I think I'll stay human for a few more years."

"I'm sure your family will be glad to hear it."

"I guess." She sighed. "Would you mind if I talked to Kadie?"

He shrugged. "Why would I mind?"

"Your name might come up."

"Ah. You're going to ask her what it's like, being married to a vampire. What it's like *being* a vampire."

Rosa nodded. "I'd like a woman's point of view."

"It's okay with me if it's okay with her."

"Thanks."

⚜ ⚜ ⚜

Rosa drove into town in the afternoon. She had been here over a week and to tell the truth, she missed being home. Saintcrow could be good company. And she loved spending time with Kincaid, but she spent a great deal of the day alone, and even she got tired of movies and eating out and shopping. She missed working. She missed her own place. Maybe she would cut her vacation short and go home early. Maybe putting some distance between herself and Jake was a good idea. She was falling for him way too hard, way too fast, and if she decided not to be a vampire, then what?

She pulled up in front of the restaurant to deliver the cake, and decided to stay for lunch. She had just ordered a ham sandwich and a bowl of potato cheese soup—the house specialty—when Paul Rhinehart entered the restaurant. A moment later, he was striding toward her.

"Mind if I join you?" he asked.

Rosa bit down on her lower lip. He was a hunter and there were two vampires in town. Saintcrow had warned her to be careful.

"I just want to talk," Rhinehart said with a reassuring smile. "I'm not stupid enough to try anything in Morgan Creek. Truce?"

Rosa nodded, wondering if she could trust him. She hadn't forgotten that he had lied to her about who he was.

He pulled out a chair and sat down.

"Are you still hunting Saintcrow?" Rosa asked.

"Yes. And no."

"What does that mean?"

"He's no longer a priority."

"Oh?" She felt a sudden chill, an overwhelming certainty that he was now hunting Jake instead. "Are you after someone else now?"

"I can't tell you."

"I guess whoever it is must be another vampire."

"Like I said, I can't discuss it."

"It's Jake Kincaid, isn't it?"

Rhinehart hesitated a moment, then nodded.

"Why?"

"I can't tell you that, either. Do you know where I can find him?"

"Even if I did, I'd never tell you."

"I don't want to destroy him."

Rosa uttered a very unladylike snort. As if she would ever believe that!

"I mean it." Leaning forward, the hunter lowered his voice and said, "I need to ask him something."

"Like what?" Seeing the look on his face, she said, "I know. You can't tell me."

"It's better for both of us if I don't. Believe me, you don't want to be involved in this."

She was already in it, Rosa thought as the waitress came to take Rhinehart's order

"Coffee," he said. "Cream, no sugar. And a slice of apple pie."

"I'm thinking about going home," Rosa remarked, when the waitress left. "There's nothing much to do here. At least not when you're alone most of the time. Are you married?"

"Yeah. Fifteen years."

"Kids?"

"Three."

"Does your wife know what you do for a living?"

"No. She thinks I sell life insurance."

Rosa laughed. "Life insurance? That's a good one."

The waitress brought their orders a few moments later.

An uneasy silence settled between Rosa and the hunter while they ate. She was dying to know why he wanted to talk to Jake, and he seemed equally determined not to tell her.

Rhinehart was reaching for his wallet when Saintcrow pulled out the chair next to his and settled into it.

Rhinehart stared at the vampire, then glanced around the crowded restaurant. Rosa saw him visibly relax, apparently feeling he was safe when surrounded by so many people.

"What are you doing here, hunter?" Saintcrow asked, a predatory growl in his voice.

"I wanted to ask Miss Ravenwood a question, which she refused to answer."

Saintcrow grunted softly. "You think Kincaid has a way to avoid Luca."

Rhinehart glared at him. "Dammit, stay out of my mind, bloodsucker."

"Stay out of my town."

"Does he have some way to hide his presence from Luca?"

Saintcrow shrugged one shoulder. "Even if he does, I'm pretty sure he wouldn't tell you what it is or where he got it. One more thing, hunter. If you destroy any of my acquaintances, I'll hunt *you* down and you won't like what happens next. Are we clear?"

Looking visibly pale, Rhinehart swallowed hard. And then he nodded. "I've been thinking about changing my line of work anyway."

Rosa glanced from the vampire to the hunter, all interest in her lunch forgotten as tension filled the air around them. Strange, no one else in the place seemed to notice, but maybe that was Saintcrow's doing.

Rhinehart dropped enough cash on the table to cover Rosa's check and his own, then stood. "It was nice seeing you again, Miss Ravenwood," he said, politely.

Rosa nodded, wondering if Saintcrow would let the hunter simply walk away. She could see from Rhinehart's expression as he turned toward the door that he was wondering the same thing.

She breathed a sigh of relief when the hunter left the restaurant. "What was he talking about?"

"From what I gather, Luca can't locate Kincaid. And Rhinehart thinks Kincaid has some kind of magical talisman to protect him."

"Is that possible?" As soon as she asked the question, Rosa remembered the gold band Jake wore. He'd told her it protected him from a necromancer.

"Oh, yeah. Black witches can conjure all manner of enchanted trinkets for all manner of things."

Too much information, Rosa thought, with a shiver. Black witches sounded even scarier than vampires. "Do you know any?"

"Not anymore."

"But you did?"

"A few. There aren't so many of them now as there used to be. Of course, there aren't as many vampires, either."

Well, that was good to know, Rosa thought, and felt a rush of guilt when she saw the knowing look in Saintcrow's eyes. As always, he knew exactly what she was thinking.

"Why do you let Rhinehart stay in town when you know what he is?"

"He's no threat to me."

"What about Jake?"

"Kincaid can take care of himself. If the hunter becomes a problem, I'll handle it."

She was trying not to picture how he would do that when her cell phone rang.

Rising, Saintcrow said, "Tell Kincaid I want to see him."

She waited until he left the table before answering the call.

"You busy tonight?" Jake asked.

"What do you think?"

"Can I hope you've been sitting at home, just waiting for my call?"

"No."

"Alas, another hope crushed," he said, a grin in his voice. "What time should I pick you up?"

"Whenever you want," she said, wondering if she should play hard to get. And then she grinned. It was really too late for that. And she only had a few more days of vacation left.

"I'll be there at six."

"I'll be ready. Oh, wait! Saintcrow wants to see you."

"Yeah?"

"That's what he said."

"All right. See you soon."

Smiling, Rosa ended the call. She sat there a moment, just feeling happy, then decided to go to the beauty parlor, treat herself to a manicure, and perhaps a new dress.

After all, she had a hot date with a smokin' hot guy.

Chapter Fifteen

Late that afternoon, Kincaid found Saintcrow in the graveyard, one shoulder propped against the tall, marble cross. "What the hell are you doing here?"

Saintcrow shrugged. "It's quiet and peaceful."

"It's creepy."

Saintcrow laughed. "You're a vampire, for crying out loud. Don't tell me you're afraid of ghosts."

"Of course not." Kincaid glanced at the rows of wooden crosses. Must be a hundred or more, he mused, men and women who had mysteriously gone missing, never to be heard from again. "Doesn't it bother you to come here, knowing you're responsible for the deaths of most of the people buried here?"

"Think of it as my penance. I come here to remind myself of what I was before I met Kadie." Of course, he wasn't personally responsible for all the deaths, but the guilt was his.

"Well, she's changed you, that's for damn sure. So, what did you want to see me about?"

"Rhinehart's looking for you. He wants to know why Luca can't find you."

Kincaid rubbed his thumb over the wide gold band on his left wrist. "Tell him to keep looking. I've got nothing to say to him."

"I kinda thought you'd say that."

"Why don't you just exterminate the man and be done with it? Or let me do it? He's getting to be a pain in the ass."

"He's one of the best, but he's no real threat to either of us," Saintcrow replied with a shrug. "Besides, I can't just kill him out of hand. Kadie would never forgive me."

"I'd gladly do it for you, but I don't think Rosa would be happy about it, either," Kincaid said dryly. "Looks like we've both changed."

"Yeah, well."

"What about Luca?" Kincaid asked. "Can you take him, too?"

Saintcrow shrugged. "Maybe. Witches are hard to read. I don't know if he's as powerful as Rhinehart thinks."

"And if he is? The two of them together could make a formidable foe."

"Let's not go looking for trouble." Saintcrow pushed away from the monument. "I guess you're going out with Rosa tonight."

"I can't seem to stay away from her."

"Things seem to be getting serious between you two."

Kincaid nodded. "I've never felt this way about any other woman. To tell you the truth, I don't know what to do about it."

Saintcrow arched one brow. "There's only two things you can do. You either try to make it work or you cut and run. Either way, you'll likely break her heart."

"Fat lot of help you are."

"You need to decide what you want before things go too far. She's a nice girl. I'd hate to see her get hurt."

"Yeah, me, too."

"Just take it slow. Although time might solve your problem. She's only going to be here another couple of days before her vacation's over and she goes back home. If things don't work out between the two of you, she can write it off as a summer fling and move on. No harm, no foul."

Kincaid nodded slowly. She *was* young. Likely she would go home and forget all about him. Oh, she might miss him for a day or two, maybe a week, but the young recovered quickly.

As for himself, he wasn't sure he would ever forget her.

⚜ ⚜ ⚜

Rosa's heart did a crazy little flip flop when she saw Jake that night. Was it her imagination, or did he get sexier and better looking every time she saw him? He reeked of masculinity. Her insides turned to mush when he smiled at her, her legs went weak when he drew her into his arms for a kiss. She leaned into him, wanting more, even as she told herself to slow down. There was so much about him she didn't know, so many decisions to make, so much uncertainty in their future. Even as her affection for him grew stronger, deeper, the gulf between them seemed to grow wider. What kind of life could they have together when he was a vampire and she wasn't? The more she thought about being turned, the less appealing it seemed.

"Where would you like to go tonight?" he asked, still holding her close.

"I don't know," she replied, as her stomach growled.

He laughed. "I think I'd better feed you before we do anything else."

"I think you're right."

"What are you in the mood for?"

"Lasagna and garlic bread," she said and then frowned. "Does garlic bother you?"

"No. It only affects movie vampires, like Dracula. And it was only the flowers that were effective."

"But why garlic?"

"In ancient times, garlic was used as an herb and a medicine. Somewhere along the way, people began to believe it possessed magical healing powers against the plague and some supernatural evils, like demons and witches. I guess it was only natural that people thought it would keep vampires at bay, too."

Rosa mulled that over on the drive to the Italian restaurant in town. She ordered lasagna and Kincaid ordered a bottle of red wine. She glanced around, admiring the paintings on the walls, enjoying the rich smells of garlic and basil and oregano that filled the air. Italian music played softly over the speakers.

She sighed as she bit into a slice of garlic bread warm and fresh from the oven. How did vampires survive without bread? There were so many varieties and she loved them all. And pasta.

She tilted her head to the side when she noticed Jake watching her intently. "Is something wrong?"

"No. I was just trying to remember what bread tasted like. Of course, it looked different when I was young, probably tasted a lot different, too."

She tried to imagine not being able to remember what her favorite foods tasted like. It didn't seem possible that she could forget the taste of chocolate, or her dad's spaghetti sauce, or her sister, Delia's, apple pie. Kincaid had been alive for centuries, existing on nothing but a warm liquid diet.

"Are you sure watching me eat doesn't bother you?" she asked when her dinner arrived.

"I'm sure. Does it bother you?"

"Well, sometimes. I mean, I feel guilty enjoying my dinner when . . ."

"When all I can have is blood and wine?"

She nodded.

"I'm used to it."

Feeling suddenly self-conscious about eating in front of him, she decided to forego dessert.

They made small talk over dinner, chatting about movies and music. Rosa told him a little about her brothers and sisters and how fun and chaotic it had been, growing up with so many older brothers and sisters.

Kincaid let her do most of the talking. There wasn't a lot in his past he wanted to remember, no happy memories, no laughter. Nothing that had mattered to him except his mother and his brothers, who had all died too soon. "What would you like to do now?" he asked, as they left the restaurant.

"It's such a pretty night. Let's just go for a drive."

"Okay by me," he said, handing her into the convertible.

Rosa turned the radio to a soft rock station, then sat back. It really was a beautiful night, she thought as they drove across the bridge to the highway. Millions of stars twinkled overhead. The air was warm but not hot, the man beside her dark and mysterious and oh, so sexy. Dark hair, dark eyes, taut muscles beneath his black silk shirt.

They traveled in silence for a few miles, and then Kincaid pulled onto a dirt road that led through a stand of timber. She felt a little thrill of anticipation when he turned off the engine.

A moment later, he opened her car door.

"Come on," he said, taking her by the hand. "Let's go for a walk."

Anticipation turned to trepidation as she got out of the car. Thoughts of wild animals flashed through her mind.

They strolled along the twisty dirt path, their feet making little sound on the soft earth.

Rosa let out a huff of surprise when they came to a small clearing. The remains of a house stood between a ramshackle barn and what was left of a peeled-pole corral. "What is this place?"

"Back in the early 1800s a family lived in that shack. They did all right for a while, but then they fell on hard times. The husband was killed by a mountain lion and the woman packed up her kids and moved away. This is all that's left."

"A mountain lion?" Rosa said, glancing around.

"Relax, love, they won't come near me."

"You mean there might be some here?"

He shrugged. "There could be, but I doubt it."

"Did you know the family who lived here?"

"No. Saintcrow told me about them years ago."

She tried to imagine what it had been like to homestead in the wilderness, to endure hot summers and freezing winters, to raise children in such lowly circumstances. Back then, everything had to be made from scratch. Food had to be hunted or raised. A bad crop, a dry season, could make the difference between life and death. It made her all the more grateful that she had been born in the present time, when food and medical care were readily available.

"You said you were a cowboy for a while. Did you like it?"

"Yeah. It gives you a kind of freedom, even when you're working for someone else. Days spent in the saddle, riding across the country. Rounding up strays, driving a herd to market, sitting around a campfire at night swapping lies. It was hard work, but I liked it."

"Was it like it is in the movies?"

"Depends on the movie," he said, with a shrug. "Not many of them got it right. I never saw two men stand in the street and shoot it out to settle their differences. There were a lot of gunfights, but usually over a game of poker or a woman."

"Did you have a woman back then?"

"Dozens," he said, with a grin. "But none as pretty as you."

She forgot all about the past when Jake took her in his arms. Her eyelids fluttered down as his mouth covered hers in a long, slow kiss that gradually grew longer, deeper, and more intense. She clung to his shoulders, her fingers digging into him as she pressed her body to his.

Kincaid swore under his breath as his desire to bury himself in her sweet flesh warred with his desire to sink his fangs into her throat.

He swore again as he put her away from him. "Damn, girl," he muttered. "What are you trying to do to me?"

"I was about to ask you the same thing."

"I'd better take you home before one of us does something she'll regret."

He was right, she thought sadly. And wondered if she was lamenting the fact that he had stopped before it was too late, or sorry that he hadn't.

It was fairly early when Kincaid dropped her off at Saintcrow's house. He kissed her good night, a rather chaste kiss when compared to the last one.

Rosa stood on the porch as he drove away, sighed as she opened the door and stepped inside. What was she going to do about Jake Kincaid?

She paused in the living room doorway when she saw Kadie sitting on the sofa, reading a novel. They had met on a few occasions in the past, some good, some bad.

Come on in," Kadie said, laying her book aside. "Rylan told me you had questions."

Rosa nodded as she settled into the chair across from the sofa.

"You can ask me anything," Kadie said, smiling.

"Are you happy as a vampire?"

"Most of the time."

"Most of the time?"

"There are moments when I regret being turned," Kadie said, choosing her words carefully. "I haven't been a vampire so long that I've forgotten what it was like to be human. I still remember the taste and texture of food and sometimes I miss being able to walk in the sunshine without wearing a hat and sunglasses and long sleeves. But those times are rare, and getting rarer every day. I love Saintcrow more than you can imagine. I wouldn't change a moment of our time together for anything in the world."

"And the blood?"

Kadie shrugged. "It's a fact of life. And it's not so bad. Once you get used to it, you really don't want anything else."

Rosa didn't say so, but she found that hard to believe. "But you steal it from people. It's not like they want you to take it."

"It doesn't hurt them if you do it right. And we don't take enough that they miss it. I mean, people give more when they donate to the Red Cross than the small amount we take. Have you tasted Kincaid?"

Rosa stared at her, horrified by the very idea. "No! Why would I want to?"

"Has he tasted you?"

"No." But even as she said the word, she wondered if it was true. Saintcrow had told her vampires could mesmerize her, drink from her, and she would never know it. "At least I don't think so."

"You should let him," Kadie said, her eyes filled with understanding. "You'll like it."

⚜ ⚜ ⚜

Later that night, lying in bed, Rosa thought about what Kadie had said. Was it possible to enjoy being bitten by a vampire? It seemed unlikely. Impossible, even. Try as she might to put the thought out of her mind, it not only followed her to sleep, it was her first thought when she woke in the morning.

Sitting up in bed, she hugged her pillow to her chest. Would she like being bitten by Jake?

Did she want to know what it was like badly enough to let him bite her? Could she trust him not to take too much? Not to take it all?

What if one bite turned to two and he made her a vampire? The thought gave her pause. Wasn't that why she had come to Morgan Creek in the first place? To find a vampire who would change her?

Somehow, the thought wasn't as exciting as it had been. Certainly not a decision she wanted to make in the few days she had left. She would have to go home the day before her vacation was over to give herself time to unpack and get ready for work. She had been employed as a receptionist in a dentist's office for the last year or so and she loved it. The pay was better than average, the hours were good, she got holidays off, and they offered medical and dental benefits. Plus, she got to meet new people every day, and her coworkers were friendly and easy to get along with.

Throwing the covers aside, she headed for the bathroom. What if she pretended to be a vampire on a weekend, she mused, and then frowned. Sure, she could sleep days and only go out at night, but she would still have to eat. And pretending to hunt would be silly. She couldn't go around following people, pretending they were prey. Besides, she had a pretty good idea of what hunting was like from going out with Jake.

Brushing the idea aside, she showered and dressed, indulged in a big breakfast because she was human and she could eat anything she liked.

Only two more days to spend with Jake, she mused with a sigh. She was going to miss him dreadfully, she thought as she loaded the dishwasher. And Saintcrow, too. If Jake would transport her home, and Saintcrow would return her rental car to the airport, she could stay three days instead of two.

She spent the rest of the morning catching up on her laundry. Would Jake miss her when she was gone? Probably not as much as she was going to miss him, she thought, as she folded her tee shirts and sweaters, hung up her jeans.

When it was done, she decided to go into town and pick up a few souvenirs so she'd have something to remind her of her visit. As if she'd ever forget the time she'd spent here. Little chance of that, she thought.

One of the novelty shops carried a variety of mugs and shot glasses embossed with the name of the town. There was also a shelf of bobble heads. She grinned when she found one of Dracula. The perfect memento, she mused, plucking one off the shelf. She bought a pair of mugs, too, a dish towel with Morgan Creek embroidered on the hem, and a bright blue tee shirt with the town logo on the front. She also bought a Morgan Creek magnet for her fridge.

Saintcrow was up when she returned to the house. "Been souvenir shopping, I see."

She shrugged. "I'll be leaving in a couple of days. Some of us have to work for a living, you know."

He grunted softly. He had never held a job in his life. In the old days, whenever he'd needed money, he had taken it from his prey. When he needed clothing, he'd stolen it. He had taken his rest in caves, abandoned warehouses, empty tombs, and bombed-out buildings. Over time, he had invested some of the money he'd stolen. Now, he owned all the stores and the hotel in town, as well as a dozen prime stocks, all of which provided a tidy profit.

Dragging his mind from the past, he asked, "So, have you made up your mind?"

Rosa sank down on the sofa. "I think so. I like the good things about being a vampire—not getting old or sick, living a long, long time, all those neat supernatural powers. But giving up the sun and food and living a normal life, having kids… " She shook her head. "For now, I'm happy to be what I am."

"I'm glad to hear it. Come on, I'll take you to lunch."

⚜ ⚜ ⚜

Rosa had just finished her Cobb salad when Kincaid strolled into the restaurant.

Her heart immediately skipped a beat. Tall, dark and dangerous, she thought, and sexy as the day was long. Between Jake and Saintcrow, she felt small and helpless and yet protected at the same time.

Kincaid nodded at Saintcrow as he took the chair beside Rosa. "I hope this isn't a private meeting," he remarked.

"It was," Saintcrow said, but there was no animosity in his voice. "I'm guessing you're not here to see me."

"Right the first time."

"I can take a hint," Saintcrow said, pushing away from the table. "I'll take care of the check, Rosa."

"Thank you." She hadn't paid for a meal—or anything else—since she'd been here.

"No problem. See you back at the house later." He sent a look she couldn't decipher toward Kincaid, then headed for the door.

"Any plans for today?" Jake asked.

"No."

"Good."

"What did you have in mind?"

"Nothing, really. I just wanted to spend it with you."

She was melting inside, she thought. How was she going to tell him goodbye when the time came?

"Are you ready to go?"

Rosa nodded. She had been thinking about a slice of banana cream pie for dessert, but being alone with Kincaid was far more tempting.

He followed her out of the restaurant, held the door while she slid into the Mustang's passenger seat. Settling behind the wheel, he gunned the engine, then pulled away from the curb and headed for the bridge. Moments later, they were driving down the highway. It felt like flying, she mused, with the wind blowing in her hair and the countryside speeding past.

"Where are we going?" she asked as the miles slipped by.

"Wherever you want."

"I don't care."

Another five miles passed before he turned onto a side road which led to a grassy picnic area with wooden tables and a couple of firepits. A narrow stream cut its way through a small stand of timber. Cottonwood trees provided welcome patches of shade.

Kincaid pulled a blanket from the back seat and spread it under the trees. As soon as they sat down, he took her in his arms. "I can't seem to stay away from you."

"Do you want to?"

"No. That's the trouble." He rubbed his cheek against hers. "I can't think of anything but you."

His scent surrounded her as he pulled her down on top of him, his hands stroking up and down her back, along her thighs. She rested her cheek on his chest and closed her eyes.

"Rosa." He trailed his fingers along the side of her neck. "Let me."

She rolled off of him and sat up, hands clenched in her lap.

Muttering, "Sorry," Kincaid jackknifed to a sitting position, his eyes dark, his whole body tense.

"Kadie said I should let you bite me, that I'd like it. Would I?"

"Probably."

"What if I let you take a…a taste and you don't stop?"

"I guess you'll have to trust me."

"Should I?"

"Do you trust me now? We're here, alone. There's nothing to stop me from doing whatever I want."

"Are you *trying* to scare me?"

"No. But I've been with you almost every day. Have I ever hurt you?"

She shook her head.

"Come on," he said, reaching for her hand. "I'll take you back."

She tugged her hand from his. "Just one taste, okay? Promise?"

"I promise. Unless you ask me not to stop."

"I don't think there's any chance of that," she said, already regretting her decision.

Sensing her hesitation, he said, "We don't have to do this."

"I know." But she was suddenly curious to know what it was like.

Moving closer to her, he brushed her hair away from her neck. "Relax, love. I'm not going to hurt you."

She didn't know how he could bite her without hurting her. She held her breath as his tongue laved her neck. Tensed when she felt the prick of his fangs against her skin, but there was no pain. Pleasure washed through her, warm and sweet and sensual as he drank from her. Kadie had been right. She did like it.

Rosa moaned a protest when Jake lifted his head. "Why doesn't it hurt?"

"Because I didn't want it to." Leaning forward, he ran his tongue over her neck, licking a drop of blood from her skin, sealing the tiny punctures. Cupping her face in his hands, he kissed her lightly. "Thank you."

"Thank *you*," she said, grinning.

Kincaid laughed softly. Damn, but she was sweet. Sweeter than anything he had ever tasted, and he had tasted hundreds, maybe thousands. The taste of her had eased his hunger, but did nothing to satisfy his yearning to make love to her. Quite the opposite, it only made him want her more.

Rosa snuggled against him, her whole body feeling alive yet strangely lethargic. She had willingly let a vampire drink from her. And what was more amazing, she had not only liked it, she wanted him to do it again.

She grinned inwardly, thinking she had an 'I told you so' coming from Kadie Saintcrow.

⚜ ⚜ ⚜

Kincaid took Rosa dancing later that night. Every time he took her in his arms, he remembered the warmth of her blood, the way it had lingered on his tongue, sweeter than summer wine as it slid down his throat, warming the cold places deep inside, filling the emptiness that had ever been a part of him. Until now.

He held her close, every breath carrying the scent of her hair, her skin, the crimson river that flowed just beneath her skin. One taste had been amazing. What would it be like to drink his fill?

He thrust the thought away as he gazed into her eyes—her expression warm and trusting.

She fit into his embrace as though she had been designed for him and him alone. Her cheeks flushed when she met his gaze, her eyelids fluttering down when he claimed her lips with his. Sweet and pliable, they yielded to him as she pressed against him, her breasts warm against his chest, her hair like silk in his hands.

He groaned low in his throat, not sure how much longer he could hold her without carrying her away to his lair and making her his.

Kincaid knew a moment of relief as the music ended and he led her back to their table, only to find Saintcrow sitting there. "What the hell are you doing here?"

The master vampire shrugged. "Just looking out for the young woman under my protection."

Rosa stared at him. "What are you talking about? I'm not in any danger."

"You think not?" Saintcrow looked at Kincaid. "What do you think?"

"I think you showed up just in time, damn you."

Rosa glanced from one man to the other. What the heck was going on? The air between the two vampires fairly bristled with tension.

Saintcrow stood. "Rosa, let's go."

"But ... " She looked at Jake, waiting for him to protest.

"Go with him, love," he said, his voice tight.

Too proud to argue, she followed Saintcrow outside, fought back the urge to cry as he put his arm around her waist.

Moments later, they were in Morgan Creek.

Rosa turned on Saintcrow as soon as they entered the house. "What was that all about?" she demanded. "I've never been so embarrassed."

"You were in danger."

She stared at him. "I don't believe you."

"You let him drink from you today," Saintcrow said as he uncorked a bottle, poured two glasses of wine, and handed her one. "Sometimes that eases a vampire's desire for your blood. Sometimes it only increases it. Kincaid falls into the second category."

"You mean ... ?"

"I'm not sure he would have followed through on what he was thinking, but I wasn't willing to take that chance."

"I guess I owe you my thanks," she murmured, sinking down on the sofa. "If I'd known letting him drink from me would make it worse, I never would have done it."

"There was no way for either of you to know in advance how it would affect him."

"Kadie said—"

"Kadie!" he exclaimed. "What does she have to do with this?"

"She told me I should let Jake drink from me, that I'd like it. And I did."

Saintcrow grunted softly. "Most women do."

Rosa sipped her wine, thinking there was more to being a vampire than she had ever imagined. "Thank you for bringing me home. I think I'll go to bed."

"Good night."

Heavy-hearted, she set her glass aside and made her way upstairs. She undressed, pulled on a nightgown, brushed her hair, and climbed into bed. She wouldn't cry. She couldn't blame Jake. He was a vampire, wanting what vampires wanted. She could hardly fault him for that. She didn't want to think of what might have happened if Saintcrow hadn't arrived on the scene. She didn't want to believe that Jake would have hurt her, but what did she know? He had obviously been thinking about doing something that alarmed Saintcrow enough to interfere. For all she knew, the master vampire might have saved her life tonight.

Turning onto her side, she closed her eyes.

And the tears came.

Chapter Sixteen

Rhinehart let out a groan as Luca once again unleashed his power. He hadn't wanted to come here, but refusing to obey the witch's summons was never a good idea. He had learned that the hard way. Still, it was impossible to imagine anything worse than this. He let out a muffled cry as Luca's power danced over his skin, slicing into his flesh until he bled.

Gasping, he fell to the floor, folded into a fetal position in an effort to protect himself, but it was futile. And all the while, the necromancer screamed curses at him, calling him weak, a failure, an embarrassment to the community of hunters.

After what seemed like an eternity, Luca's rage cooled. Giving Rhinehart a swift kick in the ribs, he growled, "Get on your feet."

Panting, Rhinehart pushed himself up to his hands and knees, then gained his feet, one arm curled protectively around his broken ribs.

"Get out of my sight, you worthless sack of crap! You had better bring me Kincaid or his head the next time I see you, or I'll have *your* head. And those of your family, as well."

With the witch's threat ringing in his ears, Rhinehart limped out of the house. He had no hope of finding Kincaid, little hope that Saintcrow would betray the other vampire's whereabouts.

Sliding behind the wheel of his car, he slumped in the seat, his forehead resting on the steering wheel. His only hope was to follow the woman, and even the feasibility of that was questionable as long as she was in Morgan Creek under Saintcrow's protection. No matter the risk to his own life, he couldn't give up. He had a wife and three kids depending on him.

Muttering, "You play the hand you're dealt," he made a U-turn and headed for the nearest hospital, every indrawn breath a new adventure in pain.

Chapter Seventeen

Rosa woke bleary-eyed in the morning. Recalling the events of the night before, she decided to pack up and go home. She'd had enough of Morgan Creek, Wyoming. Enough of vampires.

She rolled out of bed, showered and dressed, packed the rest of her belongings, and carried her suitcases downstairs. She took a deep breath and then called Saintcrow's name.

He appeared ten minutes later. "You've decided to go home a few days early, I see," he remarked, glancing at her luggage by the door.

"Will you please take me?"

"Sure, if that's what you want."

"And would you return my rental to the airport for me? The key's in the console."

"No problem." He handed her the smaller of the two suitcases, tucked the larger one under his arm, and then wrapped his other arm around her waist.

Blinking back tears, Rosa closed her eyes. *Goodbye, Jake, wherever you are.*

All too soon, she was standing in the middle of her own living room.

Saintcrow set her suitcase on the floor, took the smaller one from her hand and dropped it on the sofa, and then took her in his arms. "I know you're confused right now. My advice to you is to put it all out of your mind for the time being. I know you care for Kincaid. You might think you're in love with him. Hell, maybe you are. But, like I said, he's an old vampire. He's never settled down, and even though he's been around a long time, he still goes off the rails from time to time. I don't think he's ever really been in love, or ever cared deeply about anyone other than his family. I don't even know if he's capable of it." He wiped the tears from her cheeks with his fingertips. "It isn't easy, being in love with a vampire. There are a lot of sacrifices to be made and you'd have to make most of them. Kincaid can't change what he is. And he's afraid that he might hurt you. Or worse."

"I take back what I said the first night I arrived in Morgan Creek," Rosa said, sniffling. "You really are nice."

Saintcrow grinned at her. "Don't tell anybody. It'll ruin my reputation. Are you going to be all right here, alone?"

She nodded. "Don't worry about me."

"Sorry, you're family now. That makes you my responsibility. If you ever need me, or just want to talk, you know what to do."

"Thank you for everything."

He winked at her, and then he was gone.

She stood there a moment, thinking how big and empty her small apartment seemed. Two weeks' worth of dust covered the furniture. Her refrigerator was empty.

And all she wanted to do was cry.

Picking up her suitcases, she carried them into the bedroom. Refusing to think about Jake, she put away her clothes and toiletries, grabbed her car keys and drove to the market. Grocery shopping had always relaxed her. She concentrated on the task at hand, buying the basic necessities, which, on this night, included a carton of double fudge ice cream, a large jar of hot fudge, whipped crème, and cherries.

Returning home, she kicked off her shoes, put the groceries away, turned the music on high, and threw herself into cleaning the house. But no matter how she tried, she couldn't put Jake Kincaid out of her mind, couldn't stop thinking of him, wanting him. How could she miss him so much when she had known him such a short time? And yet, no matter how fiercely she attacked the task at hand, no matter how determined she was to think of something else, he was there in the forefront of her mind. She remembered the deep timbre of his voice, the touch of his hands, the taste of his kisses, the way his smile turned her insides to mush.

"Darn you, Jake Kincaid! Leave me alone!"

Fighting tears, she went into the kitchen to put the cleaning supplies away when she happened to glance at the plaque on the wall over the stove. It read, *Life is short. Eat dessert first.* Thinking that was first-rate advice, she filled a big bowl with ice cream, added a generous helping of hot fudge, three cherries, and topped it off with a mountain of whipped crème. Settling on the sofa in front of the TV, she turned on her favorite sci-fi channel, determined to drown her sorrows in hot fudge and science fiction.

But it was not to be. She felt the sting of fresh tears burn her eyes when she recognized the music from *The Lost Boys.*

She cried all the way through it.

⚜ ⚜ ⚜

Kincaid knew Rosa was gone as soon as he crossed the bridge into Morgan Creek that evening. Refusing to believe it, he willed himself to Saintcrow's house.

Kadie answered the door. The look on her face told him everything he needed to know—Rosa had packed up her bags and run for home.

He started to turn away when Saintcrow came to the door. "Come on in," he said.

Kincaid hesitated a moment, then followed the master vampire into the living room.

"Where is she?"

Saintcrow sat on the arm of the sofa beside Kadie. "I took her home this morning."

Shoulders slumped, Kincaid dropped into the chair across from the master vampire. "Did she say anything about me?"

"She didn't say much of anything."

Kincaid stared at him, eyes narrowed. "What did *you* say to her?"

"I told her that in any relationship between vampires and mortals, there were sacrifices to be made, and that the mortals usually had to make them. I told her to take some time to think about what she wants. You need to give her some space, time to clear her head. She came here looking for someone to turn her, but I think she's pretty much changed her mind about that, at least for now."

"What else did you tell her?"

"The truth. That you're an old vampire, and even though you've been around a long time, you aren't always in control."

"Damn you! What right do you have to interfere in my life?"

"Rosa is part of my family now, and I don't want to see her get hurt—or make a decision in a moment of weakness that she'll regret later."

"From the sound of it, her brother and sister don't seem to have any regrets."

"Do you?"

A muscle twitched in Kincaid's jaw. "Not anymore."

"But you did for a long time. I want the decision to be Rosa's. And I don't want her to make it the heat of passion. I think you need to give her some time to think about what she really wants."

Kincaid stared at Saintcrow and Kadie and for a moment, he was so jealous of what they shared that he hated them both. He clenched his fists as rage unfurled within him. Damn Saintcrow for sticking his nose in where it didn't belong!

Muttering an oath, he vanished from the room.

"That went well," Kadie remarked dryly.

"Yeah."

"What do you think he'll do now?"

"I think he's likely to kill the first person who crosses his path tonight."

⚜ ⚜ ⚜

Kincaid willed himself out of Saintcrow's house and out of Morgan Creek. Filled with impotent rage and regret, he stormed through the night. Fearing he might rip the heart out of any mortal he preyed on, he went to the nearest national park and confronted a young grizzly bear. Most animals avoided him, but the bear charged him. With a wild cry, Kincaid flung himself on the grizzly's back and buried his fangs deep in the soft skin of its throat. The bear roared as it tried to shake him off, and failed.

Kincaid drank until his rage subsided, leaving the bear a little weak with blood loss but still alive.

Transporting himself to his lair, Kincaid stood under a cold shower for a full ten minutes.

After drying off, he stretched out on his bed and opened his senses. It took only moments to find the link between himself and Rosa. Closing his eyes, he murmured her name as he summoned her image to mind…the face of an angel framed by a curtain of ebony colored hair, dark brown eyes he had seen filled with desire, a curvy little body he longed to know better…

His fangs brushed his tongue as he recalled the sweet taste of her blood, even as his body responded to the memory of her kisses.

Saintcrow was right, he thought bitterly. She was better off without him.

⚜ ⚜ ⚜

Rosa sat up, her gaze darting right and left when she heard Kincaid's voice whispering her name. She frowned, wondering where he was hiding and how he had found her. It took her a moment to realize he wasn't really there, that she had only imagined his voice. Disappointment speared through her. His voice had been so clear, she would have sworn he was in the room beside her.

Murmuring, "I miss you," she slid back under the covers. Hoping she would dream of him, she closed her eyes…

And he came to her in the dark of the night, a shadowy figure who appeared out of nowhere and wrapped her in his embrace, his dark eyes glowing as his fangs lightly grazed her throat. His hands and his voice caressed her, begging her to be his, to let him give her the Dark Gift so they could be together forever. Vowing that he loved her. Would always love her. Unable to refuse his entreaty or the yearning in his eyes, she bared her throat to his bite…

"No!" Rosa screamed the word as she sat up. Turning on the lamp beside the bed, she lifted a hand to her neck. She felt no punctures, saw no blood on her fingertips.

Sighing with relief, she fell back on the mattress. Only a dream.

⚜ ⚜ ⚜

Returning to work was the best thing she could have done, Rosa thought at her desk the next morning. She had called first thing and let everyone know she had come home early. As it turned out, the girl who had been temporarily replacing her was out sick and the other members of the staff were more than happy to have her back.

Being at work, making appointments, answering the phones, gave her a sense of purpose. She enjoyed interacting with the patients, assuring those who were nervous there was nothing to fear, handing out lollipops to the kids. Her coworkers all stopped by her desk to let her know she had been missed. Happily, she was too busy to think about a hunky vampire with gorgeous chocolate brown eyes and a whiskey-rough voice that made her insides melt like ice on a hot summer day.

She went to lunch with Bria, the only other single girl in the office. Bria was a hygienist and a year older than Rosa. She had beautiful caramel colored skin, large brown eyes, and a mass of black hair she wore in braids because, as Bria said, "it was too darn unmanageable otherwise." She was engaged to a police officer.

They went to their favorite pizza place for lunch. "So, did you meet any attractive men on your vacation?" Bria asked, adding sugar to her iced tea.

Rosa took a bite of pizza to keep from answering right away. She should have known that would be Bria's first question.

"I'm waiting."

"I did meet someone," Rosa said. "He was very nice, but not my type."

"Did you take any pictures?"

Rosa shook her head. For a moment, she wished she had, and then she was glad she hadn't. She would never get Jake out of her mind or her heart if she could look at his image every time she missed him.

"Well, darn, girl. We'll just have to keep looking. Maybe I'll ask Tom if he knows anyone on the force who's available."

"Don't bother. I'm not ready right now."

"Uh-oh. This guy you met, he hurt you, didn't he?"

"No. No, he was wonderful—tall and dark and gorgeous, with muscular arms and beautiful eyes. Everything I ever wanted. Well, almost everything," she amended.

"He sure sounds like your type. Hell, he sounds like *my* type," Bria said with a grin. "So, what was wrong with him? Was he married? Engaged? Recently divorced?"

"No, nothing like that. We were just too different. So, have you and Tom set a date yet?"

"All right," Bria said with a grin. "We'll change the subject. But I'm not going to stop looking. I know the right man for you is out there somewhere."

I had him, Rosa thought sadly. *And I let him go.*

⚜ ⚜ ⚜

Rosa hated to see the work day end. Hated to think about going back to her lonely apartment. Maybe she should get a kitten. At least then she would have another living thing in the house, something she could spoil and cuddle. Maybe she'd stop by the pet store down the street from the office on her lunch break tomorrow.

At home, she collected her mail from Mr. Evans, the building manager, before going up the stairs to her apartment. She kicked off her shoes, dropped her handbag on the coffee table, and flopped onto the sofa. Feeling blue, she sorted through the mail, putting bills in one pile on the coffee table, ads and junk on another pile, magazines on another.

Sitting back, she stared into the fireplace. What was Jake doing tonight? Was he missing her the way she was missing him? Or had he moved on? He was a gorgeous guy and the world was filled with women—women who were a lot more beautiful and sexy than she was. Women who wouldn't hesitate to take a gorgeous hunk like Jake to bed in a heartbeat…

She dashed the tears from her eyes. Saintcrow had told her to put it all out of her mind. Easier said than done, she thought bleakly. She had spent less than two weeks with Jake, but they had been the best days of her life. She had never felt more alive. Never met anyone like him, she thought with a sigh. And she never would again.

Two fat tears rolled down her cheeks. "I miss you," she murmured. "Why did you have to be a vampire?" The thought gave her pause. Maybe part of the reason she loved him was *because* he was a vampire.

Frowning, she tried to imagine what he would be like if he was just an ordinary man. Sure, he'd still be six-foot four and handsome as sin, but would he still have that air of arrogance and self-assurance? That aura of power that clung to him like a second skin? Would she have felt as safe with him if he hadn't been a vampire? Would the attraction still have been there?

She shook her head. What difference did any of it make now?

She skipped dinner in favor of tea and toast. Turned on the TV and stared at the screen, but the images meant nothing.

She jerked awake when her phone rang. "Oh, Micah. Hi."

'Hi, yourself. How was Florida?"

"Hot," she said. "You should see my sunburn. Are you guys having a good time?"

"You bet."

"I wish I'd come with you," she said. "Did you buy me a souvenir?"

"What do you think? Are you sure you're okay? I've been worried about you."

"I don't know why. I'm a big girl now."

"Uh-huh." He was quiet a moment. "Are you all right, Rosie?"

"Right as rain. I'm thinking about getting a kitten."

"A kitten? What on earth for?"

She heard the worry in his voice. "Well, I can't leave a puppy home alone all day. But a cat… They're pretty self-sufficient. When are you coming home?"

"I'm not sure. The brothers have another two weeks before they have to go back to work. The folks can stay as long as they like. I guess Sofia and I can, too."

"Well, tell everyone hi for me."

"Will do. Behave yourself."

"Yeah, yeah," she muttered. "Stop worrying about me, big brother."

He was laughing when he ended the call.

She really should have gone to Italy, Rosa mused as she turned off the TV and the lights and headed for the bedroom. She might have met a nice Italian man who didn't drink blood.

Chapter Eighteen

Paul Rhinehart drove slowly through the streets of Morgan Creek, searching for Rosa's rental car. He didn't know much about her except her name and that she was driving a late model, beige Kia. He didn't see it anywhere. Not in front of the restaurant where she usually ate. Not in the theater parking lot, or in the driveway of Saintcrow's house.

The only other place he could think to look was the cemetery, though he figured the odds were slim to none that he would find her in such a place, especially after dark.

She wasn't there, of course.

He sat in the car with the motor running, staring at the hundreds of wooden crosses. Either she had gone for a drive out of town, or she'd gone home, which was no big deal. Finding her shouldn't be too difficult. But hard or not, he figured she was his best hope of finding Kincaid.

He hadn't seen Luca since the necromancer's ultimatum to bring him the head of Jake Kincaid or forfeit his own and those of his family. Knowing Luca wouldn't hesitate to carry out his threat, Paul had sent Nancy and the kids to visit her grandparents in Ireland.

Feeling sick to his stomach, he lifted his hand to his neck, wondering, morbidly, how Luca would separate his head from his body. A sword? An axe? The guillotine he kept in the basement?

With a shudder, he stepped out of the car, let out a startled gasp when Rylan Saintcrow materialized in front of him. "Dammit, bloodsucker, don't do that!"

"Nice to see you, too. What the hell are you doing here?"

"Looking for a burial plot?"

Saintcrow lifted one brow.

"Luca has given me an ultimatum. If I don't bring him a head, he'll take mine."

"Any head in particular?"

"Kincaid's. Although he might settle for yours."

"Too bad. I'm not finished with mine yet. Not sure Kincaid's ready to part with his just yet, either."

"This isn't a laughing matter, dammit." Paul hissed as pain from his wound speared through his side.

"Am I laughing?"

"Where's Kincaid? I just want to ask him how he's evading Luca. I'll meet him anywhere of his choosing. No weapons. Dammit, man, I'm desperate!"

"I can see that. What's wrong with your side?"

"Luca kicked the shit out of me." Rhinehart's shoulders slumped. "I should have known better than to expect any help from somebody like you."

"For a hunter who's supposed to be at the top of his game, you give up mighty quick."

"I'm not worried about me. I've got a wife and three kids to think about. Luca's threatening them, too."

Saintcrow grunted softly. "Why don't you go spend the night in the hotel? If the desk clerk says they don't have a room, tell him I sent you. I'll see if I can get in touch with Kincaid."

"You'll help me?" Rhinehart stared at him in disbelief.

"I try to do a good deed every day," Saintcrow said, his voice as dry as dust. "Try to keep out of trouble until I get in touch with you."

"I don't know what to say."

"Don't say anything."

"I can't thank you . . . "

But the vampire was gone.

⚜ ⚜ ⚜

Kincaid bent the woman over his arm, his nostrils flaring as he inhaled the warm, rich scent of her life's blood. She was young. Pretty, with golden hair and sky-blue eyes. He ran his tongue along the slender curve of her neck, then paused. He could dine on her later. Right now, he had another hunger that demanded attention.

Wrapping his arms around her, he transported them to his lair. It wasn't much. A two-bedroom house located on a small cul-de-sac. There was only one other house on the block, and it had been abandoned for more than a year.

He carried the woman into his bedroom and lowered her onto the mattress. She didn't move, simply lay there staring up at him, her eyes blank. She was his for the taking, he mused as he stretched out beside her. Dammit! He had never taken a woman by force. Never compelled one to submit to him. Was that a line he wanted to cross? What if it was the woman he loved lying there, at the mercy of another of his kind?

Muttering curses under his breath, he lifted her into his arms and transported them back to where he'd found her. Annoyed with himself, he released her from his thrall and vanished from sight.

He materialized inside *The Bloody Rose.*

Five minutes later, Saintcrow strolled into the nightclub.

Kincaid glared at him. "What the hell do you want now?"

"A drink and a kind word?"

"Shut up."

Saintcrow took the stool beside Kincaid's, signaled the bartender, and ordered a glass of wine. "You look like hell."

"I feel that way, too."

"Why don't you call her?"

Kincaid shook his head. "I killed a man last night."

Saintcrow arched one brow.

"It wasn't in your territory."

"I know that."

"It was back east." Kincaid stared into his glass. He tried to feel regret for what he'd done, but he couldn't forget what it had felt like to drink and drink, the sense of power that came with it. "He fought me and I... I just lost it."

Saintcrow twitched one shoulder. "It happens." He didn't know of any vampire who hadn't lost control at least once and taken a life. Like Kincaid, most regretted it.

"It could have been her."

"I don't think so. Until last night, you hadn't killed anyone that I know of in a century or two. Maybe longer. We all make mistakes from time to time. It's easy to get caught up in the moment."

Kincaid slid a glance at Saintcrow, confused by the master vampire's words. He had expected condemnation, not sympathy or understanding. "She deserves better than me."

"I agree."

"Fat lot of help you are," Kincaid muttered. "Why don't you just take my head and do the world a favor?"

"Is that why you came here? Hoping I'd destroy you?"

Kincaid looked away. "Maybe. I don't know."

"If you're looking for someone to take your head, go find Rhinehart. Or Luca." Saintcrow jerked his chin toward the door. "If you really want to end it, go kill someone in Morgan Creek."

Kincaid glared at him, but said nothing.

"I told Rosa to forget about you for a while, to think about something else. Ordinarily, I'd advise you to do the same thing. But I think staying away from her is wrong where you're concerned. I think she was good for you. I don't know if the reverse is true, but I think Rosa is your Kadie. She grounds you, makes you want to be better than you are."

"I think I'm in love with her," Kincaid said quietly. "And I'd rather let Rhinehart take my head than cause her any pain. You know what I'm capable of, what I've done. She deserves a better man than I ever was. Or ever will be."

"Like she's so fond of saying, she's a big girl. Maybe you should let her decide what she wants."

"And if it's not me?"

Saintcrow shrugged. "You'll never know if you don't ask."

Kincaid nodded. Saintcrow was right. But at the moment, he just didn't know if he had the nerve to face Rosa again. Or the right, after what he'd done.

"One more thing," Saintcrow said. "I saw Rhinehart tonight. He wants to talk to you." Saintcrow held up a hand when Kincaid started to interrupt. "Hear me out. All he wants to do is talk. He wants to know about that band you wear, where you got it, and how it keeps Luca from finding you. Apparently Luca is threatening to take the hunter's head if he doesn't bring him yours."

"Let him. One less hunter sounds good to me."

"The man has a wife and three kids. The witch is threatening them, too."

Kincaid muttered an oath. "Am I supposed to care about that?" He felt a sharp twinge of guilt as soon as he uttered the words. Rosa would care.

"Rhinehart said he'll meet you anywhere, any time. No weapons. He sounds pretty desperate."

"What the hell. Tell him I'll meet him here tomorrow night, around eleven. And he'd better come alone and unarmed if he wants to walk out in one piece."

⚜ ⚜ ⚜

Kadie turned off the TV when Rylan materialized beside her on the sofa. "You've been with Kincaid."

"Yeah." He put his arm around her shoulders, thanking whatever Fate had sent her to Morgan Creek.

"How is he?"

"He killed a man last night."

"Oh, no." Her gaze searched his. "You didn't…?" She couldn't bring herself to finish the question.

"No, but I have a hunch he was hoping I'd destroy him and put him out of his misery."

"He really misses her, doesn't he?"

"Yeah. Life is funny, isn't it? If Rosa still wanted to be a vampire, there wouldn't be a problem."

"Not with Kincaid. But there'd sure as hell be a problem with Micah. And likely with Sofia, too."

"I don't understand why they're so against it," Saintcrow muttered.

"Maybe they aren't. Maybe they were just warning Rosa to wait, to make sure, and she took it for disapproval."

"Maybe. After all, they both seem happy with the way things turned out." He slid a sideways glance at Kadie. "Have you ever been sorry I turned you?"

Kadie huffed a sigh of annoyance, then punched him on the arm as hard as she could, knowing it wouldn't hurt. "Rylan Saintcrow, how many times are you going to ask me that?"

He shrugged. "I guess I still feel guilty for turning you."

"Well, stop it! I love you, Rylan. I don't have any regrets. I'm perfectly happy with my life, and with you."

"Are you?"

"What's wrong?"

"I don't know."

Straddling his hips, she cupped his face in her hands. "I love you, Rylan. Even when I hated you, I think I loved you. I love our life together and I wouldn't change anything. Do you hear me? I don't have any regrets."

"Not even one?"

Brow furrowed, she tilted her head to the side. "What do you think I'm missing?"

"Kids."

"I wouldn't trade you for a dozen babies. Don't you know that?" She paused a moment. "This isn't about me, is it? It's about you not being able father a child."

He grunted softly. It was true. He didn't think about it much these days, but being around the Ravenwood family had made him realize what he had missed. They were a tight-knit group. They loved each other, loved being together, looked out for each other.

Kadie slipped off his lap and tugged him down on the floor beside her. "You're all the family I need," she murmured, as she slid her hands under his shirt. "We can adopt a baby if you want one."

He shook his head. "I'm too old and set in my ways to be a father."

"But just the right age to be my lover," she purred as she raked her fingernails down his chest.

He grinned at her as, with a word, their clothing disappeared and a fire sprang to life in the hearth. What need had he for a family when Kadie was his?

Chapter Nineteen

Rosa looked up at the man on the other side of the reception desk. "Can I help you?"

"Yeah. The doc says I need to come back in a week."

She nodded as she looked at her computer. "How about next Thursday at 10:30, Mr. Dunsmore?"

He nodded. "That's fine."

She wrote in the date and time on an appoin tment card and handed it to him. "Is there anything else?"

"Any chance I could take you out for a drink when you get off work tonight?"

"I ... um ..." She bit down on her lower lip. Jim Dunsmore was in his late twenties, nice looking, with a shock of blond hair and light gray eyes. He worked for an accounting firm.

"It's just a drink," he said, smiling.

"I guess so."

"What time do you get off?" he asked.

"Six."

He smiled again. "How about if I meet you out front?"

"All right."

He winked at her, then headed for the door.

Rosa stared after him. What was she doing?

⚜ ⚜ ⚜

"A date?" Bria exclaimed. "You actually have a date?"

"Is that so hard to believe?"

"No, I guess not. So, who's the lucky guy?"

"He's one of Doctor Jansen's patients."

"Where's he taking you?"

"Just out for a drink."

"Well, I'll expect a full report at lunch tomorrow."

⚜ ⚜ ⚜

Rosa went into the restroom after work. She washed her hands, applied fresh lipstick, ran a comb through her hair, then stared at her reflection. What on earth had prompted her to say yes to this date? Jim Dunsmore seemed like a nice guy. She had chatted with him a couple of times in the past—casual conversations while she made appointments or answered questions, but surely she had never said or done anything to make him think she wanted to go out with him. Because she really didn't.

With a shake of her head, she grabbed her handbag, waved good night to one of the techs, and left the office.

Mr. Dunsmore was waiting for her at the foot of the stairs.

It was too late to back out now, Rosa thought, as she pasted a smile on her face.

"I thought we'd go to Jack's Place," Dunsmore said. "If that's all right with you?"

"Fine." Jack's was a nice club, well-lit, not like the dreary vampire bars Saintcrow had taken her to. "Why don't I take my car?" Rosa suggested. "That way you won't have to bring me back."

"Sure, if that's what you want." He didn't sound very happy about it.

She followed him to the nightclub and parked her car beside his.

It was too early for a crowd. Rosa slid into a booth near the door, wondering what they would find to talk about. Wondering how soon she could excuse herself and go home. Jim seemed like a nice guy, but he wasn't Jake, and Kincaid was all she could think of. All she wanted.

Jim Dunsmore took the seat across from her. "Have you been here before?"

"Now and then," Rosa said. "Usually with the group from the office when someone is celebrating a birthday or the arrival of a new baby."

He nodded, then looked up when someone came to take their drink order. He asked for a scotch and soda, she opted for a glass of Merlot.

"So, what do you like to do for fun?" he asked.

Rosa shrugged. "Oh, you know, movies, dancing, bowling."

"Favorite movie?"

"Thor," she said without thinking, and immediately regretted it when Jake's image popped into her mind.

"Into Marvel, huh?"

"I like superheroes." Kincaid was built like Thor, she thought. Tall and broad-shouldered and incredibly strong. "Who's your favorite hero?"

"Batman."

"He's not really a superhero," Rosa remarked. "He doesn't have any supernatural powers like Superman or The Flash."

"True, but he's got a cool car."

"I can't argue with that," Rosa said, as their drinks arrived. She stared at the wine in her glass. The red suddenly reminded her of blood. And Jake. Always Jake.

"Rosa?"

"Oh, sorry. Did you say something?"

"I asked if you'd like to go out to dinner later?"

She was pondering her answer when something drew her gaze toward the entrance. She stared at the man standing there, felt her heart do a somersault when his gaze met hers. And then he was striding toward her, tall and dark with a dangerous glint in his eyes.

"Jake," she murmured when he stopped beside her.

Dunsmore frowned as he glanced from Rosa's face to the stranger and back again. There was no mistaking the jealousy blazing in the giant's eyes. Scooting across the length of the booth, he stammered, "Excuse me, I didn't know she… that, uh…" Leaving his sentence unfinished, he edged around the big man glaring down at Rosa and made a hasty exit.

"Who the hell was that?" Kincaid hissed.

"Nobody. Sit down. People are staring."

A low growl rose in his throat but he did as she asked.

"What are you doing here?"

"What do you think?"

To avoid answering, she sipped her wine, her mind in turmoil, her whole being yearning toward him.

"You left without so much as a goodbye," he said, his voice thick with accusation.

"It seemed like the right thing to do at the time."

He took a deep breath, held it, and released it in a long, slow sigh.

"What are you doing here?" she asked again.

"Saintcrow thinks you're good for me."

She lifted one brow. "He does, huh? And what do you think?"

"I think I was a fool not to come after you sooner. Let's get out of here."

Dunsmore hadn't paid for their drinks. Rosa was reaching for her wallet when Kincaid stood and slapped a twenty on the table.

Hoping she wasn't making a big mistake, Rosa stood and followed him out of the nightclub. "What now?"

He shrugged. "We need to talk."

"My car's in the lot." She felt like a rabbit being stalked by a lion as he followed her around the side of the building. After unlocking the door, she slid behind the wheel. Her car, a two-door Civic, had never seemed particularly small until Jake opened the passenger door and settled into the seat.

His power filled the interior. Whether he was angry or jealous or both, she didn't know. She couldn't help wondering if it was even safe for her to be alone with him in his present mood.

After a moment, she started the car and drove toward home. She wasn't sure if that was a good idea, either, but at least she could scream for help if she needed it, she thought. Although she doubted if old Mrs. Kellogg or equally old Mr. Gillespie would even hear her, let alone be of much help.

Rosa parked the car and locked it behind her. Heart pounding with trepidation, she climbed the stairs to her apartment, acutely aware of the man trailing after her. Her hand trembled as she unlocked the door and stepped inside.

She frowned when he didn't follow. "Are you coming in?"

"Vampire," he said, the word as cold as ice. "I can't enter without an invitation."

She had forgotten that little piece of supernatural etiquette. After a moment's hesitation, she murmured, "Please come in, Jake."

There was a discernable vibration in the air as he stepped across the threshold.

"Nice place," he said, glancing around. Pale blue walls, white leather sofa and chair, dark blue carpet, glass-topped coffee table. A vase of red, white, and blue silk flowers on the mantel, along with a couple of family photographs.

She gestured at the chair. "Have a seat." She watched as he lowered himself into the chair, every muscle taut, his jaw rigid.

"Who was that guy?" he asked.

"Just a patient from where I work."

"Do you often go out with the patients?"

"Only when they ask me," she snapped. "Not that it's any of your business."

A muscle twitched in his jaw.

"He asked me out and I said yes. End of story. Are you ever going to tell me why you're here?"

"Why the hell do you think?"

His voice was deep, tinged with anger and jealousy, but there was also a note of remorse and it filled her with hope. "Because you missed me?"

All the tension drained out of him as his gaze met hers. "Rosa." He huffed an irritated sigh. "I'm lost without you."

She felt her heart break at the need in his voice. Without a word, she perched on his lap and clasped her hands behind his neck. "I missed you, too." Warmth spread through her, along with a sense of being where she belonged as his arms went around her.

He groaned low in his throat as the twin talons of need and desire sparked to life at her nearness. "This is never going to work," he said. "I'm no good for you. You should ask me to leave."

"No way, mister."

"There's something I have to tell you."

Suddenly apprehensive, she leaned back so she could see his face. "What?"

He refused to meet her gaze. "I killed a man the other night. I have no excuse for what I did," he said, his voice thick with regret. "I knew what I was doing and I just didn't give a damn."

She didn't know what to say. How could she tell him it was all right? Or that she understood, when she didn't and likely never would. "Why? Why did you kill him? I thought…" Her voice trailed off.

"I was mad at Saintcrow for sticking his nose in my business and angry with myself for being mad at him because I knew he was only trying to help. And I guess I was feeling a little hurt because you'd left without a word. I was on edge and spoiling for a fight and when the guy tried to resist me, I lost it." He dragged his fingers through his hair. "Dammit, that's no excuse. It wasn't your fault or Saintcrow's. I've got no one to blame but myself. I didn't mean to kill him, but he's just as dead and the fault is all mine."

Rosa bit down on her lower lip. She knew it wasn't her fault Jake had killed the man and yet she couldn't help feeling a little guilty for the man's death. Would things have been different if she'd taken the time to tell Jake goodbye? She was torn between horror at what he'd done and pity for his anguish. How awful, to have such power at your fingertips, to know people might die if you lost control. How could she stay with him, knowing what he'd done? What he might do in the future?

He buried his face in her hair. "I shouldn't have come here."

Her conscience told her to make a clean break and be done with it. But she couldn't leave him, not when he so obviously needed her. Not when doing so would surely break her heart. "Does Saintcrow know what you did?"

"Yes," he said, his voice muffled. "I thought he'd destroy me, even though it didn't happen in his territory. I guess, deep down, I was hoping he'd do just that."

"No!" she cried, horrified by the very idea. "Don't even think that!"

She held him close, crooning meaningless words, her heart breaking for his anguish. He had been alone for centuries, she thought. People weren't meant to be solitary creatures. Surely that applied to vampires, too. "Promise me something?"

"What?" It was a foolish question. He knew the answer before she spoke.

"Promise me that you'll never go hunting when you're that upset again."

"Rosa..."

"Please, Jake. I can sort of understand what happened, but I can't condone it. If it happens again..." Her voice trailed off. If it happened again, she would have to leave him for good. Her conscience would demand it.

She didn't say the words out loud, but he heard them just the same. "I should go," he said quietly.

"Please don't." She hated to think of him out there, prowling the streets alone and feeling guilty.

He lifted his head, his dark eyes haunted as they searched hers.

"Stay the night."

"Rosa?"

"I don't mean spend the night in my bed," she exclaimed. "I just meant stay here where I can keep an eye on you."

He barked a short, humorless laugh. "You think you can stop me from leaving?"

"Of course not. I just don't want to be alone."

She didn't want *him* to be alone, Kincaid thought. "Staying right now isn't a good idea," he said, his gaze sliding away from hers. "I haven't fed yet." He should have fed first, he knew that, but he had been desperate to see her, to confess what he'd done, although he wasn't sure if he had come to her looking for condemnation, or hoping for absolution.

"Oh."

"Exactly." He lifted her from his lap as easily as if she weighed no more than an infant and set her on her feet, then stood and shoved his hands into his pants' pockets. He towered over her.

Rosa stared up at him. She had forgotten just how tall and broad he was. His long-sleeved tee shirt did nothing to hide the impressive muscles in his arms or the width of his shoulders. He could probably break her in two as easily as she broke a stalk of celery. "Will you come back after?"

His heated gaze ran over her from head to foot.

It sent a shiver down her spine. Was he thinking of her as prey when he looked at her like that? Or carrying her off to bed?

A slow smile spread over his face as he drew her into his arms and kissed the top of her head. "Both," he whispered.

And then he was gone.

She was fighting the urge to cry when her cell phone rang. Thank goodness, it was here. All day, she'd thought she'd lost it. She was breathless when she found it under a dish towel on the kitchen table. Hoping it might be Jake, she glanced at the display. For the first time ever, she was disappointed when she saw Micah's name "Hi," she said, hoping she didn't sound as depressed as she felt.

"What's wrong, Rosie?"

"I never could fool you," she muttered. "Nothing's wrong. Just ... nothing."

"That usually means something. I wanted to call and let you know we're back."

"All of you?"

"No. Dad started feeling bad, so Mom decided they should come home. Holly and I decided to come with them. So did Angela and her family, since her kids were getting homesick. I told Sofie and the others to go ahead and finish their vacation, and that I'd call if we got bad news."

"What's wrong with Dad?"

"I'm not sure. I made an appointment for him at the doctor's office for Monday afternoon at three. Mom said she'd make sure he keeps it. You know how the old man feels about doctors. So, everything okay with you?"

"Couldn't be better."

"You'd tell me if there was anything wrong?"

"Don't I always?"

"Not always. Something's bothering you, Rosie. I can hear it in your voice."

"Just a little man trouble," she said brightly. "Nothing for you to worry about."

"All right," he said. "Don't tell me. What are you doing for dinner Saturday night?"

"Eating it?"

"Very funny. I'll be by around six to take you out."

She wanted to argue, but then he would know for sure that something was wrong. "Great. See you then."

She ended the call, then stared at the phone. What was she going to do about Micah?

What was she going to do about Jake? Was it possible to fall in love with a man you'd known less than two weeks? A man who wasn't really a man at all?

She pressed her hands to her temples, thinking that her two favorite men in the whole world had given her a first class headache.

Chapter Twenty

Kincaid arrived at *The Bloody Rose* at 10:30. He walked around the perimeter twice, all his senses alert, but there were no hunters lurking in the shadows.

Going inside, he took a table in the rear and sat with his back to the wall. He wasn't sure meeting the vampire hunter was such a good idea, but he was suddenly curious to hear what the man had to say. He ordered the house special with an extra splash of blood.

He thought about Rosa while he waited for Rhinehart. As expected, she had been horrified when he'd told her about killing the man back east. Not that he could blame her, but she had tried to understand. Hell, she had even been sympathetic. He wasn't sure why he'd gone to see her. Maybe he'd wanted someone to lash out at him. Maybe he'd been hoping for solace. All he knew was that, right or wrong, he couldn't stay away. It had been all he could do not to wrap his hands around the throat of the man she had been with and break his fool neck.

But the biggest surprise had come when she climbed onto his lap, as trusting as a child, to comfort him. If she could find it in her heart to forgive him for what he'd done, maybe he'd be able to forgive himself. Saintcrow had surprised him, too. He hadn't really expected the master vampire to destroy him. After all, he hadn't killed the guy in the vampire's territory. But he'd been so damn understanding. He had always envied Saintcrow's self-control.

Kincaid drained his glass when Rhinehart came through the door.

The hunter glanced around before spotting him. He hesitated a moment before striding toward the table.

"Right on time," Kincaid remarked.

"And you came early."

Kincaid grinned. "So, what do you want to talk about?"

Rhinehart gestured at the gold band on Kincaid's wrist. "I want to know where you got that. It hides your whereabouts from Luca, doesn't it?"

"Maybe."

"He's quite mad," Rhinehart said quietly. "He's determined to have your head and Saintcrow's, too. And now he's threatening me and my family if I don't bring him what he wants."

"You're afraid of him."

"Damn right! I told you, he's stark, raving mad. I can't destroy him and unless I can find a way to hide, I'm a dead man. And my family, as well."

"Saintcrow told me you've got kids."

"A girl and two boys."

"How old are they?"

"Why?"

Kincaid shrugged. "Just curious. I've never had a family."

"My daughter's six months old. The boys are five and three."

"I got the talisman from a black witch a long time ago. I have no idea where she is now. She could be dead for all I know, although witches tend to live a pretty long time."

"Tell me about it. Luca's got to be well over a hundred if he's a day. So, you have no idea where she might be?"

"When I found her, she lived in New Orleans. She went by the name of Izabela."

"Thanks. Any chance you'd be willing to try to get in touch with her for me?"

"I'll think about it," Kincaid said grudgingly. "Careful," he warned when Rhinehart reached inside his jacket.

"I'm just getting my card," the hunter said. Moving carefully, he plucked a business card from his inside jacket pocket and handed it across the table.

Kincaid glanced at it, then shoved it into a pocket of his jeans. "I'll be in touch if I find anything."

"I appreciate it," Rhinehart said, rising.

Kincaid nodded, his eyes narrowed thoughtfully as he watched the hunter leave the club. But Paul Rhinehart was the least of his worries.

What was he going to do about Rosa?

Chapter Twenty-One

Rosa sighed as she switched off the nine o'clock news. It had been two days since she had seen Jake. In that time, she hadn't heard from him, either. Had he gone home? She frowned, thinking she didn't even know exactly where he lived, just that he had a lair somewhere in Montana. He had been constantly in her thoughts, even at work, so much so that she had mixed up several appointments and neglected to enter two of them in the computer. If she kept that up, she'd soon find herself looking for another job.

Friday night, she thought morosely, and she didn't have a darn thing to do. Especially now that Bria was engaged and rarely available for a girls' night out.

And tomorrow would be just as bad. A whole Saturday with nothing to look forward to. Well, not nothing, she amended. Micah was coming by to take her out to dinner. As much as she loved her brother, she wasn't looking forward to seeing him, worried that she might accidentally mention she was seeing someone. Once she let that slip, her brother wouldn't rest until he knew who she was seeing, where they'd met, if it was serious. She had never been good at keeping secrets from Micah. He always knew when she was hiding something and she didn't want to talk about Jake. Or come up with a lot of lies about the good time she'd supposedly had in Florida. For one thing, she was a terrible liar. For another, Micah could always tell when she was skirting the truth.

Rosa glanced at the book on the end table, but she wasn't in the mood to read. There was nothing good on TV. She hated going to the movies alone.

She wondered what Kadie and Saintcrow were doing.

She wondered what Jake was doing.

Why had she been so anxious to get back home and go to work? She wished she was still in Morgan Creek. She missed Saintcrow and that surprised her. She had been afraid of him at first. But she knew him better now. Under that gruff exterior, he was a pretty nice guy. Maybe she would quit her job and move to Morgan Creek. Saintcrow could probably find her employment as a waitress or a maid, or maybe a receptionist at the hotel.

She huffed a sigh. Admit it, she thought glumly. It isn't really Saintcrow or Morgan Creek that you miss. It's Jake. She bit down on her lower lip. If she called his name, would he hear her when they were so far apart? She frowned, thinking that if she called and he didn't answer, she wouldn't know if it was because he was avoiding her, or because he hadn't heard her.

Jake Kincaid, if you can hear this, please let me know. I... I miss you.

A minute passed. Two. Five. Nothing. Had she really expected it to work?

She went into the kitchen for a can of soda, let out a startled gasp when she returned to the living room and found Jake standing in front of the fireplace, his back toward her.

Apparently sensing her presence, he turned slowly to face her.

Murmuring, "You came," she picked up the unopened can she had dropped and placed it on the coffee table.

"Did you think I wouldn't?"

"I think you're afraid of me."

He glared at her, then lowered his gaze. "You're right, I am." He sucked in a deep breath, and slowly released it. "But I'm a hell of a lot more afraid of what I might do to you."

The tension between them was a palpable thing as they stood facing each other. She wasn't sure who moved first, but suddenly she was in his arms, those strong arms that felt like home. She rested her cheek on his chest and closed her eyes, thinking she would be content to stay there the rest of the night. The rest of her life. She shivered as he brushed a kiss across the top of her head.

"Rosa." He whispered her name, his voice raw with need.

"Where have you been the last two days? I was so afraid I'd never seen you again."

"It wasn't easy, staying away from you."

"Why did you try?"

"You know why. It's hard to be near you, want you, and not have you."

"I guess I'm the first woman to tell you no."

He laughed softly.

She looked up at him. "Am I?"

"You are, indeed, my sweet girl."

"I didn't mean to ruin your reputation."

His gaze, hot as a fourth of July firecracker, raked her from head to heel. "The night isn't over yet."

"Is that a threat?"

"Maybe a promise," he whispered, and captured her lips with his. His tongue ravished her mouth as he pulled her body closer to his, letting her feel the heat of his arousal. She flattened her hands on his chest, intending to push him away, only to lose herself in the magic of his kisses. His tongue was a flame as it dueled with her own. She felt herself sinking into him, had a vague sense of a fire crackling to life in the hearth, the feel of the floor beneath her, the welcome weight of his body wrapped around hers.

She gasped his name when she felt the prick of his fangs.

As if she'd doused him with ice water, he reared back, a look of horror on his face.

"Dammit," he growled.

She blinked at him, shocked to see blood on his lips. It took a moment to realize it was hers.

Rising, he took hold of her hands and lifted her to her feet, his gaze not quite meeting hers. "I'm sorry."

Rosa pressed her fingers to her throat, sucked in a breath when he moved her hand out of the way and ran his tongue over the tiny wounds she could feel there.

"I'm sorry," he said again. "If you're smart, you'll tell me to leave and never invite me inside again."

Going up on her tiptoes, she laced her fingers behind his neck. "I guess I'm not very smart. You stopped in time. Didn't you?" she asked, suddenly uncertain.

He nodded curtly.

"Then why are you so upset? You didn't ravish me. You didn't drink me dry." She cocked her head to the side. "Did you even come close?"

"No," he said. "But I might have."

"But you didn't. I'm willing to give you a little more, if you need it."

"Woman, you're asking for trouble. You know that, don't you?"

She shrugged. "Maybe. And maybe it would help ease your craving."

"It probably would," he agreed. "But are you willing to take that chance? Dammit, woman, you don't know how easy it would be to turn you. How tempting it is."

"Promise me," she said seriously. "Promise me you won't do that without asking me first."

"How do you know you can trust me to keep a promise like that?"

"I don't," Rosa admitted, and then grinned inwardly. She still wasn't 100 percent sure if she wanted to be a vampire or not. If Jake turned her, the decision would be out of her hands.

"I'm not sure if you're just a little crazy or totally insane," he muttered.

"Maybe both."

"Come on," he said. "Let's go someplace where there's a lot of people."

"Afraid to be alone with me?" she teased.

Pulling her into his arms, he kissed her, long and hard, then growled, "What do you think?"

Breathless from his kiss, she gasped, "A lot of people sounds like a good idea."

They went dancing at a local nightclub. The music was soft and low, the man who held her in his arms was dangerous and irresistible. And she knew she was a heartbeat away from falling head over heels in love with him. His kisses were intoxicating, his scent irresistible, his smile ... oh, what that smile did to her insides. And he needed her.

Jake grinned at her as he read her thoughts. "Still think you can tell me no?"

She stared into his dark, fathomless eyes and wondered if she still wanted to.

Leaning forward, he whispered, "Don't worry, love, I won't take advantage of you." He kissed her lightly. "Unless you ask me to."

It was late when he took her home. Standing inside the doorway, he drew her into his arms and kissed her, long and slow and deep, until she leaned into him, wondering how much longer she could resist the urgings of her own heart. She sighed when he lifted his head.

"Good night, my sweet girl. Dream of me."

"I'll try."

He kissed her again, hot and quick, and then he was gone.

Rosa grinned as she shut and locked the door, thinking it was a good thing Jake had left when he did. One more kiss and she might have dragged him off to her bed and begged him to have his wicked way with her.

⚜ ⚜ ⚜

Rosa slept late in the morning. For a time, she simply lay there, reliving Jake's kisses from the night before, replaying the erotic dreams she'd had and wondering if reality could measure up to her fantasies.

Rising, she brushed out her hair, pulled on her bathrobe, and scuffed into the kitchen in search of caffeine. She couldn't stop smiling when she thought about last night. Dancing with Jake, being in his arms, savoring his kisses…Yes, he was dangerous. Yes, he had killed a man. Probably more than one in his long existence. Was she afraid of him? She had every right to be, but she couldn't believe he would hurt her, at least not intentionally. Of course, if he drained her dry, she would be just as dead whether it was an accident or not. It was a sobering thought.

But it was a risk she was willing to take.

She fixed scrambled eggs for breakfast, changed the sheets on her bed, pulled on a pair of jeans and a sweatshirt. After sorting through her dirty laundry into piles, she dumped her sheets in the washing machine.

Later, she picked up her dry cleaning, then went to the local bookstore where she spent the better part of an hour browsing the latest bestsellers but didn't find anything that sounded promising. She stopped in at her favorite dress shop, but didn't like anything she tried on, except for one slinky little black dress that she couldn't afford.

Muttering, "I guess it's just not my day," she drove to the nearest coffee shop for a cheeseburger, onion rings, and a chocolate shake. Her last stop was the grocery store.

It was after five when she returned home. Humming softly, she put her groceries away, then went into the bathroom to shower and get ready for her dinner date with Micah. She wasn't exactly looking forward to it, still worried that she might let it slip that she was seeing someone. And that that someone was a vampire. Once that particular cat was out of the bag, there would be no putting it back.

She took a deep breath when she heard his knock at the door. Maybe if she asked enough questions about Holly and the family and the trip to Italy, she could keep Micah from asking questions she didn't want to answer.

"Hi," he said. "I'm a little early, but…" He stepped inside, took a deep breath, and swore a pithy oath.

"What's wrong?" she asked, although she was pretty sure she knew the answer.

"Who have you been with?"

"I beg your pardon?"

"Don't play games with me, little sister. You've been with Saintcrow!" Micah's eyes narrowed suspiciously. "And a vampire that I don't know has been here."

Rosa stared at him while her mind scrambled for a reply.

"Who was it? Dammit, Rosa, answer me!"

She was still trying to think of an answer when there was another knock at the door. Before she could react, Micah pulled it open and came face-to-face with Kincaid.

For stretched seconds, the two men glared at each other.

And then Micah frowned. "Who the hell are you?" he demanded.

Rosa shivered as Jake's power slammed into Micah, almost knocking him off his feet. He staggered back a few steps as Jake crossed the threshold.

"I'm Kincaid. And I would advise you to shut the hell up if you know what's good for you."

Micah didn't back down, simply stood there, his whole being vibrating with tension. "Rosa is my sister." He spoke through gritted teeth. "And I have every right to know what the hell is going on."

Kincaid grunted softly. "Point to you, Ravenwood."

"How do you know Saintcrow?"

"He's an old friend of mine." Kincaid stressed the word 'old'. "You obviously know him, too, since he's given you his blood."

Micah fixed his gaze on Rosa. "Is this guy the reason you stayed home while the family went to Italy?"

"Not exactly."

"So why, exactly?"

Rosa bit down on her lower lip. The raw testosterone bouncing off the walls was thick enough to cut with a knife. "Why don't you both sit down?"

Micah hesitated a moment, then sat in the chair across from the sofa.

"I'll stand," Jake said.

Rosa perched on the edge of the couch. "Micah, I went to Morgan Creek while you were gone."

"What the hell! Why would you go there alone?"

"I wanted to meet a vampire. You won't turn me. Neither will Sofie."

"And this guy will, is that it?"

"No. I asked Saintcrow to introduce me to some vampires. I wanted to know what being a vampire is really like and I wanted to hear it from someone who didn't know me and wouldn't try to influence me one way or the other. Saintcrow introduced me to Jake, in hopes that he would scare me off. But it didn't work. We've been seeing each other ever since." She held up a hand when her brother started to speak. "You can't tell me what to do any more, Micah. I won't stop seeing Jake. But I decided that being a vampire isn't for me. At least not right now. So stop worrying."

"And I'm just supposed to accept this… this relationship?" Micah asked, his voice tight with disapproval.

"Yes. But I promise if I change my mind, I'll call you before I do anything."

Micah nodded slowly, then glanced at Kincaid. "You might be older than I am. You might be stronger. But if you turn my sister against her will, I'll hunt you down and destroy you if it's the last thing I do."

"I can live with that."

Looking resigned but unhappy, Micah stood and headed for the door. He paused, his hand on the knob, as if he wanted to say more, then stalked out of the apartment and slammed the door behind him.

"Well, that was heaps of fun," Rosa muttered.

"You can't blame him for being upset."

"If I'd known you were coming over, I'd have called and warned you."

"We were bound to meet sooner or later," Jake said, dropping down on the sofa beside her.

"I guess so." She toyed with the hem of her sweater. No doubt she would be hearing from Sofia as soon as Micah could get in touch with her.

"Are we okay?" Jake asked.

"Why wouldn't we be?"

"Your brother's pretty strong for a vampire who's only a few years old. I guess he's got Saintcrow's blood to thank for that."

Rosa shrugged.

"Who turned your brother?"

"I guess you know all about Morgan Creek," Rosa said. "About what it used to be?"

"Yeah."

"Well, my brother was turned by one of the vampires who once lived there. He told the family about it the night he admitted he was a vampire. It happened after Saintcrow freed all the people and sent the vampires away. He told us how a female vampire had found him and turned him against his will and everything that happened afterward."

"Lilith," Kincaid said. There had only been one female vampire in Morgan Creek. "I met her a long time ago. Nobody liked her."

"That's what Saintcrow said."

"Enough talk about your brother and the past," he said, draping his arm around her shoulders.

"What do you want to talk about?"

"Talk is overrated," he said, caressing her cheek with his fingertips.

Her heart skipped a beat as his gaze moved over her. She went into his arms gladly, her eyelids fluttering down as his mouth covered hers in a long, searing kiss that drove Micah and everything else from her mind. There was only Jake, his lips teasing hers, his big hands lightly stroking up and down her back, her thighs, skimming the curve of her breast.

She stilled when she felt his tongue lave her neck.

"Rosa?"

"Just a taste," she murmured, her heart pounding. "Promise?"

He groaned low in his throat, his voice husky with need when he said, "I promise."

She held her breath as his fangs lightly pierced her throat, heard him moan with pleasure as he drank from her. One taste. Two. Three... Her fear that he would take too much faded away as pleasure took its place. What was he doing to her?

"Jake?"

He growled low in his throat as he ran his tongue over the punctures before lifting his head.

"You said just one."

"I know." He gazed deep into her eyes. "Forgive me, love?"

"I guess so." How could she refuse when she was almost sorry he had stopped.

"I'd be happy to let you drink from me."

She stared at him, only then remembering that Kadie had once asked her if she had tasted Kincaid's blood. She asked Jake the same question she had asked Kadie. "Why would I want to?"

Kadie hadn't answered her.

Jake said, "You'll like it."

"I don't believe you."

"It's true. Aren't you the least bit curious to know what it's like when I bite you?"

Was she? His bite filled her with a warm, sensual pleasure. Did drinking from her give him the same pleasure in return? It hadn't occurred to her that it might involve more than just satisfying his thirst.

He bit into his wrist and held it out to her. "What do you say, love?"

She stared at the blood, darker and redder than her own. What *did* it taste like?

"Only one way to find out."

She seemed to be standing outside herself, watching, as she lowered her head and licked at the blood. It was hot and thick on her tongue and it filled her with warmth and a surprising desire for more. Horrified, she jerked her head away. And then wished again that she had taken just a little more.

He smiled a knowing smile as he sealed the wounds, then drew her into his arms again.

She hid her face against his chest, embarrassed by what she'd done.

And anxious to do it again.

Chapter Twenty-Two

After leaving Rosa, Kincaid transported to New Orleans. It had been a good long while since he'd been there. The city had changed some—a few old buildings had been restored. There were a couple of new souvenir shops, a bookstore, a palm reader. At this time of night, only the bars were open.

He strolled down Bourbon Street, not really searching for prey, just familiarizing himself with the lay of the land. Passing by an alley, he caught the scent of another vampire, a young one. The sweet notes of soft jazz drifted from one of the nightclubs.

He headed for the last known address of the witch, Izabela, a small, two-story house located in an older section of town. A six foot wrought-iron fence surrounded the property, a thick chain secured the gate. A large Doberman prowled the grounds.

When Kincaid vaulted over the fence, the dog rushed toward him, only to come to an abrupt halt when Kincaid bared his fangs. With a low whine, the dog tucked its tail between its legs and trotted into the backyard.

Taking the porch steps two at a time, Kincaid rang the bell.

Three minutes later, Izabela pulled back the lace curtain that covered the window beside the door. She stared at him for a long moment before unlocking the door. "Kincaid."

He nodded. "Mind if I come in?"

"Do you mean me any harm?"

"No. I only want to talk."

He felt her power move over him before she unlocked the screen door. With a murmured, "Come in," she stood back to allow him entrance.

He followed her into the parlor. Little had changed since the first time he'd been there. The living room was a large space crammed with heavy wooden furniture. Several bookcases held an assortment of volumes, ivory figurines, and a variety of other knickknacks. A dozen colorful throw pillows were scattered across the high-backed sofa. Dark green carpet covered the floor. A gray Persian cat lay curled up on a pink pillow beside the fireplace. A one-legged crow sat on a perch, watching him through black beady eyes.

"Sit," she invited.

He moved a couple of pillows out of the way to make room on the sofa. She looked the same as the last time he had seen her, a tiny woman with a mass of golden hair, and pale brown eyes with yellow flecks. He had often wondered how old she was. Somewhere between sixty and a hundred and fifty, he guessed.

She settled into a large rocking chair covered by a brightly colored fringed throw. "What brings you here after so many years?"

"Someone I know has asked if you could fashion a protective band for him like the one you made for me."

"Who is this someone?"

"A hunter."

She lifted one brow. "A hunter?"

Kincaid shrugged. "He seems like a decent guy, for a hunter, but he got tangled up with Luca and now his life and that of his family is in danger."

"When did you start protecting vampire hunters?"

Kincaid shook his head. "Like I said, he's a decent guy and he's scared shitless. Can you help him?"

"What is he willing to give me in return?"

"I don't know. What do you want? The blood of his first-born child?"

She laughed, although it was more of a cackle. "Not this time. Let me think on it. Who is the woman you've been with?"

"What? Why?"

"I have never known you to spend much time with the same woman. This one must be something special."

Kincaid shrugged. "She amuses me."

The witch gave him a look that told him she knew Rosa was far more important than just a passing fancy.

"So, can you make a talisman for this guy or not?"

"Of course I can!" she snapped. "Tell him I want something of Luca's in return. Something personal. His wand. A dagger. An item of clothing. Something with his scent on it."

"That won't be easy," Kincaid remarked.

"Neither is magicking a talisman that offers protection against such a powerful witch. And since you're here…" She left the room, returning with a small, glass vial. "You still owe me for the band you wear."

Muttering an oath, Kincaid bit into his wrist and held it over the vial until it was full. He didn't know what the witch did with his blood, but giving her his blood from time to time had been the price of the protective gold band he wore.

"I'll summon you when the talisman is ready," she said, capping the vial. "Don't bother coming after it if your friend doesn't have what I require."

Kincaid stood and headed for the door.

He felt the witch's power follow him. He had often wondered which of them was stronger—the vampire or the black witch.

The sun was rising when he reached his lair. His last thought before the Dark Sleep carried him away was of Rosa.

Chapter Twenty-Three

Rosa went to church Sunday morning. Sitting there, gazing at the beautiful stained glass windows, the flowers on the altar, she wondered how vampires would be judged in the Hereafter. Would they be damned? How many times had Jake broken the Sixth Commandment—*Thou shalt not kill?* He could perhaps be forgiven for the lives he had taken to save his own, but what about the others? He had been born a slave in violent times and turned against his will. Was he responsible for all those deaths? Or did the guilt fall on the vampire who had turned him?

She had read somewhere that vampires had no soul, but she didn't believe that. How could you live and breathe, love and laugh, if you had no soul?

Had Micah killed anyone? Had Sofia? Ethan? Kadie? She knew Saintcrow had taken many lives. Did he ever wonder about meeting his Maker? Did Jake?

Forcing the dark thoughts from her mind, she focused on the closing hymn being sung by the choir, finding comfort in the words of enduring love and mercy and forgiveness.

She was supposed to go to her parents' house for dinner, she thought, as she pulled out of the church parking lot, but she felt a sudden need to be with them now. So, why wait? she thought. And made a quick turn onto the freeway.

Twenty minutes later, she pulled up in the driveway. For a moment, she sat in the car, remembering all the good times she and her siblings had had in this house—the pajama parties, picnics in the backyard, sneaking downstairs on Christmas Eve to peek into the gaily wrapped packages under the tree, hiding Easter eggs, going trick-or-treating around the neighborhood, pillow fights with her brothers and sisters, sharing secrets with Sofia.

Sighing, Rosa stepped out of the car and entered the house.

Her mother's face lit up when she strolled into the living room. "Rosa, *mia figlia*," Lena exclaimed, wrapping her daughter in a bear hug. "We didn't expect you until later."

"I hope you don't mind my coming early."

"Silly girl. Of course not. *Papà*, look who's here."

"I see her," Luciano said irritably. "I'm old, not blind."

Rosa grinned as she hugged her father. Taking a step back, she took a good look at him. Micah was right. He didn't look well at all. Hopefully, the doctor would find out what was wrong and fix it. If not, maybe a little vampire blood would help. It had done wonders for him in the past.

"How have you been?" Lena asked. "Still happy with your job?"

"You bet. I'm due for a raise next month."

"Are you seeing anyone?"

Rosa bit down on her lower lip. Should she mention Jake?

"I know that look," her father said. "Who is he? What does he do for a living? How long have you known him?"

"One question at a time!" Lena admonished with a smile.

"I have been seeing someone," Rosa said slowly. "But we've only been out a few times."

"But you like him?" her father asked, a twinkle in his eye.

"Yes, *Papà,* I like him."

"Enough questions," Lena said. "Come, Rosie. I was about to make *cannoli.*"

⚜ ⚜ ⚜

Micah and Holly arrived shortly after sundown, closely followed by Angela, her husband, Steve, and their two kids, Jane and Gina. Now eight and five, she couldn't believe how the girls had grown since she'd last seen them. Rosa missed her other sisters and brothers. They had always had such great times when they all got together. Even with half of the family still on vacation, there was laughter and good-natured joking around the table. Dinner had been awkward when Micah, and later, Holly, became vampires. At first, they hadn't come over on Sundays until after dinner, but the initial awkwardness soon passed. Now, no longer self-conscious about eating in front of Micah and his wife, the rest of the family dined on her mom's homemade pasta, her father's spaghetti sauce, and bread still warm from the oven. There was wine for the adults and sodas for the kids.

Rosa found herself missing Jake as she looked around the table. Except for her, all the other adults were happily married. It made her feel suddenly more alone than ever before. Where was Jake? If she had invited him tonight, would he have come? Or would he feel uncomfortable, being there with her family while hiding what he was from everyone but Micah and Holly?

She excused herself from the table and went into the living room when her cell phone rang. "Jake! I was just thinking about you."

"I know."

She bit down on her lower lip. Took a deep breath. And blurted, "Would you like to come over to my parents' house? We're about to have dessert."

He hesitated for a moment, then said, "If you want me to be there, I will."

"I do."

"I don't think it's a good idea."

"Please?"

"All right, love. I'll be there in five."

She smiled as she resumed her seat at the table.

"No phones during dinner," her father reminded her.

"I know, but it was my young man." She felt Micah staring at her but assiduously avoided his gaze. "He's coming over in a few minutes."

Lena and Luciano exchanged knowing glances. None of their kids had ever invited their dates to the house unless the relationship was serious.

"Can I talk to you for a minute, Rosie?" Micah asked.

"I don't think so," Rosa replied, rising. "He's here." She didn't stop to wonder how she knew that as she hurried to open the door. "Hi."

"Hi." Lowering his voice, Jake said, "Are you sure this is a good idea?"

"I don't care. I miss you. Come in." Taking his hand, she led him into the living room, where the family had gathered. As she made introductions all around, she was acutely aware of the tension humming between Micah and Jake.

When all the introductions had been made, Angela and Lena went into the kitchen to get the desserts and brew a pot of coffee while Micah opened two bottles of wine.

Jake politely declined dessert, saying he'd already eaten, but he readily accepted a glass of wine.

During the next hour, Rosa realized inviting Jake to the house had been a huge mistake. Her father asked a number of probing questions—where did they meet, what did Jake do for a living, where was his family from, were his parents still living?

Rosa held her breath as Jake answered every question—every answer a lie. She slid a covert glance at Micah, praying that her brother, who was well aware that Jake was lying, wouldn't say anything.

When the family had had their fill of dessert and the coffee pot was empty, Rosa stood. "It's been fun, guys, but I really have to run. I have to be at work early tomorrow morning for... for inventory." She hugged her parents, grabbed Jake's hand, and fled the house.

"I told you it wasn't a good idea," Jake said as he held her car door for her, then went around to the passenger side.

"One I won't make again," she muttered as she started the car and pulled away from the curb.

"Your brother knew I was lying."

"I know."

Jake grunted softly. He had been waiting for Micah to expose the truth, wondering what he would say when Rosa's brother called him a liar in front of the family.

Rosa sighed with relief when she pulled into her parking spot and switched off the engine. "I'm glad that's over."

"You and me both."

Exiting the car, she locked the door and walked down the path to the stairway that led to her apartment, keenly aware of the man trailing behind her. "Do you want to come in?" she asked as she slid the key into the lock.

"Sure." He followed her inside, shut the door, gathered her into his arms, and kissed her.

She leaned into him, her fingers locking behind his neck.

"I've been wanting to do that all night long," he said, his lips moving against hers.

"Don't stop now."

Mouths fused together, he moved toward the sofa, carried her with him as he eased down on the cushions. There was magic in his touch, in the heat of his tongue.

"Rosa, do you know what you do to me?"

She laughed softly. She knew exactly what she did to him. The laughter died in her throat when she felt his tongue slide along the length of her neck.

He sensed the change in her and lifted his head. "You have no idea how tempting you are."

Seeing the faint red glow flickering in his eyes, she was sure she had a pretty good idea.

The red faded from his eyes as he said, "I've never known anyone like you."

"Didn't you know?" she said. "There is no one like me. Ask anyone in the family."

He laughed softly as he sat up. "I believe it. You're lucky to have people who care about you."

"I know, but sometimes they treat me like I'm still a little girl. Especially Micah."

His gaze moved over her, lingering on her breasts. "You don't look like a little girl to me."

She blushed under his gaze.

"I'd better go," he said. "It's getting late and I'm getting… never mind."

"Will I see you tomorrow?"

"Count on it." Cupping her cheeks in his palms, he kissed her, and then he was gone.

Jake had no sooner left than there was a knock at the door.

Blowing out a breath, Rosa went to answer it. As she had suspected, it was Micah.

"What the hell were you thinking?" he demanded as he strode into the living room. "How could you introduce that killer to our family?"

"Excuse me?"

"Don't pretend you don't know what I'm talking about. I've heard about Kincaid." He shook his head. "All those lies tonight. What are you going to do when the truth comes out?"

"I don't know. And don't you dare talk to me about killers, Micah Ravenwood! Not when your best friend is a master vampire who imprisoned hundreds, maybe thousands, of people for his own pleasure!"

Micah stared at her. And then he grinned. Rosie had always come out fighting when she knew she was in the right. Lifting his hands in surrender, he said, "All right, you made your point, little sister. I just hope you know what you're doing."

"Me, too. I think I'm in love with him, Mikey. I've never felt this way before."

"Yeah. Well, I guess we don't have much control over who we love. Just remember, I'm on your side, no matter what."

"I know.

"Have you told Sofie about Jake?"

"No."

He grunted softly. "Do you want me to?"

"I don't know. Maybe." She frowned, and then she nodded. "I think you should. If you tell Sofie now, it'll give her time to get used to the idea before she gets home."

"I'll take care of it. Just be careful, Rosie. I don't think he'd hurt you intentionally, but…Just be careful," Micah said again.

"I will. Usually, when things start to get too hot, or Jake feels like he's losing control, he leaves."

Micah blew out a sigh. "Just don't take any chances or do anything stupid, all right? And don't be afraid to call me if you need help," he said, giving her a hug. "See you soon."

"Don't forget to let me know what the doctor says about Dad."

"I'll call you as soon as I know anything."

Rosa sighed as she walked him to the door. With Micah on her side, everything was bound to be all right.

Chapter Twenty-Four

Kincaid called Paul Rhinehart soon after he left Rosa's house.

The hunter answered the phone on the second ring. "Hello?"

"It's me. I found the witch. She said she could magick a talisman for you."

"That's great news! Thanks."

"Slow down, cowboy. She wants something in return."

"I should have known," Rhinehart said. "What does she want?"

"Something that belongs to Luca. An item of clothing. His wand. A dagger. Something he values that has his scent on it."

Rhinehart muttered a pithy oath. "That won't be easy."

"Nothing ever is."

"What did she require from you?"

"My blood. Whenever she wants it."

"Holy hell! What does she do with it?"

"I never asked. She said if you can't come up with something suitable, you can forget it."

"Thanks. All I need now is a good excuse to go see him, and steal something he treasures. How hard can that be?"

Kincaid laughed at the despair in the hunter's voice. "'Oh, what a tangled web we weave,'" he muttered, and ended the call.

Chapter Twenty-Five

Rosa had trouble concentrating at work Monday morning. She couldn't help worrying while she waited for Micah to call with news of their father. And when she wasn't worrying about her Dad, she worried about what Sofia's reaction would be when Micah told her about Jake. And yet, how could Sofia say anything against it when she was married to a vampire? Still, she and Sofia had always been close and, right or wrong, Rosa wanted her sister's approval.

At 4:30, Micah called to let her know that the doctors hadn't found anything seriously wrong with their father. "Doc Macky said the old man's got high blood pressure and high cholesterol. He said Dad had probably experienced a serious bout of indigestion, likely caused by too many rich desserts while we were on vacation. He put Dad on a strict diet to lower his salt intake and prescribed medication for his blood pressure and cholesterol," Micah said. "And he wants Dad to see a heart doctor for some other tests."

"A heart doctor!"

"It's just a precaution," Micah said. "Don't get your pantyhose in a twist."

"Nobody wears pantyhose anymore, big brother," she said. "Thanks for letting me know."

"Stop worrying. You know if it was anything serious, Sofia would be on her way home. Talk to you later."

Rosa ended the call, then stared at her phone, remembering a few years back when her father had fallen off the roof. He had been unconscious for so long, Sofia had asked Ethan to give their father some of his blood. It had worked wonders. Thinking of that now helped put her mind at ease.

She was shutting down her computer when her cell phone rang again. She snatched it up when she saw Jake's name. "Hey."

"Hey, yourself. What are you doing?"

"Getting ready to go home."

"I'll meet you there, okay?"

"Okay." Smiling, she grabbed her handbag, said a quick goodbye to Bria, and hurried out the door.

⚜ ⚜ ⚜

Jake was waiting for her outside her apartment when she got there. Just looking at him made her whole body smile. She had it bad, she thought. She'd never really been in love before. She wasn't even sure this was love, but whatever it was, she never wanted it to end.

He grinned at her as she unlocked the door and followed her inside.

She tossed her handbag on the sofa and walked into his arms.

He closed his eyes as he wrapped her in his embrace. Just holding her made his existence worthwhile. Her warm, womanly scent, the rapid beating of her heart, the fragrance of her hair and skin all combined to enflame his senses. He captured her lips with his, his tongue plundering the sweetness of her mouth. Heaven help him, but he wanted her in ways he had never wanted any other woman, needed her beyond words. Dammit. He had never needed anyone.

Didn't want to need her. But he couldn't let her go. Would never willingly let her go.

She moaned softly as he rained feather-light kisses along the length of her neck.

"Let me." It was a plea, a prayer, for relief.

She pushed her hair out of the way, tilted her head to the side, and closed her eyes. As always, there was no pain, only warm, sensual pleasure as he drank from her. Lost in the wonder of it, she clung to his shoulders, not caring if he took it all.

A sharp curse brought her back to reality. She stared up at him. His eyes were red and angry.

"Don't ever let me do that again."

"Do what?"

"You have to be strong for both of us, love. Sometimes, when I drink from you, I lose all sense of time. I want only to drink and drink and never stop."

Suddenly alarmed, she asked, "Was I in danger?"

"Not this time, but you might have been."

She shivered with delight when he ran his tongue over the wounds in her neck. "It feels so good when you drink from me, the last thing I want is for you to stop."

"I know." He held her close. Keenly aware of how tempting her blood was, he usually fed before he came to her. Tonight, he'd been so eager to see her, he hadn't taken the time. He wouldn't make that mistake again.

He took her out to dinner, insisted she have several glasses of wine.

When he would have filled her glass again, Rosa held up a hand in protest. "I can't hold any more."

With a nod, he set the bottle aside. The color had returned to her cheeks, her heartbeat was strong and steady.

They left the restaurant a short time later. "Where do you live, Jake?" Rosa asked as they walked to the car. "All I know is that it's some place in Montana."

"I have a house in Butte." He opened the car door for her, closed it behind her before going around to the driver's side.

She watched him slide behind the wheel and start the car. "Oh?"

"It's not much," he said as he pulled out of the parking lot. "But I'm rarely there."

"Where do you stay when you aren't there?"

"Wherever I want."

"I thought maybe you lived near Morgan Creek since Saintcrow wanted me to meet you."

"It only takes a thought to get there no matter where I am."

She nodded. How could she have forgotten that? "Where does Rhinehart live?"

"Somewhere in Wyoming."

"And the necromancer?"

Kincaid shook his head. "I don't know. But I suspect he lives in Wyoming, too."

"Is Rhinehart still hunting you?"

"Yes. And no. I guess you could say we have a truce."

"What kind of truce?"

"A temporary one. He's afraid of Luca, and he wants a talisman like mine, something that will hide his presence from the witch. He asked me to help him get one."

Rosa stared at him. "He's a hunter and he asked for your help? Doesn't that sound kind of fishy?"

"Yeah. But he seems like a decent guy, for a hunter. Enough talk about Rhinehart," Kincaid said. "I can think of more interesting things to do."

Rosa batted her eyelashes at him. "Can you?"

"Can't you?"

"Definitely."

"Damn girl, don't look at me like that."

"Like what?" she asked innocently.

"You know like what," he growled, and stomped on the gas.

They made back it to her apartment in record time. After parking the car, Kincaid lifted her into his arms and carried her swiftly up the stairs. Once inside, a thought closed and locked the door. And then they were lying on the floor in front of the fireplace and he was caressing her, kissing her, whispering that he adored her. She couldn't think when he was kissing her like that. Right and wrong didn't seem to matter when every fiber of her being was on fire for his touch. She had a sudden yearning to give him anything and everything he wanted.

She had no idea what would have happened if the ringing of her phone hadn't penetrated the haze of passion that engulfed her. She grabbed the phone as if it was a lifeline, gasped, "Hello?"

"Rosie! What's this I hear about you dating a vampire?"

Kincaid swore a silent oath when he heard a woman's voice on the other end of the call. Sitting up, he raked his fingers through his hair. Of all the lousy timing, he thought.

"Sofie, can I call you back? Oh, hang on a minute," Rosa said, as Jake tugged on her arm.

"Take your call. I'll see you tomorrow." He kissed the tip of her nose. "It's for the best."

When she frowned at him, he said, "Things were getting a little out of hand."

She couldn't argue with that. Still, she was sorry to see him leave. With a sigh, she put the phone to her ear again. "Sofie? I'm back."

Her sister cut right to the chase. "So, a vampire." Sofia drawled. "Seriously?"

"If it's good enough for you, it's good enough for me," Rosa retorted.

"Where did you meet him?"

"Saintcrow introduced us."

"Saintcrow! When did you see him?"

Rosa blew out a sigh. "I hope you're sitting down, sis. It's a long, long story."

Chapter Twenty-Six

With nothing better to do, Kincaid transported himself to *The Crimson Rose,* where he ordered the house special. He couldn't decide if he was relieved or angry with the way the night had ended. As badly as he wanted to make love to Rosa, he was worried that he might lose control and drink from her at the same time. Then, too, she was a virgin. He still found that hard to believe. They were a rare breed in this day and age. No doubt her sister's call had come at just the right time.

He tossed back his drink and ordered another. One downside of being a vampire was that it was damned near impossible to get drunk. He had never intended to fall in love with Rosa, but he'd been hooked the minute he looked into those guileless, dark eyes. And once he'd kissed her, all thought of a brief fling had been forgotten.

"Women," Saintcrow said, taking the barstool beside him. "How they mess with a man's mind."

"Yeah. Why aren't you home in bed with yours?"

"She was watching some mushy love story on TV."

Kincaid grunted.

"So, trouble in paradise?"

"No. We were going at it pretty hot and heavy when her sister called. It came at just the right time. I could have waited around, I guess, but I figured I was going to be the main topic of conversation."

"She's got a lot of family."

"No shit."

"They're good people. Give them a chance."

Kincaid nodded. For better or worse, he was willing to put up with just about anything to make her his.

"Have you heard anything from Rhinehart?"

"Not since the other night. I found the witch who made my talisman. She said she would magick one for Rhinehart in exchange for something that belongs to Luca. Maybe the hunter hasn't been able to get ahold of anything. It's only been a couple of days."

Saintcrow grunted. "Can't be easy, stealing from a guy as powerful as Luca Sasan. Let me know if you hear anything. And tell Rosa 'hey' for me when you see her again."

⚜ ⚜ ⚜

Sofia blew out a sigh as Rosa came to the end of her story. "I can't wait to meet him."

"Aren't you going to tell me I'm making the biggest mistake of my life?"

"I was," Sofia admitted. "But who am I to tell you what to do? We've always supported each other. The other night, I was remembering when Ethan turned me. I'd been injured but it wasn't a fatal wound. I knew I'd want him to turn me sooner or later, so I just told him to do it. I've never regretted it, and yet, sometimes I wish I'd waited a few years. So, my only advice is to be sure it's what you want if you decide to let Kincaid turn you. Once it's done, it's done."

Rosa nodded, remembering that Saintcrow had said the same thing. They talked a few more minutes, sharing their worries about their father, promising to get together soon.

Rosa smiled as the call ended and she set her phone aside. She had to admit, she felt a lot better after talking with Sofia. And more determined than ever to make things work with Jake, no matter what.

She was debating whether to call him and ask him to come back over when there was a knock at the door, and a sexy male voice called, "Mind if I come in?"

Rosa's heart skipped a beat. Had he been reading her mind? "Silly question," she replied, and a moment later, Jake was on the couch beside her and she was in his arms again.

"So, what did your sister have to say? Did she threaten to lock you up if you didn't stop seeing me?"

"Hardly," Rosa said, laughing. "She said she didn't have any right to tell me what to do. Just told me not to do anything that couldn't be undone until I was sure it was what I wanted."

"Quite a change in her tune, I'd say."

"I know, right? It wasn't at all what I expected."

"I want this to work between us," he said, caressing her cheek with his knuckles. "I'm going to try my damnedest to keep my hunger and my lust under control. I know every time we get close, I head for the door, but it's only because I'm afraid of hurting you."

"I know. And I can't say it doesn't scare me every now and then. But I really don't think you'll hurt me."

"Well, next time you're worried, just mention Saintcrow's name. I have a healthy respect for his threats."

Rosa grinned at him, thinking it was a good sign that they could joke about it. "Can I ask you something?"

"Anything. Any time."

"I know you don't work, but..." She paused, wondering how to delicately phrase her question.

"You want to know how I pay for things when I have no income."

She felt herself blush as she nodded.

"The way most vampires do. We steal what we need. At least I used to. Decades ago, I found a man's wallet. There was no identification in it, nothing but a thick wad of hundred-dollar bills. I went to a broker and invested it in the stock market. He advised me to buy into a few things that really paid off. Things like Apple and Amazon and Microsoft. And Disney."

"So I'm dating a billionaire?"

"Are you thinking of marrying me for my money?"

"Are you calling me a gold-digger?"

He kissed the tip of her nose. "Let's just say I have enough to keep you comfortably for the rest of your life. And mine, too."

He must really be rich, she thought, since vampires lived for hundreds of years. "Is that how Saintcrow made his money?"

"I never asked."

"Tell me about your house in Montana. What's it like?"

"You wouldn't like it. It's an ugly little two-bedroom house on a cul-de-sac. I only go there to rest."

"Where do you spend the rest of your time?"

"Lately, I spend most of my waking hours with you."

"Just me?"

He nodded. "I don't want anyone else."

"Me, either."

"What do you think about quitting your job and moving to Morgan Creek with me?"

She blinked at him. "Are you serious?"

"Yeah."

"Funny you should say that. I was thinking about that very thing not long ago."

"Is that right?"

She nodded, then frowned at him. "Were you reading my mind?"

"No."

"Where would we live?"

"I think Blair House is empty."

"Blair House! Where the vampires used to live?" she exclaimed, and then remembered that Ethan had remodeled the place from top to bottom and modernized everything before he married Sofia. "My sister used to live there."

"You can change anything you don't like," Kincaid remarked. "And it has a secure lair in the basement."

"You want us to live together?"

"I'm not suggesting we share a bedroom," he said with a sly grin. "Unless you want to. And if you're not happy in Blair House, I'll build you a place of your own."

Rosa bit down on her lower lip, surprised at how attractive his offer sounded. Sofia, Ethan and their adopted daughter, Jenny, lived in Morgan Creek. Micah and Holly had a place there, too, although they spent a good part of their time in Arizona these days. And, of course, Saintcrow and Kadie lived there.

Thinking about Rhinehart and the necromancer, it occurred to her that there was probably no safer place to be than in Morgan Creek, surrounded by vampires who cared about her.

"What about Saintcrow?" she asked. "He might not like the idea."

"Leave that to me." Jake's gaze searched hers. "What do you say?"

"I'll think about it for a day or two."

But in her heart of hearts, she knew the answer would be yes.

Chapter Twenty-Seven

Luca frowned when he opened the door and found Rhinehart standing on the porch. "I don't recall summoning you. Have you good news?"

"I believe so."

Luca took a step back. "Enter."

Paul took a deep breath as he crossed the threshold into the witch's house.

"Speak."

"I've managed to make friends with the vampire, Kincaid. I think he trusts me."

"You came here to tell me that?"

"Hunting him was pointless. I could never take him unawares. But if he trusts me, it will be easier to take his head."

Luca grunted. "You mentioned a woman before."

"Yes. But she's of no importance. She isn't with Saintcrow any longer."

"Where is she now?"

Paul shrugged. "I imagine she went home, wherever that might be."

"I think she may be the answer."

An icy knot formed in the pit of Rhinehart's stomach. "How so?"

"Saintcrow was looking after her. He must care for her. Perhaps enough to bargain for her life."

"I don't know where she is. I don't know anything about her," he said, hoping the witch couldn't detect the lie.

"Her name?"

"I think it's Rosa something."

"Find out."

Rhinehart nodded, his gaze moving around the room, searching for something he could take for Kincaid's witch. Something that wouldn't be missed right away. A crystal ball? The silver pocket watch lying on the coffee table? The delicate figurine of a sea nymph carved from ivory? The long, gray cloak hanging by the front door?

"We're through here," Luca said. "Bring me Kincaid's head or the woman. Now be gone."

Paul swallowed hard, trying to think of a way to get Luca out of the room, but nothing came to mind. He went cold all over when Luca's gaze trapped his. Oh, Lord, he had to get out of here, now!

"I'll find the woman," he called over his shoulder, his words tripping over each other as he dashed toward the door. Only to be halted by Luca's voice calling his name.

Swallowing hard, he turned to face the witch.

"I've decided I want Kincaid alive," Luca declared. "I want to take his head myself."

Chapter Twenty-Eight

Once Jake planted the idea of moving to Morgan Creek in her mind, Rosa couldn't think of anything else. She liked the town and whatever it didn't have could be found in Custer or Cheyenne or one of the other major cities. Distance was no problem, not when Jake could quickly transport her anywhere she wanted to go.

Rosa smiled as she headed home on Friday night. With work taking up her days and Jake taking up her nights, the time seemed to fly by.

⚜ ⚜ ⚜

On Saturday, she asked Jake if they could go visit Blair House before she made her decision about moving to Morgan Creek.

Five minutes later, they were there. Rosa wasn't sure what she had expected, but it wasn't this. The front door opened onto a small foyer, which led to a large, rectangular living room, also empty of furniture, as were all the other rooms but the kitchen, which held all the modern appliances, but nothing more. Rosa guessed that, once Sofia was turned, they had no further use for a stove, a refrigerator, microwave or dishwasher.

"Guess we'll have to furnish the place," Kincaid remarked as he followed her from room to room.

"We can use my furniture," Rosa said, "unless you'd rather buy…"

"Maybe you'd better ask me before you start moving in," Saintcrow said, materializing in the doorway. "Last time I looked, I still owned this place."

"I planned to ask for your approval," Kincaid said. "Once Rosa agreed to live here."

Saintcrow glanced at her. "You want to move to Morgan Creek?"

She shrugged. "Jake asked me about it, but he was supposed to talk to you before we did anything."

"Uh-huh."

"I didn't think you'd mind," Kincaid said. "What's one more vampire?"

Saintcrow shook his head. "You beat everything, you know that?"

"So, do we have your blessing?"

"Why the hell not?" Saintcrow glanced at Rosa. "How do your folks feel about it?"

"They don't know yet."

"Well, I'm sure Kadie and Sofia will be glad to have you here," Saintcrow said. "When do you plan to move in?"

Kincaid looked at Rosa, one brow raised.

"I don't know," she said. "I should probably give them at least a weeks' notice at work."

"Well, I'll leave the two of you to work out the details," Saintcrow said. "While you do that, I'll go tell Kadie we're going to have some new neighbors."

⚜ ⚜ ⚜

Rosa called Micah later that night after Jake brought her home.

"Hey," he said, "what's up?"

"Oh, nothing." Rosa nibbled on her lower lip. She had intended to tell him she was moving in with Jake, but she'd lost her nerve as soon as she heard Micah's voice. "Dad seems to be doing okay. I've talked to him a couple of times."

"Uh huh. I went by your apartment three times today and you weren't there."

The perfect opening. "I went to Morgan Creek."

"What the hell for? And what's that got to do with anything?"

"I went with Jake. He asked me to move there with him."

"What? Are you out of your ever-lovin' mind?"

"I don't think so."

"I'm not so sure. How long have you known Kincaid? A couple of weeks? And you're ready to move in with him?"

"I like it there," she said defensively. "And Ethan and Sofie live there."

"Yeah, yeah. What's the real reason?"

"I love him, Micah. We aren't going to share a room or anything. I won't have to pay rent. I'll have a bigger house. And I'll be close to my favorite sister and her husband."

"At least there'll be someone around to keep an eye on you," he muttered.

"Very funny, big brother. Say hi to Mom and Dad and Holly for me."

"Any chance I can talk you out of this?"

"I don't think so."

'Well, at least I can tell mom and dad I tried." He was silent a moment. "Rosie?"

She frowned at the serious tone of his voice. "What?"

"You haven't done anything stupid, have you?"

"No. Stop worrying. I promised I wouldn't do anything without telling you first."

"Yeah, well, see that you remember that."

"Love you, Mikey."

"Love you, too."

Smiling, Rosa tossed her phone on the sofa. Maybe everything would work out, after all. Sofia and Micah didn't seem as upset about her dating Jake as she had expected. Maybe Jake and Micah would even become friends. With that thought in mind, she went up to bed.

Chapter Twenty-Nine

Rosa went to church Sunday morning, spent the afternoon with her parents, and a quiet evening with Kincaid.

"When's the last time you went to church, Jake?" she asked during a lull in the conversation.

He looked at her, one brow raised. "Not since I was a slave in Drakos' house."

Astonished, she said, "The vampire took you to church?"

"He was a very religious man."

"I don't believe it."

"It's true. He'd been a strong Catholic before he was turned, and ... " Kincaid shrugged, "he dragged me to Mass every Sunday morning, until he turned me. Since he could be awake during the day, I imagine he went without me while I was at rest."

"Did you ever go after that?"

"Once or twice." Kincaid shook his head. "But it just didn't seem relevant to me anymore. You go often, don't you?"

"Not as often as I should." She paused a moment before asking, "Would you go with me?"

"You must know I'd go anywhere you want."

Rosa sighed as she snuggled against him. He really was the most amazing man.

⚜ ⚜ ⚜

Monday morning, Rosa let it be known she was quitting on Friday. She apologized for the short notice, saying there was no help for it, she was leaving the state. Everyone in the office said they would be sorry to see her go.

She went to lunch with Bria that afternoon.

"I can't believe you're leaving us," Bria said. "What happened? I thought you liked your job."

"I do, but, well, you might say I had a better offer."

"Oh?" Bria leaned forward, her dark eyes alight with curiosity. " From who?"

"Jake. We're going to move in together." She grinned as her friend's eyebrows shot up to her hairline. "We're going to share a house, not a bedroom."

Bria rolled her eyes. "How long do you think *that* will last?"

"As long as I want it to," Rosa said with a laugh.

"Well, I'll miss you. And I'll still expect you at my wedding. You *and* Mr. Right. I've gotta see this guy. Are you sure you don't have *any* pictures?"

Rosa shrugged. She needed to remedy that, she thought, and then wondered if it was even possible to photograph vampires.

⚜ ⚜ ⚜

It was the first thing she asked Jake when she saw him that night. She was surprised when he laughed. "What's so funny?"

"You're the first one whoever asked me that."

"Well, what's the answer?"

"Yes. We photograph."

"I have a friend at work who's dying to see what you look like. Would you mind if I took your picture and sent it to her?"

"Okay by me, as long as she's not a hunter."

"She's a dental hygienist."

"That doesn't mean she doesn't hunt vampires in her spare time."

"Very funny," Rosa said, reaching for her cell phone. "I won't send it to her if you'd rather I didn't, but I would like one for me."

"With or without fangs?" he asked dryly.

Rosa burst out laughing. When she caught her breath, she said, "Without is fine."

She took a couple of Jake by himself and a selfie of the two of them. She decided not to send them to Bria, thinking it would be more fun to see her friend's reaction face-to-face when she got a look at Jake.

"So, what would you like to do tonight?" he asked.

"Go bowling?"

"Bowling?"

"Don't you know how?"

He snorted. "My average is about 270."

She should have known. He'd had centuries to practice. "You're on."

"Have you had dinner?"

"No, but I can grab something at the bowling alley."

⚜ ⚜ ⚜

It was Monday night, but early enough that the lanes were mostly empty. They rented shoes, picked a couple of colorful bowling balls from the racks, and walked down to their lane.

"I think I should get a handicap," Rosa said as she tied her shoes. "My average is only about 130."

"I'll spot you fifty pins. How's that?"

"How about a hundred?"

"All right," he said, grinning. "A hundred."

They were about half-way through the first game when Rosa noticed that the women on the lanes at either side of them couldn't stop staring at Jake. Not that she could blame them. He was clad in a pair of faded jeans and a black, short-sleeved tee shirt that emphasized his broad shoulders and impressive biceps. And not only was he gorgeous, but he moved with a kind of lithe grace that was beautiful to watch.

She was somewhat surprised when a teenage girl approached her.

"Miss? Can I ask you a question?"

"I guess so."

"Is he a movie star?" the girl whispered.

Rosa bit back a laugh. "No, sorry."

The teenager sighed. "You sure are lucky."

"I think so, too."

"What was that all about?" Jake asked as the girl returned to her own lane.

"She wanted to know if you were famous."

"Seriously?"

"Well, you are rather handsome, you know."

"Yeah, right. You're up."

They bowled three games. Jake rolled a 260, a 275, and a 280. With her handicap, Rosa bowled a 250, a 245, and a 230.

"You could have let me win once," she muttered as they returned their shoes to the desk.

"You wouldn't want me to throw a game, would you?"

"Well, maybe just one."

"Next time," he said, as they left the alley. "Where would you like to go now?"

"I don't care. Anything you'd like to do is fine with me."

"Anything?" he asked with a wicked grin.

"*Almost* anything," she amended when they reached the car.

He opened her door for her. "Let's go home and neck."

"Neck? Nobody uses that word anymore."

"I'm an old-fashioned guy," Kincaid said as he closed the door.

"Well, I guess you have been around a very long time," she teased.

"Hey," he growled, as he settled behind the wheel. "I'm very sensitive about my age."

"I didn't know." she said, choking back a laugh. "I won't mention it again. But just for the record, how old were you when you were turned?"

"Thirty-two," he said, as he pulled out of the driveway onto the street.

"Wow, you really *are* old."

She was grinning when they pulled up in front of her apartment. She would have to let the manager know she was moving. Being a stickler for rules, Mr. Evans would probably refuse to return her deposit, since she wasn't giving him thirty days' notice. But it couldn't be helped. She also needed to hire a truck to transport her furniture to Morgan Creek.

Kincaid parked in the allotted visitor's space, then turned to face her. "So, you've decided to move to Morgan Creek with me."

She huffed an annoyed sigh. "I wanted to tell you."

"Sorry. Sometimes your thoughts are so loud and clear, I can't help reading them."

"Well, stop it."

"I'll try." He got out of the car and came around to open her door. Now that they had exchanged blood, it was almost impossible not to read her thoughts.

Inside, Rosa flipped on the lights, kicked off her shoes, and settled on the sofa.

"Are you mad at me?" Jake asked, sitting beside her.

"Terribly." She wasn't, of course.

He lifted one brow. "You can't lie to me, you know? I can smell a lie at a hundred paces."

"Seriously?"

"Seriously."

"That's amazing."

"So are you." Sliding his arm around her shoulders, he drew her closer. His kiss, when it came, was warm and infinitely tender. "You know I'm crazy about you, don't you?" he murmured.

"I had an inkling you might be."

"Can I hope you feel the same about me?"

"I wouldn't be moving in with you if I didn't."

"I know. I just wanted to hear you say it."

"Next Friday is my last day at work."

"I'll call a mover to pick up your furniture Saturday morning. If you pack your clothes and whatever else you need, I'll transport it to Morgan Creek."

Rosa sighed. Next week, she would be starting a whole new chapter in her life. She couldn't help wondering how it would end.

⚜ ⚜ ⚜

Tuesday after work, she stopped to pick up some packing boxes, then made a quick trip to the bookstore, thinking she'd need something to read in Morgan Creek. There was no bookstore in the town, and the library didn't always get new books right away. She had always loved to read, especially historical romances set in the Old West. She grinned as she remembered Jake telling her he had once been a cowboy. She would have loved to have known him then, she thought. She'd always had a weakness for horses and men in cowboy hats.

She picked up two historical romances and a new mystery and then went to O'Shay's and bought a pair of black jeans. She was about to leave the store when she saw a tee shirt featuring the very sexy Damon Salvatore on it. Unable to resist, she grabbed one off the rack, wondering what Jake would say when he saw it that night.

⚜ ⚜ ⚜

Jake laughed when she opened the door. "I guess you probably drooled over him, although he was such an unrepentant killer, I'm surprised you didn't like his brother better."

"Oh, Stefan was nice," Rosa said. "But not nearly as sexy as Damon."

Kincaid snorted.

"You probably didn't even watch the show," Rosa said, leading the way into the living room. Of course, she'd been a little girl when the series had first aired, but she had seen it in reruns on TV.

"Of course, I did," he said. "It was as entertaining as it was unrealistic. I've never seen vampires make such a mess when feeding."

Rosa grimaced. She had forgotten about that. "Well, I loved the show. I had quite a crush on Damon."

He jerked his chin toward her tee shirt. "Looks like you still do."

Rosa shrugged. "Well, I don't think he's nearly as sexy as you are, if that makes you feel better."

"You can have a crush on as many fictitious vampires as you like," he growled as he pulled her into his arms. "As long as I'm the only flesh-and-blood one in your life."

Chapter Thirty

Paul Rhinehart hadn't been able to find an address for Rosa Ravenwood, which he thought was strange, although he'd found one for a Luciano Ravenwood. The same address was on her driver's license, and since she wasn't married, he assumed the address was her family home, and that she'd never taken the time to change her residence on her license.

Now, as he drove by the house, he considered how he might convince her parents to tell him where she lived without arousing suspicion or sounding like a stalker.

He drove around the block and parked in front of the house. He was still trying to think of a believable reason to knock on the door when a man stepped out onto the front porch.

Rhinehart frowned. The man was too young to be her father. A brother, perhaps? There was a definite resemblance.

Taking a deep breath, he exited the car and strolled up the walkway. "Excuse me, I'm looking for Rosa Ravenwood. This is the last address I have for her."

The man eyed him suspiciously. "How do you know my sister?"

"I'm a reporter. I met her in Morgan Creek while I was there doing a story." The truth, even a partial truth, was always better than an out-and-out lie, when possible.

"Why are you looking for Rosa, hunter?"

Rhinehart tensed with the realization that the man in front of him was a vampire. What the hell was he going to do now? He reached into his coat pocket, his fingers curling around a wooden stake. And then he paused. Taking a head in broad daylight, with curious neighbors watching from across the street, probably wasn't a smart idea.

"I asked you a question, hunter. I can force you to answer me, if I have to."

Deciding the truth would serve him best, Rhinehart said, "I'm looking for a vampire who goes by the name of Kincaid. I'm in deep shit with a necromancer who's threatened my life and that of my family if I don't bring him what he wants."

"Not my problem. What has any of this to do with Rosa?"

"I was hoping she'd tell me where to find Kincaid."

"She's not here."

"Who are you?"

"Smart enough not to tell you my name. If *you're* smart, you won't come sniffing around here again. I've got your scent now. Finding you won't be any trouble at all. Now, get the hell out of here. If I see you again, I'll break your neck."

With a curt nod, Rhinehart turned and walked slowly to his car, slid behind the wheel, and laid rubber as he peeled away from the curb.

Micah stared after him. And then he pulled out his cell phone and called Saintcrow.

The master vampire answered on the second ring. "What's up?"

"Some hunter came to my parents' house looking for Rosa. I read his mind. His name's Rhinehart. Does that mean anything to you?"

"Yeah. Did he say why he's looking for Rosa?"

"He was hoping she could tell him where to find Kincaid. Do you know Rhinehart?"

"I've met him a couple of times. He's supposed to be one of the best, but I have my doubts. He just doesn't seem like a stone-cold killer to me."

"Is he likely to turn up in Morgan Creek?"

"Probably. He's been here before."

Micah grunted softly. It was likely a good thing Rosie was moving there. Five vampires ought to be able to protect her, especially when Saintcrow was one of them. And, if need be, he could be there in no time at all. "If I hear anything else, I'll let you know. Oh, maybe you should warn Kincaid and let him know Rhinehart is looking for him, and for Rosa, too."

"Consider it done."

⚜ ⚜ ⚜

Paul Rhinehart drove around aimlessly after leaving the Ravenwood house. He hadn't had any luck in stealing from Luca. Even if he had, he didn't know how to get in touch with Kincaid. And on the off chance he secured talisman to protect him from the necromancer, it wouldn't keep Luca from finding his family.

He swore as a new thought occurred to him. Taking anything from Luca would be just plain stupid. Unless he could hand the object off as soon as he got it, it would lead Luca right to him. *Shit!*

He slammed his fist against the steering wheel. And then he frowned. Saintcrow seemed like a decent sort, for a vampire. What were the odds that he'd let him hole up in Morgan Creek until he could figure a way out of this mess?

The idea made him laugh. No vampire was going to give aid and comfort to a hunter. And yet Saintcrow was the only man he knew who had a chance of standing against Luca.

What the hell, he thought as he made a U-turn and headed for the freeway. There was nothing for him at home, what with Nancy and the kids out of the country. And Morgan Creek was as good a place as any to hide out, and better than most.

Chapter Thirty-One

For Rosa, the next few days flew by. She packed a few things each night after work—books and pictures in one box, shoes and handbags in another. Shirts and skirts and pants in one carton, dresses in another. Kitchen stuff in one plastic container, towels in another. She made sure to label each one in bold, black letters.

She scrubbed the sinks and the appliances, cleaned out her refrigerator, washed the windows, mopped the floors, and shampooed the rugs, determined to get her five hundred dollar cleaning deposit back. She'd also filled out a form at the post office to have her mail forwarded to her new address.

And every night, Jake was there. He rubbed her back and her feet, brushed her hair, ordered takeout when she felt like eating in. He had taken care of the moving van, which was scheduled for Saturday morning, with a guaranteed delivery to Morgan Creek no later than Monday afternoon. He had also arranged for the movers to tow her car, since he could get her there in moments rather than days. And he had already transferred most of her clothes and shoes to Blair House so they would be there waiting for her on Saturday when she arrived.

The best part of every night was cuddling on the sofa with Jake, sharing their thoughts, getting to know each other better as they traded stories of their youth. Of course, his adventures were far more dangerous and exciting than hers had ever been.

"You've lived so long," she remarked. "What decades did you like best?"

"That's easy. The 1870s and 80s. The west really was wild back then. The only laws were the ones men made for themselves. I liked working on the ranch with the horses. I miss the simplicity of those times, the freedom."

"I guess you were able to be awake during the day back then, too?"

"Pretty much."

Rosa wondered who he had preyed on. Certainly not the cowboys he worked with. People in town, then? "I thought you looked like a cowboy the first night we met."

"Comfort over fashion," he drawled with a grin. "Tomorrow's your last day at work. You're not having any second thoughts are you?"

"No." She was finally having an adventure of her own, she thought. Moving to Morgan Creek, joining her life with Jake's, perhaps for the rest of her life. Surely moving in with a vampire was the most dangerous and exciting thing she had ever done. And she could hardly wait.

"I won't let anything happen to you," he murmured.

And then he pulled her into his arms and there was no more time for talk

Kincaid kissed and caressed her, careful to keep his desire for her blood in check. It had gotten easier with time, mostly because he made sure to feed, and feed well, before he came to her. He loved holding her in his arms, loved the warmth of her skin, the heat of her kisses, the way she melted against him, her willingness to let him take a little of her blood from time to time, the trust she had in him not to take too much.

Knowing she had to get up early for work in the morning and that it was her last day, he didn't stay late. "I'll see you tomorrow night."

Rosa nodded. "Come early."

"Can't live without me, huh?"

"Don't be silly."

"I guess you don't want me to kiss you good night then," he said, and headed for the door.

Rosa stared after him. Was he really going to leave without kissing her good night?

Grinning, Kincaid turned around and pulled her into his arms. "I love you, my sweet girl," he murmured. "More than you can imagine."

The way he kissed her left no doubt in her mind that he meant every word.

⚜ ⚜ ⚜

The girls in the office took Rosa out to lunch on her last Friday at work and pestered her for information on the man who had stolen her heart.

"I'm still waiting for a picture," Bria reminded her.

Rosa smiled as she pulled her cell phone out of her handbag and scrolled through her photos. "Here you go," she said, and slid her phone across the table.

Bria's eyes widened. "Oh, girl, you really hit the jackpot, didn't you?"

The other girls all clamored to see his photo.

"Is he as nice as he is gorgeous?" Franny asked.

"Who cares," Evie murmured, practically drooling.

"He's a hunk, that's for sure," Lana said, returning Rosa's phone. "I'd go anywhere he asked."

"Me, too," Rosa said, smiling. "And I am."

The rest of the day passed quickly. At closing time, she packed up her few personal belongings and bid a last, tearful goodbye to Bria. She was almost home when she decided to go see her folks. They had been less than thrilled when they learned she was moving to Morgan Creek, but knowing that Ethan and Sofia would be there had put most of their misgivings to rest.

As Rosa pulled into the driveway, it occurred to her that she had never lived more than a few miles from home. Always, in the back of her mind was the knowledge that if she lost her job or her apartment, if she got sick or into trouble, home and help were only a few minutes away. That wouldn't be true once she moved to Morgan Creek.

It was a sobering thought.

Chapter Thirty-Two

Saintcrow muttered an oath as he sat up. Careful not to wake Kadie, who slept peacefully beside him, he slipped out of bed, tugged on a pair of jeans and a sweatshirt, and willed himself to the hotel where he found Paul Rhinehart standing at the registration desk.

"What the hell are you doing here?" Saintcrow growled.

"I was hoping you wouldn't mind if I stayed here for a few days."

"Don't you have a home of your own?"

"Yeah, but it's kinda lonely there right now. I sent Nancy and the kids to Ireland to stay with her grandparents until this mess with Luca is settled."

Saintcrow grunted. "Weren't you supposed to sneak off with something that belongs to Luca to give to Kincaid's witch?"

"Yeah, well... " Rhinehart shrugged. "He never left me alone. Besides, it occurred to me that having Luca's property would lead him right to me."

Saintcrow frowned, wondering why neither the witch or Kincaid had thought of that.

"So, can I stay?"

"I don't know. The last thing I need is for Luca to come here looking for you."

Shoulders slumped, Rhinehart picked up his suitcase.

"Shit, I guess you can stay," Saintcrow decided. "But if Luca shows up, you're on your own."

"What about my family? Any chance I can bring them here?"

"I think it might be smarter if you stay away from them until this thing with Luca is resolved."

"Yeah, you're probably right."

"As long as Luca doesn't have anything that belongs to them, they won't be easy to find, not with an ocean between them."

Rhinehart nodded. "Is Kincaid here?"

"If you're still after his head, you can leave now."

Rhinehart signed the register and stepped away from the desk.

"What aren't you telling me?" Saintcrow asked sharply.

"Luca doesn't want Kincaid's head anymore. He wants him alive."

Saintcrow snorted. "If you think you can take him, you're out of your mind."

"I'm not foolish enough to try. I came here hoping you could shield me from Luca."

"Probably not. But I can ward the bridge against him, although as strong as he is, it might not stop him for long."

"I'm willing to chance it."

Saintcrow regarded Rhinehart through narrowed eyes as his mind brushed the hunter's. He was missing something, he thought, but the man seemed sincere. Hoping he wasn't making a mistake in giving the hunter sanctuary, he said, "I want you out of here by next Friday."

Rhinehart nodded. "I appreciate your help."

Saintcrow stared after Rhinehart as the hunter crossed the lobby and stepped into the elevator. Muttering, "I've got a bad feeling about this," he headed back home.

Chapter Thirty-Three

The apartment felt strangely empty when Rosa woke on Saturday morning. Everything had been packed except her furniture, the clothes she intended to wear that day, a mug and the coffee pot, a spoon and a fork, and a small frying pan she used to scramble a couple of eggs for breakfast.

The movers showed up at nine. It didn't take them long to load the furniture, since she didn't have much more than her living room set, her bed, dresser, and nightstands, and the table and two chairs in the kitchen. All the appliances had come with the apartment.

The movers had just loaded the last of her things when Jake arrived. "Ready to go?"

"As soon as Mr. Evans comes up to look the place over. I'm hoping he'll refund my cleaning deposit even though I didn't give him thirty days' notice."

"Oh, he will," Jake said with a wink.

"How can you be so sure?"

Kincaid shrugged. "Just a feeling."

Rosa was wondering what he meant by that when Mr. Evans knocked on the door, even though it was open. He was a short, rotund man, with a receding hairline and a perpetual frown.

"I just came by to have a quick look around," he said.

Rosa nodded, her fingers crossed behind her back, as he ambled from room to room.

"Not bad," he said, "but since you neglected to give me the thirty days' notice specified in your rental agreement, I'm afraid you've lost your deposit." He smiled wolfishly. "In any event, we rarely return cleaning deposits. We like to repaint when our tenants move out, so it's spotless when the new ones move in. The way it was for you. You understand?"

"I suppose so."

With a brief nod, he headed for the door, only to stop after a few steps. Pivoting on his heels, he said, "I suppose I can make an exception in your case, Miss Ravenwood. We're sorry to lose you." Pulling his checkbook from his back pocket, he quickly wrote out a check and handed it to her. Then, looking somewhat confused, he hurried out of the apartment.

Rosa glanced at Jake, her brow furrowed thoughtfully. "Did you have anything to do with his sudden about-face?"

"Who? Me?" Jake asked, looking affronted. "Why would you think that?"

"I don't know. You tell me."

"He wasn't going to use your deposit for paint. He was planning to buy himself a new TV."

"How do you know that?"

"Darlin', I read his mind, and I decided you needed the money more than he did."

Rosa shook her head, not sure if she should be feeling grateful or guilty.

"So, are you ready?" Jake asked.

Grabbing her handbag and her cell phone, she took a last look around the room. She had expected to feel at least a little sadness—after all, it had been her first apartment—but she had no real ties here, no memories worth keeping except the hours she had spent with Jake. "I'm ready."

Rosa closed her eyes when Jake wrapped his arm around her waist. When she opened them again, they were standing in the living room at Blair House.

Rosa shivered as she glanced around. The room was lovely, the walls a pale gray, the carpets a darker shade. There was a large fireplace. White drapes covered the windows. She knew it was only her imagination, but she had the creepy sensation she was being shadowed by ghosts as she moved from room to room. There were six bedrooms, a large, rectangular kitchen, and two bathrooms.

"How many vampires lived here?" she asked.

"Eight, I think. Seven men and a woman."

"Did someone die in this house?"

"I don't know. Why?"

Rosa shook her head. "No reason." She opened a small door located at the far end of the hallway next to a linen closet. "What's down there?" she asked, staring into the darkness below.

"The basement. I think Saintcrow used it as a lair at one time, but I'm not sure."

Rosa felt a chill as she closed the door and made her way back to the living room, where Jake had stacked her boxes and suitcases against one of the walls.

Noting her discomfort, Kincaid took her in his arms. "Are you gonna be all right here? If not, we can go somewhere else."

"I'll be okay. The house is beautiful." And it was. The smaller bedrooms and bathrooms were all painted in pastel colors—pink, blue, lavender, or green. The master bedroom was pale blue, the carpet a darker shade. The kitchen was a sunny yellow. "It's just a little disconcerting, knowing a bunch of vampires used to live here."

"Well, there's just one now," he said, his gaze caressing her. "I'm thinking I should check you into the hotel for a couple of days."

"Probably a good idea" she agreed. "Since the furniture—and the bed—won't be here until Monday." It took only a few minutes to throw a couple of changes of clothes and a few other necessities into a small bag.

Reaching into his pocket, Kincaid withdrew a rather ornate brass key. "This is to the front door."

Smiling, she slipped it into the pocket of her jeans.

"I'm ready to go when you are," he said. "I left my car out front last time I was here." It was faster to transport from one place to the other, but that didn't give him the same kick as driving the Mustang.

"Let's go," she said, when her stomach growled. "I could really use something to eat."

⚜ ⚜ ⚜

They drove into town and checked into the hotel, then went into the restaurant where Rosa ordered a blueberry waffle and orange juice. She glanced at Jake. She had rarely seen him so early in the morning. "If you want to go and rest for a while, I'll be all right."

"Are you sure?"

She nodded.

He looked doubtful a moment, then nodded. "I'll be in the basement at Blair House if you need me."

"Are you going to sleep on the concrete?"

"I could, but I'm not. There's a good-sized bed down there." Standing, he dropped a twenty-dollar bill and the key to the Mustang on the table, then bent down to kiss her cheek. "I'll see you later this afternoon."

"All right." Rosa smiled as she watched him stride out of the restaurant. Coming here had been the right thing to do, she thought, and wondered when Sofia and Ethan and their daughter would come home. Sadly, Sofia couldn't be awake very long during the day the way Micah and Ethan could. Kadie was also able to be awake when the sun was up, but only for short periods of time

Rosa sighed as she sipped the last of her orange juice. She had once promised Micah that she would let him turn her if she ever decided she wanted to be a vampire, but she wondered now if that was her best option. The older the vampire who made you, the stronger you would be. And Jake was a lot stronger and older than Micah. And Saintcrow was older than Jake…

She shook her head. What was she thinking? There was no way she would ever get used to the whole blood thing. Tasting Jake's had been pleasant, but it was her understanding that vampires only rarely drank from each other. And she definitely didn't want to give up all the food and drink she enjoyed to exist on a warm liquid diet stolen from strangers.

⚜ ⚜ ⚜

Kincaid took a detour to Saintcrow's house after he left the restaurant. The master vampire was waiting for him when he arrived.

"Tell me I didn't sense Rhinehart's presence in the hotel," Kincaid growled. "Tell me you're not stupid enough to let that hunter stay here."

"Nice to see you, too."

"Dammit, what were you thinking?"

"I'm thinking I'd rather have him here, where I can keep an eye on him."

"So you invited him?" Kincaid asked incredulously.

"Of course not. He came looking for sanctuary."

Kincaid snorted.

Saintcrow crossed his arms over his chest. "I've got good news and bad news."

"Yeah?"

"He told me Luca no longer wants your head."

"What's the bad news?"

"Luca wants to kill you himself. One other thing. Rhinehart said he'd decided stealing something from the witch wasn't a good idea, since whatever he took would lead Luca straight to him unless he could hand it off right away."

That made sense, Kincaid mused, and wondered why he hadn't thought of it. Had his whole conversation with the hunter been a ruse? If so, to what end? And what about Izabela? She must have known whatever Rhinehart snatched from Luca would lead the necromancer right to him.

"He's up to something," Saintcrow remarked. "I just can't figure out what the hell it is. Anyway, I told him he could stay until Friday."

Kincaid grunted. "It's your town. I just hope you know what you're doing."

"Anything else bothering you?"

"When there is, I'll let you know."

"Yeah, I'm sure of that," Saintcrow muttered. "Are we done here? My side of the bed's getting cold."

With a shake of his head, Kincaid transported himself back to the restaurant. As long as Rhinehart was in town, he wasn't going to leave Rosa's side.

⚜ ⚜ ⚜

Rosa glanced up, startled, when Jake slid back into the booth. "I thought you were going home to rest?"

"Yeah, well, I changed my mind."

She lifted an inquiring brow.

"Rhinehart's in the hotel."

"What?" she exclaimed. "Why?"

"He came here looking for sanctuary and Saintcrow decided it was better to have him here, where he could keep an eye on him. Can't say as I agree with him. The man's hiding something. I just wish I knew what the devil it is."

"Maybe I should talk to him."

"You stay the hell away from him, you hear me?"

Rosa stared at Jake. He was worried about her. She understood that, but she didn't like him telling her what to do, or the tone of his voice. Asking was one thing, but this?

Kincaid swallowed his rage. It wasn't directed at her. And it was mostly concern, not anger. "He's up to something, love. I don't know what it is. And I know I don't have the right to tell you what to do, but please do as I ask. If anything happened to you . . . "

Reaching for his hand, she twined her fingers with his. "Nothing's going to happen. But I love it that you care. I'm done here," she said, pushing her plate aside. "You should go to Blair House and get some rest."

"I'm not leaving you alone. Let's go upstairs. I can rest in the smaller bedroom."

"All right."

They took the elevator up to their room. Once inside, Kincaid wrapped her in his arms and held her close for a long moment. No one in his life had ever been more important to him than she was. Never had he felt this protective, this responsible, for anyone. He breathed in her scent, kissed her lightly before going into the second bedroom and closing the door.

Rosa stared after him. Was he overreacting? Or was she really in danger? She had to admit, she found it a little disconcerting, knowing Paul Rhinehart was in the hotel. She knew Jake was worried about her, but he was in far more danger from the hunter than she was.

Sitting on the sofa, she grabbed the remote and switched on the TV, determined not to think about it. After a few minutes, she glanced at the bedroom door. What was it like, the Dark Sleep of his kind? Was it like being asleep? Or was it like death? Did it come over him gradually? Or all at once? Did he dream? Was he aware of his surroundings? If she peeked into the room, would he know? If she kissed him, would he feel it?

So many questions. Would she ever know everything about him?

Did she want to?

⚜ ⚜ ⚜

Rosa wasn't in the mood to go out for dinner. Earlier, she had pulled on a comfy pair of sweat pants and a baggy shirt and didn't feel like changing clothes. After a moment's thought, she ordered a shrimp dinner from room service.

She ate while watching an old Clark Gable movie. She had been a fan ever since she'd seen *Gone With the Wind* on cable as a teenager.

The guy from room service had just left with the tray when Jake emerged from the bedroom. Her gaze ran over him. Clad in nothing but a pair of jeans riding low on his hips, he looked sleepy-eyed and so sexy it made her mouth water. She bit down on her lower lip, sorely tempted to take his hand and lead him back to bed.

As always, he knew what she was thinking. She could see it in his eyes, those dark, all-knowing eyes that saw way too much.

Silence stretched between them. He was waiting, she thought, waiting for her to make a decision. He knew before she did what the answer was.

"How was your day?" he asked, dropping down on the chair beside the sofa.

She shrugged. "I stayed in. Watched TV. Took a nap. Called room service for dinner."

Jake raked his fingers through his hair. He needed to feed, but he was reluctant to leave her alone, even for a few minutes. His gaze slid to her throat, to the pulse throbbing there, slow and steady. The beat of her heart, the enticing scent of her blood, called to him.

He stood abruptly and turned his back to her.

Rosa stared at him. He was so tense, every muscle in his back and arms were starkly defined. She frowned, and then she knew what the problem was. "Go," she said. "I'll be all right until you get back."

He shook his head. How could he leave her when Rhinehart was in the hotel?

"I'll go with you."

He turned to face her. "Are you sure?"

"I can't let you starve," she said with a wry grin.

"Rosa." Drawing her into his arms, he held her close, inhaling the fragrance of her hair, the unique, feminine scent that was hers alone.

⚜ ⚜ ⚜

They left the hotel ten minutes later. Jake had pulled on a long-sleeved black tee shirt and his cowboy boots. Rosa had changed into jeans, a navy blue sweater and a pair of sneakers.

Outside, Jake slipped his arm around her waist and transported them to a small town in Montana that housed little more than a gas station, a seedy motel, and a ramshackle nightclub.

Rosa shivered as they waited in the shadows. How did he do this night after night? How did any of them do it? Did it ever bother Sofia or Holly? Somehow, it seemed more nauseating for a woman than a man.

"Stay here," Jake whispered.

Rosa clenched her hands as she watched him approach his prey. She had gone with him once before, but it wasn't any easier to watch this time.

The woman he'd chosen was middle-aged and she smiled when she saw him. Rosa grunted softly. What woman wouldn't smile when Jake looked at her like that? He said something to the woman, took her by the hand, and led her behind a parked car near where Rosa waited.

She glanced away as he bent his head to the woman's throat. But morbid curiosity drew her attention and she watched as he cradled the woman in his arms and bent his head to her neck.

It was over in a matter of moments. Jake released the woman from his thrall and she walked to her car and drove away as if nothing had happened.

"You okay?" Jake asked, returning to her side. "It's not the first time you've come with me."

"I know." She made a vague gesture with her hand. "It's just... I don't know. Hard to imagine doing that night after night. Have you ever fed on the same person twice?"

He shook his head as he wrapped his arm around her. "Not to my knowledge."

"How do you know their blood is safe? I mean, what if they're sick with something contagious? Or their blood is tainted in some way?"

"It doesn't matter."

"Really?"

He nodded. "We're pretty much impervious to disease."

She mulled that over as he transported them back to the hotel.

In their room again, Rosa curled up in a corner of the sofa. "Remember when you said I could ask you anything, any time?"

He nodded as he settled beside her.

"What's it like when you rest? Is it like mortal sleep?"

"No. Vampires don't dream. There's no sense of time passing."

"So, you just close your eyes and you're asleep? Or at rest, or whatever you call it?"

"Pretty much."

"Is it like being... dead?"

"I don't know. I've never been dead, at least not in the way you mean. But even at rest, I'm aware of my surroundings."

She thought that over for a moment. "So, if you were sleeping and I touched you, you'd know it?"

"Yeah."

"I've always heard hunters try to kill vampires while they're at rest because they're vulnerable."

"Fledglings are less aware of their surroundings in the beginning. Less likely to sense the presence of danger until it's too late."

"How long did it take before you could be awake during the day?"

"I don't remember. The vampire who turned me was ancient, so it didn't take as long as it takes most fledglings. All I remember is that it happened gradually."

"But Saintcrow's blood made it possible for Micah and Ethan to be awake during the day."

Jake nodded. "Ancient blood."

"Like yours?"

He nodded again. "Anything else?"

"No. It's just all so fascinating. So unbelievable. Like a fairytale."

"More like a nightmare," Jake muttered.

Her gaze searched his. She had asked him before if he liked being a vampire. He'd said he wouldn't be human again if he could, but she couldn't helping wondering if that was really true.

"Rosa." He caressed her name as he drew her gently into his embrace. "None of the past is important now. All that matters is that you're here now, with me." His hand massaged her nape as his lips moved over hers, evoking images of the two of them writhing in each other's arms. He fell back on the sofa, drawing her down on top of him as his kisses grew longer, deeper.

She reveled in the taste of him, in the touch of his hands sliding seductively over her back, down her thighs, the whiskey-rough sound of his voice as he moaned her name. She stilled as his tongue stroked up and down the length of her neck.

With a low growl, he whispered, "One taste?"

Lost in the wonder of his kisses, she turned her head to the side, brushed the hair away from her neck, sighed as she basked in the warm, sensual pleasure of his bite.

Ignoring the urge to take more than he should, Jake lifted his head and rolled onto his side, carrying Rosa with him.

She smiled at him, her eyes hazy with desire, her lips swollen from his kisses. "Why did you stop?"

"If I hadn't, you'd be a vampire when you woke up tomorrow," he said, his fingers stroking her cheek. "And likely not a virgin anymore."

She blinked at him, speechless. "Did you mesmerize me or something?"

"No."

"I guess I should thank you for your self-restraint," she murmured, suddenly embarrassed. And then she frowned, wondering how he'd managed to caress her, drink from her, and still keep a tight rein on his self-control.

Jake's eyes narrowed as he read her thoughts. This was the first time he hadn't been tempted to drink her dry. Sure, the urge had been there, but he had easily ignored it. Why? The only explanation he could think of was that he had tasted her often enough that it had somehow eased his desire to take it all.

Chapter Thirty-Four

Sunday was a long, lazy day. Rosa slept late. Not wanting to wake Jake, she called for room service again. Feeling famished, she ordered bacon, eggs, hash browns, toast, and orange juice. And when breakfast was over, it was only 11 a.m.

She called her Mom and Dad and assured them that she was fine and promised to visit them soon.

At noon, she pulled on a pair of jeans and a tee shirt. Barefoot, she went to the window and gazed out at the town. It was a beautiful day, the sky a bright, clear azure dotted with a few fluffy white clouds in the distance. A faint breeze stirred the leaves of the trees. The afternoon stretched ahead of her. What was she going to do until Jake got up? It was, she thought, the perfect time to go sit in the park and read for an hour or two. And then she sighed. Jake didn't want her going anywhere alone as long as Paul Rhinehart was in Morgan Creek. As much as she hated to admit it, he was probably right.

But what if the hunter had left town?

She was about to call the front desk and ask the clerk if Mr. Rhinehart had checked out when there was a knock at the door.

Rosa frowned, wondering who it could be. All the vampires she knew were likely at rest this early in the day. Going to the door, she called, "Who is it?"

"I have a floral delivery for Miss Rosa Ravenwood."

Flowers? "Who are they from?"

"A Mr. Kincaid."

Flowers from Jake? That sweet man. Had he sent them as an apology for almost turning her into a vampire last night?

Smiling, she opened the door, let out a startled gasp when Paul Rhinehart yanked her out the door, pulled her into his arms and pressed a foul-smelling rag over her nose and mouth. Before she could scream for help, blackness descended on her.

⚜ ⚜ ⚜

Rhinehart drove across the bridge. Then, feeling a little sick to his stomach at what he was doing, he pulled to the side of the road. Last night, he had come up with an idea that had seemed plausible at the time. Convinced it would work, he had gone to see Luca and outlined his plan. The witch had screamed that he didn't give a damn how he accomplished his task but he'd damn well better get it done.

"Bring me the vampire!" Luca had roared, his voice like rolling thunder. "I know where your family is! This is your last chance!"

Rhinehart shivered with the memory. He had nothing against Kincaid. Nothing against Rosa. But with his family's life and his own neck on the line, he had no choice but to do as he was told.

It had been no easy task, getting Rosa out of the hotel. He had confiscated a wheelchair, settled her in it, and covered her legs with a blanket, hoping anyone who saw her would think she was asleep. He'd taken the service elevator down to the ground floor and wheeled her out the exit to the parking lot where his car waited, praying the whole time that no one would see him. He had folded her into the backseat of his car and driven out of town as fast as he dared.

Fighting off a wave of regret, he pulled onto the highway. As the miles slipped past, regret turned to concern, which quickly coalesced into a hard knot of fear in the pit of his belly as the town fell behind him. If things with Luca went south, if Kincaid survived, his own life wouldn't be worth a plug nickel.

⚜ ⚜ ⚜

Kincaid woke with the setting sun. He knew immediately that Rosa wasn't in the room, nor was she in the hotel. He frowned. Surely she wouldn't have gone out alone, not with Rhinehart in town. Opening his senses, he bit out a vile oath when he realized Rhinehart wasn't there, either. Were they together? He swore under his breath. She wouldn't have left the hotel without letting him know. He would have heard if she'd called for help.

Rising, he pulled on a pair of jeans and a shirt, tugged on his boots and took the stairs down to the lobby three at a time. The desk clerk confirmed what he'd feared. Rhinehart had checked out several hours ago.

"Have you seen Rosa Ravenwood?" Kincaid asked, his voice tight with worry.

"No, sir. Not since last night." He turned to his assistant. "Have you seen her?"

"I might have. I didn't see her face, but I saw a woman with dark hair being wheeled out of the service entrance a little after noon."

A wheelchair! What the hell was she doing in a wheelchair? Kincaid spewed a string of curses as he left the hotel, his gut churning with fear as he made his way around to the rear of the hotel. If Rhinehart had harmed a hair of her head, he'd tear the hunter apart with his bare hands! Fighting for calm, he drew in a deep breath. He sorted through the myriad scents, some fresh, some fading. Rosa's was barely discernable.

He swore again as he caught Paul Rhinehart's scent. Both traces disappeared in the same place in the parking lot. Had Rosa driven away with the hunter? That seemed unlikely, and yet it was the only answer that made sense. The question was, why? Why would she get in Rhinehart's car and go off with the hunter? Had she gone with the hunter willingly? If so, why hadn't she let him know? And if not, what the hell was Rhinehart up to? And why had Rosa been in a wheelchair?

Pulling his phone out of his back pocket, Kincaid punched in her cell number. The phone rang several times, then went to voice mail.

Dammit! He tried to open the link between them, but there was only emptiness. Fear tightened his gut. Was she dead?

He was trying to decide what to do next when Saintcrow materialized beside him. "What's got you so uptight?"

"Rosa's gone."

Saintcrow lifted one brow? "Gone? Where?"

"I don't know. But I'm pretty sure she's with Rhinehart and that can't be good."

Saintcrow lifted his head, nostrils flaring. "Do you smell that?"

Kincaid frowned. "Chloroform?" That explained the wheelchair, he thought. And why he was having troubling sensing her whereabouts.

Saintcrow nodded. "Maybe she didn't go willingly."

"Shit!" Kincaid knew a moment of hope when his phone buzzed. Felt that same hope vanish when the number was unfamiliar. Something told him to answer it anyway. "What?"

"It's Rhinehart. Rosa's with me."

"Is she all right? Dammit, if you've hurt her…"

"She's fine, I swear it."

"She'd damn well better be."

"I haven't touched her. I give you my word."

"The word of a hunter." Kincaid snorted his disdain. "Where the hell are you?"

"You know I can't tell you that. Don't try to track my phone. I'm using a burner."

"You're a dead man when I get my hands on you."

"I didn't want to do it," Rhinehart said quietly. "But Luca knows where my family is, and he's out of patience. My back's against the wall."

"What do you want?"

"I want you to surrender to Luca. He has a spell that will render you powerless when you enter his house. Rosa will be there with me. Tell Saintcrow to call me when Luca has you." He rattled off the number of his phone and Luca's address. "I'll take Rosa home with me after you surrender. Saintcrow can pick her up there."

"Why the hell would I trust you?"

"Luca doesn't want her. Just you."

Kincaid glanced at Saintcrow, who shrugged.

"Let me talk to her."

"She's unconscious right now."

"He's telling the truth," Saintcrow said.

Fighting down an impotent sense of rage and frustration, Kincaid growled, "Where should I meet you?"

"Luca's place, in an hour," the hunter said. "Come alone. Luca will know if Saintcrow or anyone else is with you. Oh, and leave that gold band behind. One hour. Don't be late."

Rhinehart disconnected the call.

"An hour doesn't give us much time," Saintcrow remarked.

"Go to New Orleans. Find Izabela. Tell her you need an edge of some kind in fighting Luca. Promise her my blood or your blood or both," Kincaid said curtly. "Whatever the hell she wants."

Saintcrow snorted. "What makes you think I'll have time to do that? Luca's likely to take your head as soon as you walk in the door."

"I don't think so. He's waited for this for over a century. He'll want to drag it out. Make me suffer. I don't think he'll execute me right away," Kincaid muttered. "Where's the fun in that?"

"You're putting a lot of faith in Rhinehart."

"What other choice do I have?" Slipping the talisman off his wrist, Jake handed it to Saintcrow. "If he doesn't keep his word, kill him."

Saintcrow nodded. "With pleasure. Where can I find the witch?"

⚜ ⚜ ⚜

Kincaid went in search of prey. He put everything else from his mind but the need to feed before he faced Luca. He had to trust Rhinehart to keep his word, had to trust that Izabela wouldn't refuse Saintcrow's request for help.

And if she refused? He could live with that. He could live with anything, as long as no harm came to the woman he loved.

⚜ ⚜ ⚜

Rosa regained consciousness slowly. She had a bad taste in her mouth, and when she tried to sit up, she discovered she was lying on a sofa and that her hands and feet were bound.

Struggling to sit up, she glanced at the unfamiliar surroundings.

"Here, drink this."

She stared at Paul Rhinehart. "Where am I? How did I get here?" Fighting down a wave of panic, she glanced around again. Maybe she was dreaming. The room was large and dark, crammed with furniture and bookcases that were obviously antiques. A Persian rug covered the hardwood floor. A large cage housed a parrot. A black cat slept in front of the fireplace. An owl perched on the back of a chair. Strange looking objects were scattered across the mantel. A skull that had been turned into a lamp occupied a small table. A long, curved sword hung on one wall. A gray cloak embroidered with silver lightning bolts had been carelessly tossed over the back of a ladder-back chair.

She shivered as a tall, thin man with long, gray hair and blue eyes so pale they were almost white entered the room. She had never felt dark magic before, but she felt it now, crawling over her skin, invading her mind. She flinched when the grandfather clocked tolled the hour. Six-thirty p.m.

"It's been an hour," Luca said.

Rhinehart drew back the edge of the curtain and peered out the front window. "He's here."

Rosa flinched when the hunter picked up a knife, felt her blood run cold when he moved toward her. Was he going to kill her?

"Relax. I'm just going to cut the ropes," he said quietly. "Don't say or do anything. Do you understand? Your life and mine depend on it."

She nodded, her throat thick with fear, her skin icy.

"Open the door," the witch said.

Rhinehart crossed the room and unlocked the heavy front door. Black clouds hung low in the sky.

The witch went to stand beside the hunter. "Come in, vampire."

Rosa reeled back as a wave of black magic rolled through the room, let out a gasp when Jake walked in the door. As soon as he crossed the threshold, the witch waved his hand and a pair of thick silver manacles shackled Jake's wrists and ankles. He didn't move, didn't look at her.

"My debt is now paid in full," Rhinehart said. Taking Rosa by the hand, he lifted her to her feet.

"Be gone," Luca said, his full attention on the vampire in front of him.

Rosa started to protest, but the warning look in Rhinehart's eyes stilled her tongue.

As soon as they were out of the house and on the sidewalk, she turned on the hunter. "What's going on?"

"I'll tell you later. Let's get out of here while we can."

"But..."

He dragged her down the path that led to the street, shoved her into his car and slammed the door.

A moment later, they were speeding away from the necromancer's house.

"Where are we going?" Rosa asked.

"My place. You'll be safe there."

At the moment, her own safety was the last thing on Rosa's mind.

"Saintcrow called me a few minutes ago," Rhinehart said. "All I know is that he and Kincaid have some sort of plan. I'm a little fuzzy on the details."

"What about Jake? We can't just leave him there at Luca's mercy. The witch wants his head."

"Listen to me. I don't like this anymore than you do. But Luca threatened to kill my wife and kids if I didn't bring him Kincaid. Originally, he just wanted Kincaid's head. Be glad he changed his mind."

"What does he want now, I'm afraid to ask?"

"He said he wants to take it himself."

"How is that any better?" Rosa exclaimed.

"I don't think he'll do it right away."

"You don't *think?*"

"I admit, it's a gamble."

"With Jake's life!" She turned to look out the rear window but the necromancer's house was no longer in sight. "Where's Saintcrow?"

"Hopefully in New Orleans."

Chapter Thirty-Five

Saintcrow felt the witch's power as he approached her house. It overshadowed the dwelling like a heavy, invisible weight. A black, wrought-iron fence surrounded the property, a thick chain secured the gate. A large Doberman slept on the porch. It stood stiff-legged at Saintcrow's approach, hackles raised. Saintcrow unleashed a bit of his power and the dog lay back down.

"Some guard dog," he muttered as he vaulted over the fence.

The witch answered the door before he knocked. "I have been expecting you, Rylan Saintcrow."

He lifted one brow.

"Do you mean me any harm, vampire?"

"No. Only a favor to help a friend."

"Come in."

She unlocked the screen door, stood back to let him enter.

Saintcrow glanced around the room, which was cluttered but clean. A gray cat stared at him through unblinking yellow eyes. Most witches had familiars, usually cats.

Izabela gestured for him to sit, then settled into a large rocker. The cat jumped onto her lap.

"What do you want?" she asked. "And what are you willing to give in return?"

She was a tiny thing, with a wealth of golden hair streaked with silver. Her eyes were an unusual shade of brown with yellow flecks.

"I need a talisman that will not only protect me from Luca's Dark Magic but turn any spell unleashed on me back to its maker."

Her laughter was like the tinkling of silver bells. "What have you done to rouse the necromancer's anger?"

"Nothing. But Kincaid is his prisoner and I fear for his life."

Her brow furrowed. "I am sorry to hear that. I am rather fond of Jake."

"We're wasting time. Will you help me?"

"Kincaid paid me in blood. Will you do likewise?"

"Yes."

"You understand your blood is mine whenever I ask?"

"Yes," he said impatiently. "How long will it take to make the talisman?"

"Magic cannot be rushed."

"How long, dammit?"

"As long as it takes!" Setting the cat on the floor, she eased out of the rocker. "But I'm very good at what I do," she said with a touch of arrogance, and glided out of the room. The cat padded in her wake.

Saintcrow stared after the witch, trying to judge her age. It wasn't easy with witches. They had the ability to change their appearance. She could be twenty, she could be a hundred.

He tensed as wisps of black magic crawled over his skin.

Five minutes passed.

Ten.

Saintcrow paced the floor, his agitation growing. He tried to contact Kincaid, let out a shudder as excruciating pain exploded through him. What the hell was Luca doing to him? Muttering an oath, he closed the link.

Twenty minutes later, Izabela reappeared with the cat at her heels. She carried a small, clear bottle in one hand, and a copper band etched with runes similar to the one Kincaid wore in the other. "Hold out your right arm."

He did as she asked, flinched when she locked the talisman onto his right wrist. He muttered, "What the hell!" as magic slammed into him.

She uncorked the bottle and held it out.

Saintcrow stared at it a moment. When comprehension dawned, he bit into his left wrist and held it over the small flask, which slowly filled with his dark, red blood. "What are you going to do with it?"

"Whatever I wish. Kincaid's blood is very powerful. I can tell yours is even stronger."

"My thanks."

"If you need help with Luca, call me. As I said, I'm very fond of Kincaid."

Saintcrow ran his hand over the copper band on his wrist. "If this doesn't work, I'll be back," he said, and vanished from the house.

Izabela frowned. He was a powerful vampire. More powerful than she had suspected, she mused, for his threat lingered in the air like thick, black smoke even after he was gone. She would be wise not to underestimate him.

⚜ ⚜ ⚜

Kincaid stared at the thick iron bars that imprisoned him. In spite of what he'd said to Saintcrow, he had expected to be dead by now. It would have been preferable to this. He flinched as Luca jabbed a needle into a vein in his arm and began draining his blood into a large, brass container.

Helpless to resist, Kincaid lay there, watching his blood flow through the tube.

He didn't know what spell the witch had conjured, but it had left him unable to move. Was the magic in the spell itself, or in the manacles that shackled him? The silver had drained his strength as surely as the needle that was stealing his blood.

Pain clawed at his vitals as his need to replace the blood he was losing became overpowering. His insides turned to fire even as he grew steadily weaker. Being drained of blood wouldn't kill him. It was worse than that. He would truly be a living corpse then, a dried husk with no power to move or speak, an empty shell aware of what was going on around him but unable to respond.

He glared at Luca, who smiled wolfishly. The witch hadn't drained him completely, only enough to leave him weak and helpless, the pain of his hunger excruciating and unrelenting.

"Rest well," Luca cackled as he stood. "In a week or a month, my guillotine will take your head." Laughing wildly, he picked up the blood-filled basin and vanished from the cellar.

It was only then that Kincaid noticed the guillotine standing in the corner. It was old, the wood faded, the steps cracked and uneven. But the deadly blade at the top shone brightly even in the dark.

Kincaid groaned low in his throat at the thought of lying there for another minute, engulfed by the worst pain he had ever known. A pain that would only grow worse as the hours and days passed by.

"Rosa." Closing his eyes, he summoned her image. If she was safe, whatever price he had to pay was worth it.

⚜ ⚜ ⚜

Rhinehart took a deep breath, hoping he wasn't making a fatal mistake as he invited Saintcrow into his house.

Rosa ran toward him. "Where's Jake?"

"Still at Luca's."

"Aren't you going after him? Jake's been there too long already."

"All in good time." Saintcrow looked at Rhinehart. "Tell me about Luca's house. Where's he likely to keep Kincaid?"

"Probably in the basement. He has a couple of holding cells down there, a few ancient instruments of torture, including a working guillotine."

Rosa felt the blood drain from her face. "A guillotine?"

Rhinehart nodded.

"I need to figure out how to get into the house," Saintcrow said. "One thing for sure, he's not going to invite me inside. Even if you could sneak in, that wouldn't do me any good. I need Luca to invite me in and he's not going to do that."

Rhinehart stared at him. "So we're at a stalemate."

"Not exactly. You need to get him outside," Saintcrow said.

"How am I supposed to do that?"

"I don't know. But we wouldn't be in this fix if you hadn't told Luca about Kincaid."

"Hey, I didn't know he was after Kincaid until I inadvertently mentioned his name. Until then, the only head he was after was yours. Hell, none of that matters now. My family was at risk and I did what I had to."

Saintcrow nodded. "It was your choice to save them. Now I'm making the choice to go after Kincaid. And you're going with me, willingly or not. But you're going. Just as soon as we can come up with a plan that has a chance of working."

"I'm going, too," Rosa said.

"Like hell," Saintcrow said. "Kincaid will have *my* head if anything happens to you."

"Assuming any of us survive," Rhinehart muttered.

Chapter Thirty-Six

Kincaid stared at the witch. He had lost all track of time, had no idea if it was morning or night, if he had been in the witch's power a day or a week. He was aware of nothing but the excruciating pain that clawed at his vitals and spread outward to every inch of his body, a cold, relentless agony. There was no respite, even when he was lost in the Dark Sleep of his kind.

The witch, sadistic monster that he was, had hung a bag of fresh blood from the bar above his head. The smell of it drove him wild, but he couldn't move, couldn't reach it.

Luca grinned at him. Malevolence and satisfaction rolled off the man in waves. He came down to the cellar every hour, stood beside the cage, a faint smile creasing his weathered face as he watched his prisoner writhe in endless torment.

"Do you see, Katya?" the witch murmured. "Do you see his agony? Can you feel it? I swore on my life that I would avenge you, my best beloved one. Soon, I will take his head and your soul will be able to rest in peace."

With a last, triumphant glance at his prisoner, the necromancer snapped his fingers and disappeared.

Kincaid let out a long, anguished sigh as he summoned Rosa's image, wishing he could hold her in his arms one last time, taste the sweetness of her kisses, hear the sound of her voice. "Rosa. Rosa." He murmured her name like a prayer as he closed his eyes and wished for death.

⚜ ⚜ ⚜

Rosa bolted upright in the chair, her eyes wild as she glanced around the room. Rhinehart was dozing in a recliner. Saintcrow sat on the sofa, long legs stretched out in front of him. She frowned when she looked out the window. The sun was up. How long had she been asleep?

"What is it?" Saintcrow asked, though his eyes remained closed.

"Jake. He's calling my name. He's in agony. We have go to him now, before it's too late!" Maybe it was already too late, she thought. The witch could be killing him an inch at a time while they sat around doing nothing. "We've got to do something!" They had stayed up all night trying to come up with a workable plan. Saintcrow had shot them all down.

"As soon as we come up with an idea that has a chance in hell of working, we'll be on our way," Saintcrow said mildly. "But not until then."

Rosa stared at him. How could he be so callous? "I don't care about a plan!" she exclaimed. "Rhinehart and I can sneak into Luca's house."

"Yeah?" Saintcrow snorted derisively. "How do you intend to do that? The place is heavily warded against intruders of every stripe. And what are you going to do on the off chance you make it inside alive?"

"I don't know. But we can't just sit here staring at the walls." She told herself Jake couldn't be dead. She would feel it if he were.

Saintcrow swore softly. She was right. They couldn't wait much longer. Last night, they had stayed up to the wee hours of the morning suggesting and rejecting ideas. Rhinehart had proposed setting the house on fire, an idea Saintcrow had quicky rejected. Vampires were hard to destroy, but fire was one sure way to do it. He had considered challenging the witch to a fight, but it was doubtful Luca would agree. The witch had nothing to gain and everything to lose.

He glanced at the clock on the DVD player. It was 9:15 a.m. Black Magic tended to be more powerful after dark. It was the reason so many spells were cast at midnight. If they were going to strike, it was best to do it when the sun was up. And they'd better do it soon. Kincaid had been in Luca's power for almost fifteen hours.

Saintcrow grinned as a new thought occurred to him. "I have a plan, after all," he said. "Listen up. This is what we're gonna do."

⚜ ⚜ ⚜

Two hours later, Rosa hid behind the large bush at the end of the witch's driveway. Saintcrow had been opposed to her coming along, but she had insisted. He had relented on her promise that she would stay outside and she had reluctantly agreed. She had no supernatural abilities but she could feel the evil that resided within the house. It crawled over her skin like some hideous infection seeping into her pores, making her stomach churn with revulsion.

Rhinehart stood on the front porch holding a thick silver chain fastened to the silver collar around Saintcrow's throat. Shackles also bound his wrists. Saintcrow stood with his head bowed, his jaw clenched against the pain of the silver burning his skin. This had to work, she thought. She could feel Jake's agony, sense his yearning for death.

She was beginning to think the witch would never answer the door when it swung open and he stood there, the scowl on his face quickly turning to stunned surprise.

"I have another favor to ask." Rhinehart jerked his head in Saintcrow's direction. "I brought you this in payment."

The witch's pale blue eyes narrowed. "I only wanted his head," Luca snapped.

"You never told me why," Rhinehart said.

"And I never will. What do you want in return?"

"Lasting wealth."

Luca grunted. "Easy enough. Bring the bloodsucker inside."

Rhinehart crossed the threshold and gave a sharp tug on the chain.

Saintcrow stumbled after him, as if he was too weak to move.

"Shut the door," Luca said.

Rhinehart kicked it shut with his heel.

"This way." Luca smiled as he led his guests down the dark, narrow stairway to the cellar. "Put him in the other cage," he said, his gaze on Kincaid. "And leave the collar and the shackles in place."

Rhinehart walked the short distance to the second cage and made as if to open the door.

At that moment, Saintcrow tore the collar from his throat, a collar that had not been locked, and tossed it aside. The irons on his legs followed.

The sound of the shackles hitting the concrete floor drew the necromancer's attention. "What is this?" Lifting his hand, he spoke a few words as he snapped his fingers. Rhinehart collapsed where he stood.

For a moment, Saintcrow and the witch glared at each other.

"My Katya lies in her grave all these years because of your friend," Luca hissed. "Now you will die. And then her murderer will die."

The witch lifted both arms overhead as he chanted in a language Saintcrow recognized as ancient Egyptian.

Dark Magic filled the air. Saintcrow took a deep breath as it swirled around him. Damn, he hoped Kincaid's witch knew what she was doing. He felt Luca's power slam into him like a tornado. It stole the breath from his body and drove him to his knees, but after a brief moment, he felt it withdraw.

Luca's eyes widened, his mouth opening in a silent scream as the Death Magic he had unleashed ricocheted off the vampire and hit him with full force. It ripped through his body like a scythe. Blood-stained bits of flesh, bone, and hair flew through the air.

Saintcrow glanced over his shoulder when he heard a horrified cry from the top of the cellar stairs. "Dammit, girl, you were supposed to wait outside."

Rosa didn't seem to hear him as she made her way down the stairs, eyes wide, face devoid of color. He was sure she was going to faint. When she saw Kincaid, her face turned even whiter. She stared at Jake a moment and Saintcrow felt Rosa pull herself together before she ran toward the cage.

"Jake? Oh, Lord, Jake, can you hear me?" She tugged on the door, but it was locked.

Stepping forward, Saintcrow ripped it off its hinges and tossed it across the room.

Rosa hurried inside and knelt beside Kincaid. "Jake! Jake, can you hear me?"

His eyelids fluttered open, his eyes as red as flame.

"Jake?" She let out a shriek when he pulled her down on top of him and buried his fangs in the side of her throat.

Chapter Thirty-Seven

Muttering an oath, Saintcrow darted into the cage. He dared not pull Rosa away for fear Kincaid would rip out her throat. *Shit.* "Rosa? Listen to me. Talk to him. He's half out of his mind with pain. He doesn't know it's you."

"Jake? Jake, it's me. Rosa. Remember? You love me, Jake. And I love you. You're hurting me. Please let me go so I can take you home. Please, Jake."

Retracting his fangs, he lifted his head. "Rosa?"

"Yes. It's me. I'm here with Saintcrow to take you home. Luca is dead." She glanced at Rhinehart, still lying motionless on the floor, and wondered if he, too, was dead.

"Rosa?" Kincaid put her away from him, his pain-filled gaze moving over her face.

She let out a sigh of relief as recognition lit his eyes.

"Rosa, come out of there," Saintcrow said quietly. "Stay where he can see you."

She stepped out of the cage, watched as Saintcrow broke the thick shackles that bound Jake as if they were made of tissue paper.

Saintcrow held out his left arm. "Drink."

Kincaid didn't argue. He grabbed hold of Saintcrow's arm and sank his fangs into a vein.

Saintcrow looked over his shoulder at Rosa. "You saved his life," he said, hoping to ease the worry in her eyes. "This is just to make him recover a little faster."

Kincaid drank for several moments, then fell back on the concrete, his eyes closed.

"Is he ... is he all right?"

"The sun's up, that's all. He's still a few pints low. I imagine he'll sleep until nightfall."

Saintcrow licked the bite marks in his arm and left the cage to kneel beside Rhinehart. The man looked like death, but he was still breathing. Biting into his right wrist, Saintcrow pried the hunter's mouth open and let a few drops of his blood drip onto the man's tongue.

Rhinehart swallowed convulsively, then grabbed hold of Saintcrow's arm and took several long swallows. He looked horrified when he came to himself. Jackknifing to a sitting position, he exclaimed, "What the hell? You didn't ... dammit, tell me you didn't."

Saintcrow chuckled. "Stop worrying."

Rhinehart glanced around the basement. He grimaced when he saw what was left of the necromancer's body. "Is that ... ?"

"Yeah. Kincaid's witch cooked up one hell of a spell." Rising, he offered Rhinehart his hand and pulled him to his feet.

Rosa's gaze darted from Saintcrow to Kincaid and back again, a question in her eyes.

Stepping into the cage, Saintcrow picked up Kincaid and draped him over his shoulder. "Give me your hand, Rosa. Rhinehart, put your arm around her waist and let's get the hell out of here."

⚜ ⚜ ⚜

Saintcrow dropped Rhinehart off at his home, then transported Rosa to Blair House. Standing on the porch, he said, "I'm taking Kincaid home with me."

"But..."

"Don't argue with me. He'll be out the rest of the day, and most likely through the night. He's been as close to death as you can without going over the edge, but he'll be okay, in time."

Rosa wanted to argue. She had questions that needed answering, but the master vampire was already gone.

Vampires! Heaving an exasperated sigh, she opened the door and went inside.

⚜ ⚜ ⚜

Kadie was still at rest when Saintcrow got home. Their lair was the only secure place in the house and that was where he took Kincaid. He lowered him onto the floor in the walk-in closet and shut the door. He hadn't wanted to worry Rosa, but he had no idea what condition Kincaid would be in when he woke. Few vampires had the strength to fully recover after something so traumatic. Some went rogue, becoming a danger to themselves and everyone around them. Some just faded away, their will to live gone. Some went mad and had to be destroyed.

One thing was certain, Kincaid would need blood when he woke. A lot of blood.

Saintcrow just hoped Kincaid would be in his right mind, able to control the overwhelming need to feed. It had been a long time since he'd had to destroy a friend.

⚜ ⚜ ⚜

Rosa glanced around the living room, at the boxes piled to one side. She had completely forgotten about the movers. Fortunately, she had given them a key to the house in case no one was home when they arrived.

She stood in the middle of the room, at a loss as to what to do. How was she supposed to worry about what piece of furniture to put where when all she could think of was Jake? Was he still at rest? Would he be all right when he woke? She knew Saintcrow was worried about him, too, but no more than she was.

She dragged her thoughts back to the present, tried to focus on the here and now. They definitely needed to buy more furniture to fill up the room. Hers didn't take up much space.

Was Jake still at rest?

She wandered down the hallway, wondering what to do with all the extra bedrooms. There would be no children to fill them up, no grandchildren to spend the night.

Luca had put him through hell. Would Jake be the same man she'd fallen in love with? Would she be safe with him now, after what he'd been through?

The movers had carried her bedroom set into the largest bedroom. Too bad they hadn't assembled the frame. She might have tried to do it, but she had no tools and lifting the mattress was out of the question.

How long until it would be safe to see Jake again?

She drifted into the kitchen. All the boxes marked "Kitchen" had been piled in a corner of the room. She stared at them. What was the point in thinking about furniture or where to put what when it might never be safe for her to be alone with Jake again?

She didn't have the will to do anything except sit at the table and worry and wonder what would happen when Jake woke from the Dark Sleep. Would he remember what had happened? Would it change him? Had it affected him mentally as well as physically? How could it not? Would Saintcrow be able to control him?

Was it even safe for her to be in Morgan Creek right now?

⚜ ⚜ ⚜

Kincaid woke abruptly. Hunger clawed at his vitals as he glanced around. Where the hell was he? A deep breath carried Saintcrow's scent. And Kadie's. Why was he on the floor in their closet?

Rising, he opened the door and stepped into the bedroom. It was empty, but he knew the vampires were somewhere in the house.

Where was Rosa?

He clenched his hands as pain knifed through him. He needed to feed. But when he tried to leave the house nothing happened.

Muttering an oath, he willed himself into the living room.

Saintcrow looked at him, one brow raised. "So, you're finally back in the land of the living."

"Let me out of here."

"Not right now."

"I need to hunt."

"Not right now," Saintcrow said again. "Kadie, get out of here."

She didn't argue but made a hasty retreat.

"What the hell's going on?" Kincaid demanded.

Saintcrow stared at him. Kincaid's eyes were blood-red, his cheeks sunken, the skin of his face taut. "What do you remember?"

"About what? Dammit, let me the hell out of here!" he roared.

Saintcrow grunted softly as he rolled up his shirtsleeve, bit into his wrist, and held it out. Kincaid's nostrils flared, the red in his eyes growing brighter as he lunged across the room and buried his fangs in Saintcrow's arm.

A minute passed.

Two.

Three.

"Enough," Saintcrow said.

Kincaid growled low in his throat but didn't lift his head.

"Enough." The master vampire spoke quietly but his power slammed into Kincaid, knocking him across the room.

Kincaid sprang to his feet, murder in his eyes, and then discovered he couldn't move.

"Relax," the master vampire said. "You've been at rest for two days."

"Two days?" Kincaid shook his head. "That's impossible."

"What do you remember about going to Luca's house?"

Kincaid frowned at him. Luca's house. The cage. The silver manacles that had burned his skin like fire and rendered him helpless. The thirst—the excruciating thirst that had turned his insides to flame. The malice in the necromancer's pale blue eyes as he had drained him to the point of madness. The welcome threat of the guillotine.

And then the blood. Rosa's blood. Warm and sweet as it eased his thirst and made the excruciating pain bearable. He needed more. Much more to restore his strength, to satisfy his hellish thirst. "Let me go."

Saintcrow shook his head. "I know you need blood. I'll take you hunting."

"I don't need you to go with me."

"Oh, yes, you do. You're ready to drain the first mortal you see and I'm going to be there to make sure it doesn't happen."

"Go to hell."

"Not tonight. Are you ready?"

Kincaid glared at him, fangs bared, eyes blood-red, hands clenched into tight fists. "I want Rosa's blood."

"That's not happening tonight, either. You can go hunting with me, or you can stay here and go without. The choice is yours."

"Why are you doing this?"

"Because you love her. Because destroying her would destroy you. And because I'm your friend. Now, what's it to be?"

"I need to feed, dammit. Now!"

"Behave yourself," Saintcrow said, releasing Kincaid from his power. "You won't like what happens if you don't." He tossed a shirt and pair of jeans at Kincaid. "Change your clothes first. You smell like blood and death."

⚜ ⚜ ⚜

Kincaid was tempted to try his luck at escaping the master vampire's watchful eye, but what was the use? The man was unbeatable, unstoppable, and as tenacious as a bulldog. But the real reason was that he was just too damn thirsty to waste time trying to elude Saintcrow.

They left Morgan Creek and headed for New York. Known as the City That Never Sleeps, the moniker was certainly true that night. The streets were crowded with people—men, women, and couples crowded the sidewalk along the theater district, panhandlers plied their trade, homeless people and drug addicts huddled in front of shoddy tents. The air reeked of urine.

Kincaid strolled through the throng. It took all the self-control he had—and that was damn little—to keep from attacking anything that moved, and only the knowledge that Saintcrow was trailing behind him kept him from pushing the nearest mortal against the side of a building and surrendering to the need that burned like hellfire inside of him.

It took a surprisingly long time to find a woman alone, and by then, his nerves were raw. He practically dragged his prey into a dark alley, had to concentrate to mesmerize her before he sank his fangs into her throat.

Eyes closed, he drank. And drank.

Until Saintcrow forcibly stopped him. The master vampire sealed the ghastly wounds in her throat and sent her away.

He should have felt regret, Kincaid thought. Should have felt something other than the driving need to take it all. *Rosa.* He needed her blood. It soothed him, eased his hunger, his pain, as nothing else. Just a few sips to ease the torment. The awful thirst.

"Rosa." He murmured her name, unaware that he had spoken it aloud.

"Do you think that would be wise?" Saintcrow asked.

"I don't know."

"I can't let you see her alone, you know that?"

Kincaid nodded curtly.

"Well, what the hell," the master vampire muttered. "Maybe it will help."

Thinking of the brutal way he had fed on the woman, Kincaid murmured, "Don't let me hurt her."

"Count on it."

⚜ ⚜ ⚜

Rosa woke to the sound of someone pounding on the front door. Pulling on a robe, she padded into the living room. "Who's there?" she called, switching on the porch light.

"Saintcrow. And Kincaid."

"Jake!" She unlocked the door, her heart pounding with relief. "I'm so glad ... " Her voice trailed off when she saw his face, the skin pale and stretched taut, the faint red glow in his eyes. Tension radiated from him like heat off a city street in mid-summer. She glanced at Saintcrow. "What's wrong with him?"

"He's in a bad way. I'm not sure bringing him here was a good idea. But I think maybe your blood is the only thing that will help."

She stared at Jake. He stood beside the master vampire, his head down. He refused to meet her gaze. For the first time, he looked like what he was. "Oh, Jake," she murmured, her heart breaking, "what has he done to you?"

And still he wouldn't look at her. "I'm sorry," he said, his voice barely audible.

"Come in."

She led the way into the living room, perched on the edge of the sofa, then looked up at Saintcrow. "You won't let him ... ?"

"No. That's why I'm here."

When she brushed her hair away from her neck, Saintcrow said, "Let him drink from your wrist." When she looked at him askance, he said, "It's less intimate. Less dangerous."

With a nod, she rolled up the sleeve of her robe and held out her arm.

Kincaid's eyes went dark red as he knelt in front of her. She froze as he grasped her arm in both hands and bent his head to her wrist. His bite was sharp and painful.

Saintcrow stood immediately behind Jake, eyes narrowed. After what seemed like forever but was only a few moments, he said, "Enough."

For stretched seconds, she thought Jake wouldn't stop, but then he lifted his head and ran his tongue over the tiny punctures in her arm. Rising in one lithe moment, he muttered, "Thank you," and vanished from the room.

Rosa rubbed her arm as her gaze searched Saintcrow's. "I've never seen him like that. Is he going to be okay?"

"I don't know. I hope so."

"He seemed almost afraid of me."

"He's afraid of himself. His control is hanging by a thread. Probably best if I don't leave him alone too long. Try not to worry."

Rosa nodded. Far easier said than done.

Chapter Thirty-Eight

Kincaid stood outside Luca's house, his hands knotted at his sides. Even with the necromancer's death, the place reeked of evil. Taking a deep breath, he mounted the stairs and stepped inside. It had once been a grand place, he mused, as he walked through the rooms. Now, it was filled with magical implements, old bones, a small skeleton under a glass dome. One room held the desiccated body of a cat. Another held ancient instruments of torture. The upstairs held four bedrooms. The largest one looked like a shrine. It had been the woman's room, he thought. Dresses from another age filled the closet. A satin quilt covered the bed. An old-fashioned, white cotton nightgown was spread across the quilt, as if waiting for the owner to step into the room and put it on.

He descended the stairs to the cellar. The stink of blood and death hung heavy in the air. He stood over what was left of the witch. "You should have killed me," he muttered, his voice laced with bitterness. "It would have been kinder."

Going back upstairs, he found a box of matches in the kitchen and went from room to room, setting fire to anything that would burn.

When he left the house, he found Saintcrow standing on the sidewalk.

"Feel better now?" the master vampire asked.

"No. I just feel empty inside."

"Give yourself time. It takes a while to recover from a trip through hell."

"What would you know about it?"

"I've been there myself a time or two."

"Good for you."

"Kincaid ..."

"Just let me be alone for a while, all right?" He stared at the front windows, at the bright orange flames licking at the dusty curtains. Small explosions sounded from inside the house.

The master vampire nodded. "If that's what you want."

"It is." Kincaid cocked his head at the *whoop-whoop* of an approaching fire truck. "Time to go."

"Come home with me for a few days."

"No." The thought of watching Saintcrow with Kadie was more than he could bear.

"Don't do anything stupid," Saintcrow warned and vanished into the darkness.

A moment later, Kincaid did likewise.

⚜ ⚜ ⚜

Rosa spent a restless night on the sofa in the living room. Sleep eluded her and all she could think of was Jake, the way he had looked, his face drawn, his eyes blood-red and haunted, the way he had avoided looking at her, talking to her, as if he had something to be ashamed of. She didn't understand why he felt that way. He hadn't done anything wrong. Luca had tortured him, practically destroyed him.

She tossed and turned most of the night, only to fall into a troubled sleep, where she was the one locked in a cage and the necromancer was draining *her* blood. She could feel it slowly being leeched from her body, feel the chill it left behind. And she felt the hunger, the same kind of hunger Jake must have felt, the agony of it, the way it had burned through his veins like cold fire. And then Jake was bending over her, his eyes hellfire red, his fangs long and sharp as he savaged her throat over and over again. There was no pleasure in his bite, only excruciating pain. And when she was writhing with fear and anguish, he was leading her up the steps to the guillotine, forcing her to her knees…

She woke with a start, her body covered with sweat and shaking violently as she whispered his name.

Scrambling off the couch, she went through the house, checking every lock, turning on every light.

She spent the rest of the night curled up in a chair by the fireplace huddled beneath a quilt.

⚜ ⚜ ⚜

In the morning, Saintcrow surprised her with a visit.

"Is something wrong?" she asked anxiously. "Is Jake…?"

"As far as I know, he's all right. For now." His gaze moved over her, missing nothing. "How are you holding up, kid? You look like hell."

She shrugged. "I miss him."

Saintcrow nodded. "I'm sure he misses you, too."

"Then why isn't he here?"

He looked at her, one brow raised. "You must know why."

"He's afraid of hurting me. I get it. But last night, he seemed ashamed to face me."

"He is."

"Why? He didn't do anything wrong."

"I suspect it's his pride, his masculinity, that's suffering."

"His pride?" She stared at him. "What the devil does his pride have to do with anything?"

"Luca came near to breaking him. Hell, maybe he did. You don't understand what it's like for a man like Kincaid to find himself locked up and helpless. And it's not the first time."

She nodded slowly. "The vampire who turned him kept him locked up and fed off of him."

"He told you about that?"

She nodded again.

"I'm surprised. It's not a story he usually shares. I suspect he relived that while Luca had him caged. No doubt he remembered what it was like when Drakos fed off of him all those years ago. But as bad as that was, he wasn't locked up all the time, or drained to the point when he couldn't move or speak. Drakos showed him the world, taught him to read and write. He was a harsh master, but he wasn't needlessly cruel."

Rosa sighed.

"My only advice is to give him time to heal. To regain some sense of… of balance, I guess. I told you any sacrifices made would have to be made by you. I guess the question is, are you up to it?"

"I honestly don't know." She had come to Morgan Creek wanting to meet a vampire, thinking she wanted to be a vampire. Now, she wondered if she wouldn't have been better off going to Italy with her family.

"It's not too late to go home," he said quietly.

It would be admitting defeat, Rosa thought, admitting she might have made the biggest mistake of her life. Maybe love wasn't enough, would never be enough, for two people who were so different. Suddenly, home sounded like heaven.

"Anything I can do for you while I'm here?"

She started to ask him to take her back to Arizona, then bit down on her lip. She couldn't give up on Jake. Not yet. Not when he needed her.

With a faint smile, she said, "Do you think you could put the bed together for me?"

⚜ ⚜ ⚜

Kincaid muttered a string of curses in a dozen languages as he stalked the Montana night. He wanted Rosa Ravenwood as he had never wanted anything in his life—not sex, not his lost humanity. He wanted the woman—body and soul. He wanted to make love to her and know her love in return. He wanted to spend the rest of his existence making her smile, hearing her laugh, fulfilling her every wish, her every desire. He wanted to be her sire, so that she would be his forever.

And it was wrong. All of it. So damn wrong on so many levels. She was a beautiful young woman with her whole life ahead of her.

He might have killed her the other night.

She had seen him at his worst, a pathetic creature locked in a cage, unable to move or speak. Helpless. Weak.

He bit off a pithy epithet as Saintcrow appeared beside him. "What the hell do you want now? Don't you have better things to do than follow me around?"

"Rosa's worried about you."

"She tell you that?"

"In a way."

"You read her thoughts?"

"I didn't have to. They were loud and clear. She thinks you're afraid of her."

"So, what if I am?"

Saintcrow shrugged. “I don’t give a damn one way or the other.”

“Then what are you doing here?”

Saintcrow snorted. “I hate to see you making the biggest mistake of your life.”

“Yeah? Well, it’s my mistake to make. So leave me the hell alone.”

“Don’t do something you’re gonna regret.”

“Why not?” Kincaid asked bitterly. “I’ve been doing it my whole life.”

“Maybe it’s time to stop.”

Kincaid drove his fist into a block wall. The force of it split the wall in half and shattered his knuckles. “I almost killed her the other night.”

“But you didn’t.”

“But I could have. Don’t you understand? Dammit! I can’t be with her and not want her. All of her. And she deserves better.”

“I understand better than you think.”

Kincaid stared at his hand, which had already healed. “Tell her I’m sorry,” he said, his voice thick. “Now, leave me the hell alone.”

Saintcrow came to a halt. He stood there until Kincaid was out of sight, then willed himself back to Morgan Creek.

Chapter Thirty-Nine

Paul Rhinehart stared at his face in the mirror. He had been feeling strange in ways he couldn't explain ever since leaving Luca's house. His wife and kids had noticed it as soon as they returned home. He told them he was just overly tired, that he'd been working a lot of overtime. He could hardly tell Nancy the truth. How could he explain that he felt as if someone else was sharing his body with him? And his dreams... nightmares, really... ghastly images of death and destruction, of places he had never been, people he had never met. And yet they were all familiar, like old friends. He dreamed of a golden-haired woman, stood helpless as he watched her die at the hands of a vampire, as he bathed his hands in her blood and vowed vengeance... Katya. Pain stabbed his brain as he tried to remember the name of the vampire who had killed her. Gradually, the monster's face appeared in his mind. He had changed his name over the years... what was he calling himself now? Kinsey? Kingman? Kincaid? Yes, that was it. Jake Kincaid.

He went cold all over as his eyes slowly changed color, his normal light brown fading until they were a blue so pale they were almost colorless. His hair, too, slowly faded, until it was no longer thick and brown but long and white and wispy.

Horror engulfed him. Luca!

The necromancer's image smiled back at him.

And then he passed out.

Chapter Forty

When Rosa scuffed into the kitchen in the morning, she was surprised to find Saintcrow sitting at the table waiting for her. "You're up early."

"And you were up late."

She didn't ask how he knew that. She had come to realize that Rylan Saintcrow knew practically everything about everyone in Morgan Creek.

"Are you still determined to stay here and hope Kincaid comes to his senses before it's too late?"

"Do you mean before I'm old and gray?"

Saintcrow snorted, and then he laughed.

"I thought about going home," she said, turning on the coffee pot.

"But?"

"I can't leave, not yet." Leaning against the counter, she folded her arms. "Not until I'm sure there's no hope for us." She blew out a sigh. "Any chance you could find me a job?"

"You don't need one. Just tell everyone to charge your purchases to me. I'll let the staff know you're here as my guest."

"I can't let you support me."

"Why not?"

"It's not right. And I can't just sit around doing nothing all day, hoping he'll come back."

He shrugged. "I'm sure I can find you something to do if you want to work."

"Thanks." She poured a cup of coffee, added cream and sugar, and sat down across from him.

"You might be wasting your time staying here," Saintcrow remarked. "Kincaid went home to Montana last night."

Rosa stared at him as if he'd spoken in a language she didn't comprehend. "Is he coming back?"

"I don't know. He's still afraid of you. Of hurting you."

"Do you think he'll get over it?" She had accused Jake of being afraid of her once before.

Saintcrow dragged his hand across his jaw. How could he make her understand? "Maybe afraid *for* you would be a better way to put it. He's an old vampire and he's lived alone most of his life, taking what he wanted when he wanted, with little regard for the consequences. And he wants you."

She stared at him blankly. "What's wrong with that?"

"He wants all of you. Your heart. Your soul. Your blood. He wants to make you his in every way, so that you'll never leave him."

It took her a few minutes to understand what he was saying.

Saintcrow watched her eyes slowly widen with comprehension. "He wants to turn me so he can be my sire. My master."

"He's scared he won't be able to control what he feels. Being Luca's prisoner changed something inside him, weakened his confidence and his self-control. He damn near killed you."

"He surrendered to Luca because of me. I couldn't just stand there and watch him suffer when I could help."

"I know. And he's grateful. But, like I said, he came damn close to killing you. He knows that and it's tearing him apart. So he left. He loves you, Rosa. He's never really been in love before. I think part of the problem is that he just doesn't know how to handle it."

"What about the woman in Mexico?"

Saintcrow chuckled. "That wasn't really love for either one of us. She was a beautiful, desirable female and we both wanted her. She was like the spoils of war, a prize for the winner. Only neither of us won. And neither one of us gave a damn."

Two fat tears slid down Rosa's cheeks. She made no move to wipe them away, just sat there staring at the floor. "Maybe I should have let him turn me that night."

"Is that what you want?"

"I thought I did," she said slowly. "Now I'm not so sure. But what if it's the only way we can be together?"

⚜ ⚜ ⚜

Rosa sat in the kitchen long after Saintcrow had gone home. Did she want to be a vampire? Did she love Jake enough to give up her humanity so they could be together? She could wait a few years. She was young yet. Maybe the promise of letting him turn her would be enough. Was that really the only way they could be together? If her blood was such a temptation, couldn't he just drink a little from her every night? Too bad she couldn't find a way to make her blood taste bad so he wouldn't want it… She frowned. Was such a thing possible? If a witch could conjure a way to hide Jake's presence, why couldn't the same witch give her a potion or something to make her blood unpalatable?

Maybe she would ask Saintcrow if that was possible the next time she saw him.

Where was Jake? Was he at rest in his lair in Montana? Was she ever going to see him again?

"Tune in tomorrow, same Bat time, same Bat channel, for the answer," she muttered darkly.

She had just dressed for the day when her phone rang. "Micah, hi! I'm so glad to hear from you."

"You won't be when I tell you why I called."

The tone of his voice was like a punch in the gut. "What's happened?"

"You'd better come home right away. Dad's in the ICU. It's not looking good. I can't leave Mom. Ask Saintcrow to bring you."

"I will!"

She called Saintcrow's name as soon as Micah said goodbye.

He arrived within seconds. "What's wrong?"

"My dad . . . ," she said, blinking back her tears. "He's in the hospital . . . "

"Are you ready to go?"

"As soon as I change clothes."

Ten minutes later, she closed her eyes as Saintcrow wrapped his arm around her waist.

When she opened them again, they were standing in front of the hospital.

"Do you want me to go in with you?"

"If you don't mind."

⚜ ⚜ ⚜

Time seemed to move in slow motion as Rosa signed in to the hospital, had her picture taken, produced her ID. She didn't know what vampire voodoo Saintcrow used, but no one seemed to notice him as they made their way upstairs to the Intensive Care Unit.

The family was in the waiting room, except for her mother and Micah, who were in her father's room, and Sofia and Holly, who were home at rest.

"Ethan, what happened?" Rosa asked anxiously.

"I'm not sure. I think he had a heart attack. They took some tests. We're waiting for the results." Ethan looked at Saintcrow. "Any chance you can help?"

Saintcrow shrugged. "You don't need me. You gave him your blood once before. No reason why it won't work this time."

"Have you talked it over with Mom?" Rosa asked.

"Not yet. I figured if she wanted me to help, she'd ask."

"Maybe she's too upset to think about it."

"Maybe," Ethan agreed. "They're only letting us in two at a time. I'll send Micah out and take his place and talk to Mom."

"If she's in favor, Ethan, just do it," Angela said. "I've got a bad feeling about this."

She had barely spoken the words when the call Code Blue came over the loud-speaker.

Rosa bit down on her lower lip. Was that for her father? Were they too late?

Moments later, Micah and Lena returned to the waiting room. Lena leaned heavily on Micah, her eyes brimming with tears.

Looking at Ethan, Rosa mouthed the word, "Go!"

⚜ ⚜ ⚜

Ethan drifted into the ICU. Several doctors were clustered around Luciano, trying to revive him. Exerting his supernatural power, he mesmerized the doctors and nurses, then materialized beside the bed. He bit into his wrist and held it to his father-in-law's mouth, letting his blood drip onto the old man's tongue, stroking his throat in an effort to make him swallow.

Ethan swore softly as he closed the wounds in his wrist. It wasn't working. He was about to call Saintcrow when the master vampire appeared beside hm.

"He's pretty far gone," Saintcrow said. "But maybe I can help."

He bit into his wrist and held it to Luciano's lips. "Drink!" he commanded, and although his voice was little more than a whisper, it resonated within the room.

Ethan watched his father-in-law's face as the master vampire's dark red blood dripped steadily into his mouth. In moments, a hint of color returned to the old man's face, his heart began to beat slow and steady. Five minutes passed, and Luciano's breathing returned to normal.

"That should do it," Saintcrow said, licking the punctures in his wrist.

Ethan freed the doctors and nurses from his thrall and the two vampires vanished from the room before anyone knew they had been there.

⚜ ⚜ ⚜

The family was ecstatic when the doctor came into the waiting room thirty minutes later. "It's a miracle," the surgeon said. "I can't explain it, but his heart rate is as strong as that of a twenty-year old. There's no blockage, no damage." He shook his head. "He's resting comfortably. You'll be able to visit him as soon as he's transferred from ICU to another room."

There were hugs and tears all around.

Rosa glanced at Saintcrow, who stood a little apart from everyone else. Say what you wanted about vampires, she mused. They could be cruel, they lived on the blood of others, but her family owed Ethan and Saintcrow a life debt they could never repay.

She smiled at Saintcrow as he ambled toward her.

“Ready to go home?” he asked quietly.

“Not just now. I think I’ll stay here with my Mom for a few days. I’m the only unmarried daughter she has left, and I don’t think she should be home alone right now.” The doctors wanted to keep her father in the hospital for a day or two for additional testing.

Saintcrow nodded. “Call me if you need me.”

Going up on her tiptoes, Rosa kissed his cheek. “Thank you for everything. If you see Jake … ”

“I’ll tell him where you are.” Not that it would be necessary, Saintcrow thought as he left the hospital. Kincaid already knew where Rosa was, but then, he would always know, whether she liked it or not.

Chapter Forty-One

Kincaid prowled the rooms in Blair House, his mind in turmoil as he tried to decide what to do about Rosa. He loved her. He wanted her. He needed her. He thought she loved him. But was that enough? She didn't want to be a vampire, at least not for the next few years, and that was fine. He loved her as she was. The blood she had so generously given him had cooled his rage and quieted his need to lash out. She had forgiven him for almost killing her. But could he ever forgive himself? He wasn't accustomed to worrying about or caring for anyone but himself. For centuries, he'd gone through life like a bat out of hell, doing what he wanted when he wanted, never considering the consequences, never stopping to think or give a damn about how his actions might affect others.

Until now.

Until Rosa Ravenwood drove across the bridge into Morgan Creek looking for a vampire.

He blew out a sigh. It took some doing to admit that the real problem was his pride. She had seen him at his worst, seen him locked up like some kind of wild animal, shackled and impotent, and when she had risked her life to help him, how had he thanked her? He had buried his fangs deep in her throat. Lord, he could have killed her. He had thought of little else since it happened.

He raked his hands through his hair. If not for Saintcrow's timely interference, Rosa would likely be dead now. What if it happened again? What if Saintcrow wasn't there to stop him the next time? How could he stay with her and put her life in danger? Hurting her would destroy him as surely as a stake in his heart. What the hell was he going to do?

CHAPTER FORTY-TWO

Rosa yawned and sat up. It seemed strange to wake up in her old bedroom, the one she had once shared with Sofia. Mama hadn't changed a thing—the bedspreads, the curtains, and the paint were all the same. The books she and her sister had loved remained on a shelf, along with a jar of shells they had collected at the beach one summer. Sofia's stuffed animals lined her headboard, a little dusty but as cute as always. The teddy bear that an old boyfriend had given Rosa one Valentine's Day still occupied the place of honor on her pillow.

She let out a sigh as she swung her legs over the edge of the mattress. It seemed like an eternity since she had lived at home, even though it had only been a year or so. She hadn't realized how easy she'd had it, living here with her parents. No real worries except to wonder if her current boyfriend would call, no responsibilities except for helping with the dishes and keeping her room clean.

A noise in the kitchen told her that her mother was up and making breakfast. Rosa had left a few items of clothing behind when she moved out. Now, she pulled on an old bathrobe and shuffled downstairs. "Morning, Mama."

Lena smiled at her.

She looked tired, Rosa thought. No doubt she hadn't gotten much sleep last night even though the doctors had assured them that Luciano would recover fully.

"Waffles okay?" Lena asked.

"Sounds good." Rosa set the table and poured the orange juice. And wondered where Jake was and how he was doing. Was he still in Montana? What did the future hold for them? Did they even have a future?

"The doctor called," Lena said as she set a platter of waffles on the table. "He said Papa can come home tomorrow. Now that everyone is home from vacation, we'll have to plan a big family dinner."

"Sounds like fun," Rosa said. "It's been a while since we all got together."

Lena nodded. "Do you think Mr. Saintcrow would come?"

"I don't know. I can ask him."

"He's really a very nice man, for a vampire," her mother said, taking a seat at the table.

"I think so, too," Rosa agreed, smiling as she took the opposite chair. "I'll bet you never thought you'd have four vampires in the family, did you?"

"I never thought we'd have one," Lena said drily. And then frowned. "Rosa, you aren't… ?"

"I need to tell you something."

Lena's eyes widened. "You haven't… ?"

"No. But I've been thinking about it. The reason I didn't go to Italy was because I went to Morgan Creek looking to meet a vampire."

"Why? Why in the name of all that's holy would you do that?"

"I thought it was what I wanted. Micah and Sofia wouldn't change me, so I went to see Saintcrow. But he wouldn't do it, either. But I met Jake while I was there… "

Lena's eyebrows shot upward. "Jake? That man you introduced us to? He's a vampire?"

"Yes. And I'm in love with him."

"Oh, Rosa." With a shake of her head, Lena pushed her plate away.

"You don't approve?"

"How can I?"

"But you don't have a problem with Micah or Sofia."

"They are my children and I love them," Lena said in a quiet voice laced with pain. "I will always love them. But how can I be truly happy for them, knowing what they have given up? They have chosen a way of life contrary to nature. Against the way life was meant to be. Sofia will never know the joy of having her own child. Micah will never be a father." She lifted a hand when she saw the protest in Rosa's eyes. "I know, Sofia has Jenny and I'm sure she loves her deeply, but it's not the same as feeling that child grow within you, hearing its first cry, the joy of holding a newborn baby in your arms and knowing that, with God's help, you and your husband created a new life."

"I never knew you felt that way."

"You must never say anything to either of them," Lena said. "Promise me."

"I promise. But aren't you forgetting something? Vampires saved Papa's life, not once, but twice."

"I have not forgotten," she said with a sigh. "One can only hope it was God's will."

⚜ ⚜ ⚜

Later that day, Rosa drove her mother to the hospital. The whole family was in the waiting room, patiently waiting their turn to go in two-by-two to visit Luciano.

Rosa was surprised to see how well her father looked. It was hard to believe they had all been so worried about him. He looked ten years younger, she thought, as she left his room.

Visiting hours were over by the time everyone had gone in to see him.

Her sister, Angela, had invited their mother to spend the rest of the day with her family. Lena, always happy to spend time with her grandchildren, had accepted. Angela had invited Rosa, too, but Rosa wasn't in the mood for company.

At loose ends, she took her mother's car and drove to the movies, hoping it would distract her from thoughts she didn't want to pursue.

Rosa had no sooner settled into her seat than Jake materialized beside her.

His gaze searched hers. "Do you want me to leave?"

"No." She could feel the tension in him. His hands were clenched, his jaw tight. "Are you all right?"

He shook his head.

Tugging on his hand, she said, "Let's get out of here."

He followed her out of the theater, sat stiffly beside her as she drove away from the city. Where to go? She thought it over for a moment, then drove to a small park near a housing tract still under construction. The place was deserted this time of the day. She parked the car and they walked across the grass toward a wooden bench located near a slide. They sat side by side, not touching.

"How's your father?" he asked.

"Much better. Saintcrow should open a clinic for the critically ill. I'm sure he could make a small fortune."

Kincaid grunted. "It wouldn't turn out well. Word would get out. Scientists would want to put him in a cage and test his blood. Fanatics would denounce him as evil and demand his destruction."

"You are in a dark place, aren't you?"

"You have no idea."

"Saintcrow said . . . "

"I know what he said. And he's right. I am afraid of you, but I'm more afraid of myself. And I'm . . . ashamed of what I almost did."

"You can't blame yourself, Jake. You were out of your mind with pain. I could feel it, too, you know? A part of it, at least."

He blew out a sigh. "I never wanted you to see me like that."

"It doesn't change anything."

"What if it happens again?"

"Are there any other necromancers after your head?"

He looked at her, his expression momentarily confused and then he laughed, but there was little humor in it. "Not that I know of. But there are hunters everywhere."

"Life is uncertain," she said with a shrug. "All I know for sure is that I love you. Do you love me?"

"You know I do. I also know how your mother feels about having vampires in the family."

"How is that possible?"

"I was there, outside your house earlier. I heard it all."

"It doesn't change anything," she said again.

"No? I think you'll break your mother's heart if you follow in Sofia's footsteps."

He was right, she thought. Even though her mother hadn't put it into words, Rosa knew it would hurt her mother deeply if she let Jake turn her. "I don't have to decide right away."

Tentatively, he reached for her hand, as if he wasn't sure she would welcome his touch. "You don't have to do it for me," he said quietly. "I would never ask you—or force you—to do that."

"I thought that's what you wanted. To be my sire. Saintcrow told me you wanted to be my master so that I could never leave you."

"I can't deny I thought about it," he admitted with a shrug. "To make you mine. To know you would always be mine. But I would never do it. I was not given the choice when I was turned. I would not make that decision for you." Yet even as he said the words, he wondered if it was true.

"I do love you, Jake."

With a wordless cry, he drew her into his arms and held her close. For a long while, neither of them spoke.

Rosa rested her head on his shoulder, content to be near him. He seemed strangely vulnerable for such a powerful creature. She could feel his strength, the preternatural power that radiated from him, yet she knew in her heart that he would never deliberately hurt her, just as she knew that he needed her in ways she didn't fully understand.

"Where do we go from here?" he asked.

"Where do you want to go?"

"I want to take you home and make love to you."

"And if I'm not ready?"

"I still want to take you home."

"That's what I want, too. But, what about my mom's car?"

"You can call Micah and ask him to pick it up."

She didn't even have to think it over. Murmuring, "Let's go," she grabbed her handbag and then closed her eyes as Jake gathered his power around him. When she opened them again, they were in the living room at Blair House.

Dropping her handbag on a side table, Rosa sank down on the sofa and patted the place beside her. She took Kincaid's his hand in hers when he joined her. "Do you want to talk about what happened while you were with Luca?"

"Hell, no."

"I think it might help."

Kincaid shook his head. Was she crazy? Why would he want to remember what it had been like, to be at the mercy of a mad man, to feel helpless, impotent? To relive the constant, agonizing pain? Or the way he'd felt lying there, unable to move or speak? Or recall the brutal way he had attacked her... He closed his eyes, remembering the warm, sweet taste of her life's blood flowing over his tongue, easing his agony. Rosa. Rosa.

"Saintcrow said he thought being a prisoner was so painful because it reminded you of being caged by the vampire who turned you."

Kincaid frowned, and then he nodded. He hadn't made the connection at the time, but he could see it now. He had felt weak, vulnerable, helpless while he was the vampire's prisoner. Drakos had humiliated him, humbled him, broken his will, and he had killed him for it. He had wanted to kill Luca, too. Instead, he had almost killed Rosa. Saintcrow had said he never would have bitten Rosa if he had known it was her. And he was right. Half out of his mind with pain and desperate to replace the blood he'd lost, he would have attacked anyone or anything that came near him. He grinned, thinking Saintcrow had a lot more insight than he gave him credit for.

"What are you smiling at?" Rosa asked.

"You."

Brow furrowed, she stared at him. He looked different, she thought. The tension had drained away, his beautiful dark eyes had lost their haunted look.

"Rosa, my little virgin, will you marry me?"

"What?"

"Will. You. Marry. Me?"

"I... what happened?"

"You healed my soul, if I have one," he said, giving her hand a squeeze. "I've done a lot of thinking in the last few days and I realized I'm not as lost or irredeemable as I thought I was. And it's all because of your faith and trust in me. And Saintcrow's, too. You both know me better than I know myself."

"Well, it's good to see you smile again," Rosa murmured, still confused.

"You haven't answered my question."

"Yes, Jake, I'll marry you."

He swept her into his arms, his mouth covering hers in a kiss that threatened to steal the breath from her body. She clung to him, desperate to hold him closer, closer, until there was no space between them. This was where she belonged, where she wanted to be. She melted against him, felt as if her whole being was turning to liquid fire, when, abruptly, he lifted his head.

"What's wrong?" she asked.

"How badly do you want to be a virgin on your wedding night?"

The question put out the fire.

"I'm an old-fashioned guy," he drawled. "I don't want to defile you. You're aren't just a one-night stand. You're going to be my wife." He took a deep breath. "And I'm going to ask for your father's permission."

Rosa blinked at him. "Are you serious?"

He nodded, his expression solemn.

Shoulders slumped, Rosa fell back against the sofa. Her father might give them his blessing. After all, he wouldn't be alive if not for the vampires in the family. But her mother?

Rosa sighed. She wasn't so sure about her mother.

Chapter Forty-Three

Paul Rhinehart stared at his reflection in the mirror. Why was he still seeing Luca's face day after day? The necromancer was dead. He had seen what was left of the body.

You have not fulfilled your end of the bargain! The vampire Kincaid has not been destroyed!

Rhinehart clapped his hands over his ears as he heard Luca's voice shriek in his mind. "Stop it, dammit! Get out of my head!"

If you cannot destroy the vampire, I will destroy your family.

"You're dead!" he screamed. "I saw your body!"

The image in the mirror laughed and the sound of Luca's evil cackle filled the room. He covered his ears again, but the laughter went on. And on. And then Luca's voice whispered to him.

The baby. She's asleep. Kill her now.

"Kill her now," Paul murmured. Leaving the bathroom, he took a pillow from his bed, walked down the hall to where his baby daughter slept, and leaned over the crib…

What was he doing? With a sob of despair, he hurled the pillow across the room and fled the house.

⚜ ⚜ ⚜

Kincaid sat in the living room of Blair House, his thoughts on Rosa. He could hear her humming softly as she cleaned up the kitchen after dinner. He wasn't looking forward to speaking to her father, had no idea what he would do if Ravenwood refused to give them his blessing. If her father said no, would Rosa change her mind?

He was trying to mentally compose what to say when he heard Izabela's voice in his mind.

The necromancer's body is dead but his spirit lives on.

What the hell? Reaching for his cell phone, he called the witch.

She answered immediately. "Be careful, Kincaid. My spell killed Luca's body but somehow his spirit escaped."

"How is that even possible?"

"He is very old and very powerful, with an incredibly strong will to survive. I have heard of such a thing only once before, a very long time ago, in Egypt."

"Where is his spirit now?"

"I don't know. Most likely he transferred to someone else who was in the room."

Kincaid frowned. "I was there. Rosa. Rhinehart. And Saintcrow."

"The mortal male is the weakest and therefore the most likely vessel. Be careful of him."

"Yeah. Thanks for the warning."

"It will cost you," she said, a smile in her voice.

"I'll make a deposit next time I'm in New Orleans."

There was no humor in her voice when she said, "See that you do."

"Any ideas on how to separate Luca from Rhinehart?"

"Not at the moment."

"If we kill Rhinehart, will Luca die with him?"

"Possibly. But if he had the power to leave his own body, it should not be difficult for him to leave Rhinehart's for another."

Kincaid muttered an oath.

"I shall look in my grimoire and see if I can find anything that might be of help," Izabela said, and ended the call.

Kincaid stared into the hearth. Damn. If he killed the hunter, would the witch just hop into someone else's body? Maybe his own, he thought darkly. Was there no way to kill Luca? No way to send his black soul to hell without harming Rhinehart?

Shit! Was this never going to end?

He stared at his phone, then punched in Saintcrow's number.

The master vampire answered as though he had been expecting his call. "I know," he said. "The witch sent her thoughts to me while she was talking to you."

Kincaid huffed a sigh. "What the hell do we do now?"

"Beats the hell out of me. Your guess is as good as mine."

⚜ ⚜ ⚜

"Who were you talking to?" Rosa asked as she settled on the sofa beside Jake.

"Izabela."

"The witch? Why?"

As succinctly as possible, he told her what Izabela had said.

Rosa stared at him, wide-eyed with disbelief, and then shook her head. "That's impossible."

"I always thought so."

"Poor Rhinehart. Do you think he knows?"

Kincaid shrugged. "How could he not? I mean, if you had an evil spirit inside you, I'm pretty sure you'd feel it."

"What are you going to do?"

"Hell, I don't know. Killing Rhinehart seems like the only solution."

Rosa's eyes widened. "You wouldn't? I mean, you can't. Paul hasn't done anything except try to help. And what if you kill Rhinehart and it doesn't kill Luca?"

"I have no idea. I've never heard of anything like this. I mean, disembodied evil spirits are one thing, but Luca was human. At least I thought he was." Kincaid shook his head. "I'm hoping Izabela or Saintcrow can come up with an answer."

"You'll have to find him first."

Kincaid grunted softly. Luca had been seeking vengeance against him for almost a hundred years. He doubted the necromancer would give up now.

Who would have thought there were scarier things in the world than vampires and necromancers? How many other supernatural creatures lurked in the shadows? Maybe werewolves and zombies weren't just fictional monsters but living, breathing creatures hiding in the shadows.

Rosa shivered as she snuggled closer to Jake, wondering if she would ever feel truly safe again.

⚜ ⚜ ⚜

Unable to rest, Kincaid prowled the streets of Morgan Creek after Rosa retired for the night. How dangerous was Luca if he was inhabiting Rhinehart's body? Did the necromancer still possess his own powerful magic? Was he fully in control of Rhinehart? Would Luca's power over the hunter increase day by day? Or weaken? Was there a way to destroy Luca without destroying Rhinehart? Would killing Rhinehart also kill the witch? Or would he just jump into the nearest host?

So many questions, he thought bleakly. Who the hell had the answers?

There was only one thing he knew for sure. If Rhinehart so much as threatened Rosa, he was a dead man.

A thought took him to Izabela's house.

She answered the door before he knocked. "I have been expecting you, Jake Kincaid. Do you mean me any harm?"

"Never." She asked the same question every time he came to call. He followed her into the house, sat in the chair she indicated.

"What can I do for you?"

Kincaid shrugged. "I couldn't sleep."

"Have you come for a sleeping potion?"

"Hell, no."

"I am very good at what I do," she said. "But you must know it will take more than an hour or two to solve this problem."

"I know. But lives hang in the balance."

"Have you been in touch with Rhinehart since this happened?"

"No."

"In order to understand what we're dealing with, either you or Saintcrow need to contact him. It is the only way to determine the extent of Luca's power."

Kincaid nodded. Unfortunately, at the moment, no one knew where to find the hunter.

"We need to know if Luca retains his magic, or if his spirit is merely residing in a new shell. If he cannot work his magic inside the hunter, then killing the hunter will kill Luca, as well. If he retains his power, he will merely flee the hunter's body before it dies."

"So, if his spirit leaves Rhinehart, is there a way to trap him inside a new body? Or catch him between one host and the other?"

"Perhaps. I will study the matter further. Thus far, my grimoire has revealed no answers. I may have to consult someone familiar with exorcisms as I have never performed one. Is there anything else?"

"No. Sorry I bothered you."

"There is the usual charge for a visit."

"Yeah, I thought there would be." He rolled up his shirt sleeve while she went to fetch a container. He would have given a pint of blood to know what she did with it.

When she returned, he bit into his left wrist and held it over the bottle until it was full.

"Until next time, Jake Kincaid."

He nodded. "Until then."

Saintcrow was waiting for Kincaid on the porch when he returned to Blair House. "You've been to see the witch."

"Yeah." Kincaid relayed what Izabela had told him. "Any idea where Rhinehart is?"

"No. I tried calling his cell phone. No answer."

"We should go by his house. Maybe his wife knows something."

"I doubt it, but we have to start somewhere. You're afraid he'll come after you."

Kincaid shrugged. "I'm more worried about Rosa."

"We'll go in the morning. Around eleven."

Kincaid checked on Rosa after Saintcrow left. He stood by the bed for several minutes, just watching her sleep, listening to her slow, even breathing, the steady beat of her heart.

Murmuring, "Dream of me," he brushed a kiss across her brow, then sought his lair in the basement.

⚜ ⚜ ⚜

Rosa woke slowly, wishing that Jake was beside her. Now that Luca had reared his ugly head again, their wedding had, regretfully, been put on hold. She still couldn't believe that the necromancer wasn't dead. How could anyone—any*thing*—have survived that spell? And if that hadn't killed Luca, what on earth would?

Swinging her legs over the side of the bed, she sat there a moment, wondering when Jake would rise and what she would do until then. Staying inside seemed like the wisest thing to do. And then she remembered she had lots of boxes to unpack.

"No time like the present," she mused aloud. "And I'll get to it, right after breakfast."

⚜ ⚜ ⚜

She was in the kitchen, putting silverware in a drawer, when Jake came up behind her and nuzzled her neck.

"Hey, beautiful," he murmured.

"Hey, yourself." She turned in his arms, lifting her face for his kiss.

He pulled her close, his lips moving evocatively over hers, stealing the strength from her legs and making her heart beat faster. When she felt his tongue stroke the side of her neck, she turned her head, giving him access to her throat, sighed as warmth spread through her, like a flower opening to the sun.

Murmuring, "Thank you, love," he sealed the tiny wounds. "I needed that."

"Oh? Why?"

"Saintcrow and I are going hunting."

"In the middle of the day?"

"Not that kind of hunting. We need to find Rhinehart. Saintcrow suggested we start at his place on the off chance that he'd be home, or that his wife might know where to find him." Kincaid lifted his head, nostrils flaring. "Saintcrow's here."

"Be careful, Jake."

"Always." He kissed her again, hard and quick, before striding out of the room.

⚜ ⚜ ⚜

A combined thought carried Saintcrow and Kincaid to the front porch of Rhinehart's house.

"He's not here," Saintcrow said. "But the woman is."

Kincaid rang the bell.

A few moments later, the door opened a crack and a woman peered at them. She was in her late thirties, with blonde hair and dark shadows under worried brown eyes. "What do you want?"

"We're looking for Paul, Mrs. Rhinehart," Kincaid said. "Do you have any idea where he is?"

"No. Who are you?"

"Friends of his who are worried about him."

She stared at the two of them. "I haven't seen him for a couple of days."

"Was he all right when he left?"

"No. I've been so worried. He's been acting so strangely. Not like himself at all. Talking to himself. Wandering through the house, babbling incoherently. Unable to sleep at night." She shook her head. "I'm afraid he's lost his mind."

"Do you have any idea where he'd go?" Saintcrow asked.

She thought about it for several minutes, her brow furrowed. "We have a summer place on the lake in Deer Creek."

"Could you give us the address?"

She hesitated for the space of a heartbeat. "I'll write it down for you," she said and shut the door.

Kincaid heard the snick of the lock being turned. "The woman's scared half to death."

"Yeah. Can you blame her?"

The door opened again and she slid a piece of paper through the crack.

Kincaid looked at it, then tucked the paper into his shirt pocket.

"If you find him, you'll let me know?"

"I promise."

"Tell him how worried I am," she said. "And that we miss him."

Saintcrow nodded. "If you hear from him, give us a call," he said and offered her one of his business cards.

"I will." She snatched the card from his hand, closed and locked the door.

"Well," Saintcrow said, "at least we have a place to start."

Chapter Forty-Four

Paul Rhinehart paced the cabin floor, stopping now and then to take long swallows from the bottle of whiskey clutched in his hand in a vain attempt to drown out the voice in his head. Luca's voice, whispering lies, urging him to go home and kill Nancy.

She's cheating on you, the voice said. *Has been for years. The last brat she bore isn't even yours. Kill them both. Kill them all.*

"No! Get out of my head, damn you! You're dead! Dead!"

Luca's laughter echoed in his mind. *You can't kill me. You're weak and soon you'll be mine. You want to kill her, Paul, you know you do. Only then will you be a man.*

Paul drained the last of the whiskey and hurled the bottle into the fireplace. Staggering slightly, he picked up the pistol lying on the coffee table. It nestled in his hand, promising an end to the malevolent voice in his mind.

"I know how to get rid of you," he said.

Don't be a fool.

"Scared now, are you, you vile creature? One shot and you'll be gone." Muttering, "Forgive me, Nancy, it's the only way to save you and the kids," he lifted the gun barrel to his temple and curled his finger around the trigger.

Chapter Forty-Five

Kincaid raised his hand to knock on the cabin door when the report of a gunshot echoed from inside.

"We may be too late," Saintcrow remarked.

"Maybe he solved the problem for us," Kincaid said, trying the door.

It was unlocked.

Kincaid pushed it open and glanced inside, expecting to find Rhinehart's body on the floor. Instead, the man was standing in front of the fireplace, a Glock in his hand. Smoke curled from the barrel.

Rhinehart looked up, his face pale. "Coward that I am, I couldn't do it. How did you find me?"

"Your wife advised us to look here," Kincaid replied.

"What do you want?"

"The same thing you do," Saintcrow said. "To get rid of Luca once and for all."

"He won't leave me alone," Rhinehart said, his voice ragged and filled with despair. "He troubles me day and night, telling me my Nancy is unfaithful, that Becky isn't mine, that I should kill them both. That I should kill them all."

"We'd like to help," Kincaid said.

"Why?" Rhinehart asked, and then his eyes widened with comprehension. "You don't want to help. You want to kill me in hopes it will kill Luca! You're afraid he'll use me to destroy you!"

"The thought crossed my mind," Kincaid admitted with a shrug.

Rhinehart lifted the gun and leveled it at the vampire.

"Don't be a damn fool," Kincaid snarled. "I can break your neck before you pull the trigger."

"If only you could. But you can't come in."

"Rhinehart."

The hunter froze at the power in Saintcrow's voice, power that left him motionless, helpless.

"Put the gun down and invite us in."

Moving like a zombie, Rhinehart stooped down and placed the Glock on the floor. "Saintcrow, Kincaid, come in," he said woodenly.

"Kincaid, get the gun," Saintcrow said. Crossing the threshold, he took hold of Rhinehart's arm.

"What now?" Kincaid asked, tucking the pistol in the waistband of his jeans.

"We need to find a place to keep him where he can't do any harm until we figure out a solution."

"What if we can't figure out a way to destroy Luca without killing Rhinehart?"

"He's still a hunter."

"What kind of answer is that?"

"I don't know about you, but if it's him or me, I don't have a problem getting rid of him."

Kincaid nodded. He just hoped if they had to kill Rhinehart, that Rosa would understand. "So, where are we gonna keep him?"

"I know a place."

"Yeah?"

"There's an old jail out past the cemetery in Morgan Creek."

"A jail?"

"Well, not really a jail. More like an escape-proof cage."

Kincaid lifted one brow.

"Don't ask. Are you ready to go?"

"Lead the way."

⚜ ⚜ ⚜

The cage, surrounded by tall trees and brush, was maybe eight feet by twelve. The bars were iron, thick and set close together, the top and three sides covered by heavy plywood. It held a narrow iron cot topped by a ragged quilt and a small bookcase crammed with yellowed paperbacks. A portable toilet stood in one corner.

"When did you use this last?" Kincaid asked.

Saintcrow shrugged. "Forty, fifty years ago."

"For what?"

"Nothing I'm proud of."

"Not gonna tell me, huh?"

"No." Saintcrow opened the door and gestured for Rhinehart to step inside. Still under the master vampire's spell, the hunter did as he was told.

"Rhinehart, did you see anyone between the time you left your house and arrived at the cabin?"

"I don't remember."

Once the door was locked, Saintcrow stepped away from the cell and motioned for Kincaid to follow him so Luca couldn't overhear what they were saying, should he still be inside the hunter.

"Do you think Luca's still possessing him?" Kincaid asked. "Seems like if he was, he'd object to being locked up."

"Maybe he wants us to think he's gone so we'll relax our guard."

Kincaid grunted softly. "Or maybe he's really gone. Or he could be resting. Gathering his strength."

"It's possible," Saintcrow agreed. "We need to find out if Luca still has his power, which could be dangerous as hell."

"Tell me about it." Kincaid studied Rhinehart. The hunter stood there, unmoving, unblinking. Was Luca still inside, resting? Or had he deserted the hunter's body for another? If that was the case, they might never find him.

"Are we just gonna leave him in there?" Kincaid asked.

"It's the safest place for him. He can't hurt himself. He can't get out. No one will hear him if he screams for help. I'll bring him something to eat and some clean blankets later," Saintcrow said. "He'll be all right until then."

Kincaid stared at the cage. Remembering another cage centuries ago, and the one he had recently occupied, he thought he would rather be dead than locked up again.

Chapter Forty-Six

Rosa stared at Jake. "You left him in a cage?"

"You got any better ideas?"

Try as she might, she couldn't think of even one. If the necromancer's spirit still resided in Paul, then he was dangerous, not only to himself, but to anyone who came in contact with him.

"Izabela said if Luca can't work his magic while inside Rhinehart's body, killing Rhinehart will kill them both. If Luca retains his power, he'll just leave the hunter's body before it dies."

"So there's a chance you'd have to kill Paul to kill Luca? That's murder."

"I don't know if Luca is capable of practicing his magic, but he's already controlling Rhinehart to some extent. He tried to get the hunter to kill his family."

Rosa stared at him in horror.

"Think of it as self-defense. If Luca still has the ability to practice his magic, he's going to keep coming after us. And like Saintcrow said, if it comes down to Luca or us ..." Jake shrugged.

Rosa bit down on her lower lip. It seemed wrong to kill Paul when he wasn't responsible for whatever violence he might do, but what other choice would Jake or Saintcrow have?

"We talked to Izabela. She said if Luca still has his magic, the best way to destroy him might be to catch him between host bodies. Or maybe trap him in a new one."

Seeking comfort, she went into his arms. "Is this ever going to end?"

"I hope so."

Maybe it never would, she thought bleakly. Jake and Saintcrow might spend weeks, months, years, trying to destroy the necromancer before they found a way to defeat him. Did she want to wait that long to be Jake's wife? And what if something happened to him? Wouldn't a few hours of forgetfulness in his arms be worth whatever happened next?

"What are you thinking about?" he asked when she looked up at him, her beautiful dark eyes filled with love and desire.

"Do you still want to marry me?"

"Is that a trick question?"

She smiled faintly. "Is there any place where we could get married tonight?"

"I haven't asked your father's permission yet."

"You have my permission. That's all you need."

"Reno?" Pulling his cell phone from his jeans, he did a quick search, and smiled.

"The license bureau is open until midnight. No blood tests required. Are you game?"

Was she? She gazed into Jake's eyes. The love she saw there turned her insides to mush. He loved her, he wanted her, and oh, how she wanted him. "Let's do it."

⚜ ⚜ ⚜

It was six o'clock when they arrived in Reno via a little vampire magic. It didn't take long to procure a license. A quick trip to the nearest mall provided a simple white dress and heels for Rosa, a pair of black slacks, a crisp white shirt, and a black jacket for Jake. They found a set of matching wedding rings—far more expensive than she would have chosen—and they were ready to go.

They had to try half a dozen places before they found one that was open and available. The venue was clean and neat, if not particular fancy, but Rosa only had eyes for Jake.

The ceremony was brief. Her heart pounded so loudly in her ears she hardly heard the words of the official who pronounced them man and wife. And then Jake was holding her in his arms, his gaze warm with love as he kissed her tenderly.

They left the wedding chapel hand-in-hand, their marriage license in Jake's pocket. "I'm afraid we'll have to postpone a lengthy honeymoon until this mess with Luca is cleared up," Jake remarked. "But we can spend our wedding night anywhere you want."

"I don't care where we go," Rosa replied, feeling her cheeks grow hot, "as long as it has a big bed and clean sheets."

Jake grinned at her, and the next thing she knew, they had checked into a fancy hotel and Jake was carrying her down a carpeted hallway and into the most beautiful suite she had ever seen.

He kicked the door shut behind them, his eyes hot when they met hers. "Rosa, don't make me wait any longer."

"I'm here," she said with a saucy grin. "But the bed's in there."

Somewhere between the living room and the bedroom, their clothing disappeared.

Holding her close with one arm, Kincaid tossed the bedspread aside, then lowered her gently to the mattress. He held her close, his dark eyes filled with desire as he kissed and caressed every inch of her until she was wild with wanting him, her own hands eager as she explored the width of his shoulders, his hard flat belly, the taut muscles in his arms that quivered at her touch. He was beautiful to look at, heaven to touch.

And then he was rising over her, eyes blazing, as he whispered that he loved her more than life.

She gasped, a mingled whimper of pain and pleasure as he possessed her. She writhed beneath him, desperate for something that seemed just out of reach until one last thrust carried her over the edge and there was only wave after wave of pleasure as he moved deep within her. She grasped his shoulders, her fingernails digging into him as the world seemed to explode around her in a kaleidoscope of rainbow colors.

He cried her name a moment later, shuddered violently, then collapsed on top of her.

For a moment, she couldn't move, couldn't think, could only lie there, waiting for her breathing to return to normal.

When he started to roll over onto his side, she wrapped her arms around his waist, holding him in place. "Not yet," she whispered.

"I must be heavy."

"You are," she agreed with a faint smile. "But I like it."

"Did I hurt you?"

"Only a little, at first."

Lifting up on his elbows, he brushed a kiss across her lips. "It will never hurt again."

"It was worth it."

"High praise, indeed," he murmured.

"I love you, Jake."

"And I love you, my sweet girl, more than you can imagine." In spite of her protests, he rolled onto his side, carrying her with him, their bodies still locked intimately together. He smoothed his hand over her hair, unable to believe she was his. Lawfully and legally his. He smiled faintly as, with a sigh, her eyelids fluttered down and she fell asleep in his arms.

He held her for several minutes, basking in her nearness, her warmth. She had been fire and silk in his arms, curious and eager and yet shy at the same time. He had never loved anyone the way he loved this woman, he thought as he eased away from her. Her love and acceptance had filled a need he never knew he had, healed a centuries-old ache deep inside him.

Slipping quietly out of bed, he pulled a blanket over her, kissed her cheek, then pulled on his shirt, jeans, and boots. As much as he hated to leave her, even for a few moments, making love to her had fired his hunger and he needed to feed before the temptation to drink from her while she slept became overwhelming.

He kissed her one more time, warded the room against intruders, and left the hotel, happier and more at peace than he had ever been in his life.

⚜ ⚜ ⚜

Kadie jabbed Rylan in the side with her elbow. "What are you grinning at?" she asked. They were sitting side by side in bed. She had been reading a book. He'd been going over some paperwork.

"Unless I'm mistaken," he said, "and you know I never am, our Rosa is no longer a maiden."

"What?" Kadie's eyes widened. "You mean ..."

"Yep. He's finally had his way with her."

Kadie bit down on her lower lip. "Did he … I mean … was she … ?"

"He didn't take her against her will, if that's what you're wondering."

"Thank goodness," she said, momentarily relieved. And then she stared at him.

"Micah will kill him!"

"Calm down. They're married."

"Married! Are you sure?"

He nodded.

"Well, that was kind of sudden, wasn't it? I mean, they've known each other such a short time." And then she grinned. "I guess we didn't wait very long either, did we?"

"Too long as far I was concerned."

"Men." She shook her head in mock despair. "All they want is one thing."

He put his paperwork aside, took the book from her hands and dropped it on the floor. "I'm thinking about that one thing right now," he drawled, taking her in his arms."

"Do you *ever* think of anything else?" she asked with a dramatic sigh.

"Not when you're this close," he said, his voice a low growl as he began to lift her nightgown over her head.

"What if I said no?"

His hand stilled immediately. "Are you?"

"Have I ever refused you?" she asked, fighting the urge to laugh.

He snorted. "Shall I count the ways one by one?"

"That was then," she said, her fingers tracing the line of dark hair that disappeared beneath the sheet. "This is now." Falling back on the bed, she threw her arms wide. "Have your wicked way with me if you must."

"Always my pleasure, my lady."

She sighed as he aroused her, amazed as always that she had ever thought she hated the wonderful, powerful man in her arms.

Chapter Forty-Seven

Paul Rhinehart paced the narrow confines of the cage, the food and drink Saintcrow had left for him untouched. He could feel the necromancer inside of him, a malevolent, alien presence constantly fighting him for control of his thoughts, filling his mind with vivid images of death and destruction. He felt his own will growing weaker as Luca's grew stronger and it scared the living hell out of him.

We need to get out of here, hunter.

"No, we don't."

Coward! Think of the power that will be yours if you surrender to me. You want it, you know you do.

"I don't!"

You're lying to yourself, but it doesn't matter. Sooner or later, you will surrender your will to mine and when that happens, I will be in control. I can already feel my magic coming back to life. No mere mortal can defeat me now.

Rhinehart pressed his hands over his ears as Luca's maniacal laughter rumbled in his head. Where were Saintcrow and Kincaid? Had they left him here to rot? Why wouldn't they? He was nothing to them. Vampires! He had been a fool to trust them. With Luca's power, he could...

"No!" He screamed the word as he heard the necromancer's insane laughter in his mind once more.

Chapter Forty-Eight

A blush warmed Rosa's cheeks when she woke to find Jake in bed beside her, propped up his elbow, watching her. "Is something wrong?"

"No." He ran his tongue along the curve of her throat. "I never thought you'd be mine. No matter how much I dreamed of it, I never thought it would happen."

Smiling, she pulled his head down and kissed him. "Are you convinced now?"

Kincaid laughed softly as he stretched out beside her and drew her into his embrace. Her curvy little body fit his perfectly, he mused, as he ran his fingers through the thick mass of her hair. She was here. She was his. But for how long? Unbidden, thoughts of Rhinehart tugged at his mind. What were they going to do about the hunter?

"Hey," Rosa said, tugging on a lock of his hair. "Where did you go?"

"Sorry."

"You were thinking about Paul, weren't you?"

"Yeah. We have to find a way to destroy Luca. It's the only way any of us will ever have any peace."

She ran her hands over his broad chest, slipped her fingers under the sheet that covered him from his hips down. "Can't you think about him later?" she purred, and laughed softly as his arousal became blatantly evident.

"Think about who?" he growled, as he rose over her and captured her lips with his.

⚜ ⚜ ⚜

Rosa brushed a kiss across Jake's cheek before she slipped out of bed. Caught in the Dark Sleep, he didn't stir.

She padded into the bathroom and turned on the shower, thinking she hated to wash away Jake's scent, which was all over her. She felt her cheeks heat when she remembered how she had caressed him, the pleasure it had given her to know she could touch him anywhere she wanted, that she had been able to please him. He had certainly pleased her! She had suspected he would be a wonderful lover, but wonderful didn't begin to describe the way he had made her feel, the joy she felt just looking at him. The man was gorgeous from head to foot and everywhere in-between. She blushed as she recalled how eagerly she had explored his hard, muscular body, the way he had instantly responded to her touch, the husky sound of his voice as he declared he loved her, would always love her.

She stood under the hot spray for a long time, her thoughts gradually turning toward less pleasant things, like what they were going to do about Rhinehart, and how and when to tell her family she had married Jake.

After washing her hair, she stepped out of the stall, wrapped herself in one of the fluffy hotel towels, and dried her hair with the dryer also provided by the hotel. "I could get used to this," she murmured. Everything she could possibly want was there—scented soap, hand lotion, shampoo and conditioner, the blow dryer, toothpaste and brushes, enough towels for five people.

Slipping into a bathrobe, also provided by the hotel, she called room service and ordered breakfast.

How long would Jake rest? she wondered. And what would she do until he woke? Would he want to make love again? She certainly did.

She glanced at her cell phone, lying on the coffee table. Should she call her parents? Micah? Sofia? She was still trying to decide when her breakfast arrived.

She ate at the table by the window. Reno, hailed as The Biggest Little City in the World, had an abundance of hotels and casinos, some of which were visible from where she sat.

It was near noon when she got dressed. Thinking she needed a diversion, she grabbed her handbag. When in doubt, when you had decisions you didn't want to make, shopping was always a pleasant diversion. She hesitated a moment, wondering at the wisdom of going out, then shrugged. They were miles away from Morgan Creek. Rhinehart was locked up. And no one knew where they were.

⚜ ⚜ ⚜

Kincaid went from nothingness to awareness in the blink of an eye. He knew immediately that Rosa had left their hotel room. Muttering an oath, he took a quick shower, dressed, and followed her unique scent to the elevator and down to the lobby. He stood there a moment, separating his bride's scent from the hundreds of others.

He found her in the hotel dress shop, standing in front of a mirror, turning this way and that, her brow furrowed. "I like it," he said, coming up behind her.

She whirled around, her lips curved in a smile. "Do you?"

"I said so, didn't I?"

"Do you like the color?"

"I like you."

"I like you, too." She glanced at her reflection again and nodded. "I think I'll take it."

He waited while she changed into her own clothes, then followed her to the cash register. When she pulled her credit card out of her wallet, he shook his head and paid for the dress.

"You didn't have to do that," she said, as they left the store.

"You're my wife. I intend to provide for you. And," he said with a wicked grin, "satisfy all your wants and desires."

"Like you did last night?"

"Absolutely." The look in his eyes made her whole being smile.

⚜ ⚜ ⚜

They wandered down the street, stopping in at the Peppermill Casino so Rosa could try her luck at the slots and the craps table.

"I never knew gambling was so much fun," she exclaimed.

"Especially when you're winning."

"I guess that helps. Let's go try the Blackjack table."

"I hate to cut our time here short," Kincaid said. "But we need to get back to Morgan Creek. I've got to go see Izabela and find out if she's learned anything."

Rosa wanted to argue, but she felt suddenly guilty, gambling in a fabulous casino while Paul Rhinehart was trapped in a cage, never knowing if he would ever see his family again.

"I'll make it up to you," Kincaid said as they left the casino. "I promise."

⚜ ⚜ ⚜

The witch was waiting for him when he arrived. After asking the usual question about his intentions and reminding him of the cost of her services, she said, "It is good to see you again, Kincaid. I may have found a solution, depending on Luca. Does he retain his power inside the hunter?"

"I'm not sure, but it sounds like it, at least from what Rhinehart says."

"If you can drive him out of Rhinehart's body, I may have found a spell that will imprison his spirit inside a vessel, sort of like trapping a Genie in a lamp."

"Sounds promising."

"If it fails, Luca's spirit will attempt to inhabit whoever is nearby."

Kincaid nodded thoughtfully.

"Give me a day or two to refine the spell." Reaching into the pocket of her skirt, she withdrew a familiar bottle.

And Kincaid obligingly bit into his wrist to pay for her information.

⚜ ⚜ ⚜

As usual, Saintcrow was waiting for him on the porch when he returned to Blair House. "So? What did your witch have to say?"

After muttering, "She's not my witch," Kincaid told him what Izabela had said.

"Sounds tricky," the master vampire remarked. "Seems to me the best way to get Luca out of Rhinehart is to kill the hunter."

"That's not going to sit well with my bride."

Saintcrow shrugged. "Kadie won't like it, either. Think of it as collateral damage."

"Uh-huh."

"I guess I should congratulate you on your recent marriage," Saintcrow said, changing the subject. "Happened kind of quick, didn't it?"

Kincaid shrugged. "She asked me and I said yes."

Saintcrow lifted one brow. "She. Asked. You?"

"That's what I said. I'm irresistible, didn't you know?"

"Well, I'm glad she thinks so." Saintcrow dragged his hand across his jaw. "So, back to matter at hand. You said the witch needs a day or two to work on her solution."

"Yeah. And I hope like hell it works the first time, because I doubt if we'll get a second chance."

⚜ ⚜ ⚜

Pausing outside the cage, Saintcrow set the wooden tray he carried on a flat stump. Rhinehart sat on the concrete floor, head bowed, arms dangling at his sides. Blood, now dry, had dripped from his nose and down his chin. He didn't move, didn't look up.

Saintcrow opened his preternatural senses. The hunter was alive but unaware. The signature of Luca's dark magic tainted the air.

Slowly, Rhinehart lifted his head. His face was blank, his eyes empty and unblinking.

"He is mine now." It was Luca's voice, not the hunter's. "You will not be able to hold us much longer."

"What have you done to him?"

"Only what was necessary."

Saintcrow nodded. Whatever Luca had done to Rhinehart, it hadn't been pleasant. The blood was proof of a violent internal struggle. Not knowing if it would work, he reinforced the wards around the cage, then picked up the tray and willed himself back home.

This was bad, he thought.

Very bad.

Chapter Forty-Nine

Rosa took a deep breath when her phone rang. She considered not answering then huffed a sigh. She had to talk to him sooner or later.

"Hi, Micah," she said brightly. "What's new?"

"Not much. Just thought I'd call since I haven't heard from you for several days. Everything okay?"

"Peachy."

"Uh-huh. Where are you?"

"In Morgan Creek."

"With Kincaid?"

"Of course. I know you don't approve," she said quickly, "but you'd best get used to it."

There was a long pause. "What have you done, Rosie?"

"Not what you're thinking! I told you, I wouldn't do that without telling you first."

His sigh of relief came through the phone loud and clear.

"How's Dad?"

"He's doing well. I thought you'd have come to see him by now."

"I've been meaning to."

"But?"

She bit down on her lower lip.

"Rosa, what aren't you telling me?"

"There's been some trouble," she said. "It's too complicated to explain over the phone and it doesn't directly involve me. Just Saintcrow and Jake."

"Are you in any danger?"

"No. I'm fine, just worried."

"He's no good for you, Rosie."

"I love him, big brother. Please try to understand. Remember how you felt about Holly? Well, that's how I feel about Jake."

He sighed again. "Come and see us when you can."

"I will. I promise. Tell Mom and Dad I'll be there as soon as possible." She stared at the phone after Micah said goodbye. She hated keeping secrets from him. As soon as this mess with Luca was cleared up, she'd go home and tell him everything.

She looked up when Jake materialized in the living room, frowned when she saw the troubled look on his face. "What's wrong?"

"I had a phone call from Saintcrow while you were talking to Micah."

"Oh?" Judging by his expression, it hadn't been good news.

"Saintcrow went to see Rhinehart. Luca has pretty much taken over the hunter's body. And his mind."

"Oh, no."

"Izabela thinks she might have a way to trap his spirit if we can catch him between hosts."

"How will you convince Luca to leave Paul's body?"

"That's the problem. We'll probably have to kill him."

She stared at him, her expression troubled. "Doesn't that bother you? Even a little?"

"It's him or us. You make the choice."

"That's not fair!"

"I have an idea. Whether it will work or not..." He shrugged. "Only time will tell."

⚜ ⚜ ⚜

Rosa lay in bed that night struggling with her feelings. Jake had gone in search of prey. She didn't like the tension between them. She understood where he was coming from. They had to do something before Luca got any stronger, but to kill Paul... He had a wife and three kids. She bit down on her lower lip. What if killing Paul was the only way to protect his wife and family? If Luca had taken over his mind and body, that might be the only option. But what if something went wrong? What if Luca was stronger than they thought? What if... She thrust the troubling thoughts from her mind, refusing to think the worst.

She scooted over as Jake materialized in the bedroom.

Sitting on the edge of the mattress, Kincaid toed off his boots and undressed down to his briefs, then slid in beside her, unsure of his welcome. He had sensed her thoughts on the way home. Relief washed through him when she rolled onto her side and rested her head on his shoulder.

"I'm sorry," she murmured. "I know this isn't your fault. I guess it's really Paul's fault for getting mixed up with Luca in the first place." She traced his lower lip with her fingertips. "Make love to me, Jake."

"Always my pleasure," he murmured.

She clung to him, raining kisses on his face and neck, his shoulders, moaning with pleasure as he kissed and caressed her in return. She stilled when she felt his fangs at her throat, sighed with pleasure as he bit her, ever so gently. And for that moment, all her fears of the future were forgotten. There was only Jake, telling her with every kiss and caress that he loved her.

Kincaid opened the bond between them as he held her close, heard her gasp when the pleasure between them increased as each experienced what the other was feeling.

Later, sated and satisfied, Rosa asked, "How did you do that?"

"We've shared blood," he explained. "It makes the bond between us stronger. Deeper."

"Why didn't I feel it on our wedding night?"

He grinned at her. "I wasn't sure I wanted you to know what I was thinking."

"Oh?"

"I was afraid the intensity of what I was thinking and feeling might frighten you," he admitted, somewhat sheepishly.

Rosa stared at him, not knowing if he was serious or not.

He kissed the tip of her nose, held her close until her eyelids fluttered down. When he was sure she was asleep, he slid out of bed, pulled on a pair of sweat pants, and went outside.

Dark clouds shrouded both moon and stars. With his preternatural vision, he could see the silhouettes of the buildings on Main Street, as well as a few of the residential porch lights. Standing there, he felt the night wrap around him, enfolding him in her dark embrace. He preferred the night to the day, the darkness to the light, but for Rosa, he endured the daylight hours. He smiled faintly. He would do anything for her, he thought. He, who had spent his whole existence with nothing and no one to tie him down, was now bound to a beautiful young mortal female, and he would live and die for her.

He smiled a self-mocking smile as he returned to the house and slid into bed beside the only woman who had ever captured his heart and his soul.

⚜ ⚜ ⚜

It was mid-afternoon the next day when Kincaid heard from the witch.

"I think I have what you need," she said. "You and Saintcrow may come by tonight, if you wish."

"We'll be there, say, eight o'clock?"

"Until then."

Kincaid stared at his phone. As eager as he was to get this whole mess over with, he was dreading it at the same time. There was no guarantee of success for any of them.

⚜ ⚜ ⚜

Izabela opened the door with the usual question. "Do either of you mean me any harm?" She was dressed all in black today, Kincaid noted, as if to remind them of what she was. As if he could forget. He had felt her dark power every time he entered the place, but never more so than now. A glance at Saintcrow showed he was aware of it, too.

"Maybe that's a question we should be asking you," the master vampire remarked.

Her gaze bored into him. "Spare me your insolence."

"Hey, it's a fair question," Saintcrow retorted. "And the answer to yours is no."

She stepped back to allow them entrance. "Are you both prepared to pay the price?"

Saintcrow glanced at Kincaid, then shrugged.

The witch made a vague gesture with her hands and a small glass bottle appeared in each one.

"Payment in advance this time?" Kincaid asked.

"Do you object?"

"I guess not," he said, and bit into his wrist.

Muttering an oath, Saintcrow did likewise.

A look Kincaid could not interpret flitted over the witch's face as she watched the thick, dark red liquid fill the containers. He wondered suddenly if she drank the blood. It was said to lengthen the life of mortals. Perhaps it worked on witches, too.

Izabela capped the bottles and tucked them into her skirt pocket. She left the room for a moment and when she returned, she offered Kincaid a small ebony box. It was square, the top intricately carved with Celtic runes and zodiac signs. "If you can capture his soul inside this, he will be helpless."

"How does it work?"

"As soon as he is between hosts, open the box and command him to enter. If I have performed the spell properly, he will be compelled to do so. Once locked inside, no one will be able to open the box, including the two of you."

"And if you haven't done it right?" Kincaid asked.

"Magic doesn't come with guarantees."

"That's no answer."

"If the spell fails, he will seek the nearest host. The talismans I made for the two of you should repel him."

"Then what? His spirit will wander around until it finds a new host?"

"It depends on how strong he is. If he is denied a host for more than twenty-four hours, his spirit will return to his own body."

"But that was destroyed in a fire," Kincaid said.

"Nothing is ever completely destroyed," she said. "His spirit will be compelled to seek whatever is left, wherever it may be."

"What happens then?" Kincaid asked.

"If he is strong enough, if he can find some small part of his ashes, his spirit might be able to survive in what's left for a short time. *If* he is strong enough."

"Well, hell," Saintcrow muttered. "No guarantees is right."

⚜ ⚜ ⚜

Saintcrow shook his head as they left the witch's house. "We're putting a lot of faith in a black witch and a little black box."

"She's never failed me yet."

"Yeah? Well, there's a first time for everything."

"We're gonna have to take Rhinehart to some deserted island," Kincaid said. "Some place where there's no one else for hundreds of miles."

"There's a stretch of desert in Chile that's pretty much uninhabitable," Saintcrow suggested. "It should fill the bill."

Kincaid grunted softly. "Are you thinking what I'm thinking?"

"I am if you were wondering how the hell we got mixed up in this mess? I should have killed Rhinehart the first day he wandered into Morgan Creek."

"Why didn't you?"

"For the same reason you didn't."

"Because the women we love wouldn't have approved?"

"Right the first time," Saintcrow said with a wry grin. "Sometimes they're a lot of trouble, aren't they?"

"Yeah. But mostly worth it."

Saintcrow slapped him on the back. "On that, we can agree."

"All we have to do now is decide when we're going to put this little black box to the test."

"The sooner the better," Saintcrow said, all humor gone from his voice.

"Tomorrow night?"

Saintcrow nodded. "Tomorrow night."

⚜ ⚜ ⚜

Rosa was waiting for Kincaid when he got home, her eyes filled with curiosity when he carefully placed a box on the mantel in the living room.

"What's that?"

"A soul catcher."

"A what?"

"It's some kind of spirit trap. We need to get Luca's spirit in there."

"How on earth will you do that?"

"We haven't quite figured that part out yet." Kincaid hadn't yet discussed his idea with anyone, partly because he doubted if it would work, and partly because he had no backup plan if it failed. He wondered if Saintcrow had come up with any alternative ideas.

Rosa wrinkled her nose when Jake took her in his arms. "What's that smell?"

"Dark magic. Izabela was in full black witch mode when we got there."

Rosa shivered. "Do you trust her?"

"I always have."

Taking his hand, she led him to the big chair by the fireplace, pushed him down, and climbed onto his lap. "How did you ever meet a black witch?"

He tapped the gold band on his wrist. He had taken to wearing it again soon after they apprehended Rhinehart.

"I was looking for a witch who could fashion some sort of protection against Luca. New Orleans seemed like the place to go. Back then, the place was crawling with witches and warlocks and vampires. It wasn't safe for mortals to be on the streets after dark.

"I was in a sleazy bar when a woman approached me. She was a tiny thing with lots of golden hair and brown eyes with weird little yellow specks. She said she'd heard I was looking for a black witch. I said I was and told her what I wanted and she told me what the price would be. I hadn't felt her power until then. I've never felt anything like it before or since, although Saintcrow's power is probably just as strong but in a different way. Anyway, I agreed to her terms and she said she would get in touch with me.

"About a week later, a crow showed up on the window sill of the place I was using as a lair. When I opened the window, the bird dropped a note on the floor and flew away. It was the address to her house."

"What was it like, her house? Does she still live in the same place?"

"Yeah. It's a small two-story house crammed with furniture, books, and knickknacks. As you'd expect, she has a cat."

"A black one?" Rosa asked with a grin, then shuddered, remembering the big black cat in Luca's house.

"No, it's gray."

With a sigh, she rested her head on his shoulder. "Jake, I don't like any of this."

Kincaid grunted softly. "I can't say as I do, either." He brushed a kiss across her cheek. "But I'm crazy about you." He slid his hand under her sweater as he ran his tongue along the side of her neck.

Little fires of desire kindled inside her everywhere he touched. "Jake." She moaned softly as his tongue slid across her lips, then delved inside.

The next thing she knew, they were lying on the floor, naked, in front of the hearth. The heat of the flames was nothing compared to the blaze he lit inside of her as he whispered that he loved her, would always love her. His bite was gentle, letting her feel what he was feeling. In a distant part of her mind, she wondered why she had ever been afraid of what he was, and then there was no more time for thought. There was only Jake carrying her away to heights and depths she had never dreamed of.

Chapter Fifty

Rosa paced the floor, her nerves taut. She found herself constantly glancing at the clock, as if she could make time stand still. Jake and Kincaid were taking Rhinehart to some remote desert to try to separate Luca from the hunter. They had left an hour ago to pick him up. She had begged to go with them, but Jake had adamantly refused, and Saintcrow had agreed with him.

She scowled, thinking that if she was a vampire, she could have followed them whether they liked it or not.

She tried to pray, tried to assure herself that no matter how powerful Luca was, surely he was no match for the combined power of two ancient vampires.

Fighting tears, she sank down on the sofa, hands clasped tightly in her lap as she tried to petition Heaven. But all she could do was murmur, "Please," over and over again.

Chapter Fifty-One

Rhinehart stared at them as they approached the cage. There were dark smudges under his eyes, his cheeks were sunken, his hair lank. He looked like the walking dead, Kincaid thought, as Luca's malevolence crawled over his skin.

"Do you think Rhinehart's still in there?" Saintcrow asked.

"Beats the hell out of me."

Saintcrow pulled a pair of handcuffs out of his pocket. "We need to bind him."

"How do you suggest we do that?"

"See if you can mesmerize him. I'll go inside the cage and handcuff him."

"Right."

"It'll be an adventure," Saintcrow said with a jaunty grin.

Kincaid summoned every ounce of preternatural power he possessed as he met Rhinehart's gaze, hoping all the while that the hunter was still in there, that he had some modicum of control left.

For a moment, it was touch and go and then, abruptly, Rhinehart went still.

At the same time, Saintcrow materialized inside the cage and bound the hunter's hands behind his back.

"That was too easy," Kincaid remarked.

Saintcrow shrugged. "Let's go."

They had timed it so that they would arrive in the Chilean desert three hours after sundown. It was a desolate place, not fit for man nor beast. Barren mountains rose in the distance. The sky overhead was a dismal gray, the air hot and thick.

"I did some research on this place," Saintcrow said. "One website remarked that when Hollywood wants to simulate Mars, they come here. I read that this part of the desert gets less than an inch of rainfall a year and that even insects can't survive in parts of it."

"So there's no one else around?"

"Not for miles. Are you ready to put your plan into action?"

"Not really," Kincaid muttered. "Damn, it's hotter than hell here."

"Have you got the box?"

Kincaid pulled it out of his jacket pocket and handed it to the master vampire. When that was done, he took a deep breath. "I hate to do this to you, Rhinehart. I know you've got a family. But you're a danger to your wife and kids and we've decided the best thing to do is put you out of your misery. It'll be a long time before anyone finds your body."

With a low growl, Kincaid grasped the hunter by the shoulders and buried his fangs deep in his throat.

Rhinehart shook violently as he tried to escape Kincaid's hold as he drank and drank.

A high-pitched screech filled the air, followed by Luca's voice screaming, "No!"

Saintcrow swore as a pale, white mist in the vague shape of a man emerged from the hunter. Opening the box, he cried, "Luca Sasan, by the power of earth, wind, and fire, I command you to obey my words and submit your will to mine. Come to me."

The wraith hovered in the air, seemingly being pulled apart as half of it drifted toward the box while the other half endeavored to go in the opposite direction.

Kincaid lifted his head, unable to believe what he was seeing.

Saintcrow repeated his command, And still the wraith refused to obey. Shrinking in on itself, it seemed to gain power as it moved away from Saintcrow.

Kincaid swore under his breath. Dammit! "Saintcrow, let's try saying the spell together!"

Saintcrow nodded. "On three. One, two, three."

Together, they repeated the words, their combined voices ringing in the air like thunder in the quiet of the night. "Luca Sasan, by the power of earth, wind, and fire, we command you to obey our words and submit your will to ours. Come to us."

A horrible, other-worldly shrieking rent the silence as the necromancer continued to struggle against the power of their command. The wraith stretched out, straining to refuse, but, ever so slowly, it was drawn toward the box.

Kincaid held his breath when, with one final, ear-splitting scream of denial, Luca's essence was sucked into the soul catcher.

As soon as it was inside, Saintcrow slammed the lid down. "How's Rhinehart?"

"As near death as you can get without actually dying." Kincaid bit into his wrist, pried the hunter's mouth open and let his blood drip onto Rhinehart's tongue.

At first, nothing happened, but, gradually, Rhinehart swallowed.

"I think that's enough," Saintcrow said.

"He still looks pale. Maybe a little of your blood?"

"Hell, no," Saintcrow said, removing the handcuffs from Rhinehart's wrists. "It's bad enough that the black witch has some." He jerked his chin toward the hunter. "He's awake."

Rhinehart sat up, his expression befuddled, then fearful as he glanced around. "What happened? What am I doing here? Why do I feel so… so strange? Damn, the ground is hot. Am I in hell?"

"I'll admit it looks like hell," Saintcrow agreed. "But it's just a desert."

"What happened?"

"It's a long story," the master vampire said. "Kincaid can tell you all about it someday. But right now, all you need to know is that your vampire hunting days are over."

Chapter Fifty-Two

Kincaid felt as if days had passed since they'd left home. Once they reached Wyoming, they made a phone call and three stops on their way back to Morgan Creek.

Kincaid called Izabela to let her know her spell had been a success.

With a snort, she said," Did you think it would fail? As I told your companion, I'm very good at what I do."

"Can't argue with that."

"An extra deposit of your blood and that of the master vampire would be a most appropriate thank you the next time you visit New Orleans."

With a snort of his own, Kincaid ended the call.

Their first stop was at the *Nevado del Ruiz* volcano in Colombia.

"Izabela hexed the box so that no one will be able to open it once Luca is inside," Kincaid remarked.

With a nod, Saintcrow said, "Let's hope that spell works for a thousand years."

Kincaid dug a hole fifteen feet deep at the base of the volcano. He had been tempted to toss the box into the lava, but feared that once the box disintegrated, Luca's spirit might somehow escape. And while it was unlikely the necromancer would find another host in this Godforsaken place, he wasn't willing to take the risk.

Since Rhinehart had suffered the most damage from the necromancer, Saintcrow decided they should let him drop the soul catcher into the makeshift grave. Kincaid filled it in, and Saintcrow worked a little vampire magic that would effectively repel anyone from going near the place.

The second stop was to return Paul Rhinehart to his wife and kids. They didn't wait around to watch the happy reunion.

The third was at *The Crimson Rose* where they split a bottle of wine.

"Rhinehart's got quite a tale to tell," Kincaid remarked. "Assuming he remembers any of it."

"If he does, I wonder how much he'll tell his wife," Saintcrow mused. "And how much she'll believe."

"That's his problem, not ours."

"If I never see him again, it'll be too soon," Saintcrow remarked. "So, how's it going with Rosa?"

Kincaid smiled at the mere thought of her. "I'll be forever grateful that you introduced us."

Saintcrow grinned as he refilled their glasses. "That's me, vampire matchmaker extraordinaire. But don't tell anybody. I've got a bad boy reputation to uphold."

"Yeah, right, you old softie." Kincaid held up his hands in surrender as the master vampire's power rolled over him.

Saintcrow swirled the wine in his glass. "Been a hell of a night. I think I'll go home and make love to my wife."

"Best idea I've heard all day," Kincaid said, and vanished from the nightclub.

"Newlyweds," Saintcrow muttered with a grin. "No self-control."

But a moment later, he too, was gone.

⚜ ⚜ ⚜

Rosa was lying on the sofa, asleep, her cheeks stained with tears, when Kincaid reached home. For a moment, he stood there, just looking at her, thinking how she had changed his life. He didn't know how he had survived so long without her, but as he carried her to bed, he vowed she would never be sorry for marrying him.

She stirred as he placed her gently on the mattress and eased her out of her clothes.

"Jake?"

"Hi."

"Thank you, Lord," she murmured. "What happened?"

"I'll tell you all about it in the morning." Removing his boots and shedding his clothes, he slid into bed beside her. "Suffice it to say Luca will never bother anyone again and Rhinehart is home in the bosom of his family." He grinned as he lightly nipped her breast. "And I'm in the bosom of mine."

Epilogue

It was Sunday evening and the Ravenwood family had gathered for dinner. Everyone was there. Rosa could hear their laughter as she and Jake climbed the stairs to the front porch.

"I don't know why I'm so nervous," she said, clinging to Jake's hand. "I know they love me."

"Not as much as I do. Come on, let's get this over with."

Pasting a smile on her face, Rosa opened the door. All eyes swung in their direction as she stepped into the living room. "Hi."

Lena hurried forward to wrap Rosa in a bear hug. "I'm so glad to see you, *mia figlia.* And you, too, Jake," she said, as she gave him a quick hug.

When everyone had made the two of them welcome, they looked at her expectantly.

"You said you had news," Micah said.

"Yes," Sofia said. "Tell us."

Rosa reached for Jake's hand. "We were married a few weeks ago."

"Married!" Luciano exclaimed. "Without your family?"

"There were a lot of extenuating circumstances," Rosa said quickly. "But we'd like to do it again next week, with all of you there."

Kincaid took a step back as Rosa's sisters gathered around her, all talking at once.

Micah took that opportunity to take Kincaid aside. "I guess I misjudged you," he said. "I thought…Hell, you know what I thought."

"I'd never turn Rosa without her permission. But when she's ready…"

"When she is, she'll have my blessing."

Kincaid stared at him, thinking Micah's approval was the last thing he had expected.

"I was out of line, but I didn't know anything about you except the rumors I'd heard. And none of them were good."

"Sad to say, they were all true," Kincaid said, glancing over at his wife. "But she changed all that."

Holding out his hand, Micah said, "Welcome to the family."

Rosa glanced over her shoulder, tears welling in her eyes as the two of the three men she loved most shook hands.

Life was good, she thought, and would only get better.

And because she loved Jake desperately and wanted to be with him for more than a few years, Rosa had decided that she would ask Jake to give her the Dark Gift as an anniversary present next year.

Truth be told, she could hardly wait.

~***finis***~

Dear Reader,

I hope you enjoyed Rosa's story. Of course, the real reason I wrote the book is because I'm crazy about Rylan Saintcrow. He is one of my all-time favorite paranormal heroes, and the reason I wrote *Twilight Dreams, Twilight Desires,* and *Twilight Destiny.* I hope you enjoyed reading it as much as I enjoyed writing it. With luck, I'll find a plot for one more book.

Midnight Enchantment

Liliana Falconer is hoping to find some excitement when she goes to stay with her great-grandmother Ava in New Orleans. The only daughter of a powerful Hungarian vampire and a witch, Lily has been sheltered and protected her whole life.

While strolling along Bourbon Street, Lily is drawn into a nightclub by the lyrical strains of a guitar. Something mystical and frightening happens when her gaze locks with that of the man strumming the instrument and she quickly leaves the club.

But avoiding Raedan is not in the cards and Lily soon finds herself falling in love with a man who is not only a vampire, but a vampire possessed by a blood-demon that constantly urges Raedan to take not only Lily's blood, but her life as well.

As their love grows stronger, they realize the only way they can be together is to destroy the blood-demon, a task that sends them to the Carpathian Mountains in search of a dragon.

"A sexy, mysterious hero. A dark and dangerous love affair that survives against all the odds. Amanda Ashley delivers a rousing good read!"

Vicki Crum, award-winning author of Blood Moon

Midnight Enchantment: Chapter One

Ava Liliana Falconer strolled along Bourbon Street, pausing now and then to peer into one window or another. There were so many interesting places to visit in New Orleans, known far and wide as the voodoo capital of the world. There were museums and old cemeteries, antebellum mansions and gardens. Not to mention the stores and shops where you could buy all manner of fascinating things, like voodoo dolls and tarot cards, shrunken heads and monkey paws, spell books, charms, and "gris-gris" bags. And books on magic—both light and dark—as well as volumes on the occult, and all manner of mysterious and mystical arts.

Having a vampire for a father and a witch for mother, Lily was no stranger to the supernatural world, and was, in her own right, a rather powerful witch, though her powers were not half as strong as those of her mother, or her great-grandmother, Ava Magdalena. But she was no slouch, either.

The lyrical strains of a guitar drew her toward a nightclub at the far end of the block. She made her way cautiously along the crowded sidewalk. Only months ago, the Knights of the Dark Wood had been hellbent on exterminating the vampire side of her family. Of course, the Knights weren't adverse to killing witches, as well. And although that had changed, thanks to her great-grandmother's magic, New Orleans could still be a dangerous place for a young, unescorted woman.

Lily paused outside the club, all her senses alert, but she didn't detect anything more dangerous inside than the unmistakably earthy scent of pot, something she had never experimented with, although a girlfriend in high school had once dared her to try it. But magic and marijuana didn't go together.

Taking her courage in hand, Lily stepped through the arched doorway. She found a small table near the raised dais where the guitar player sat, felt the notes of his song surround her. He had hair as black as her own, though not as long. When he looked at her, she saw that his eyes were a deep, deep blue, mesmerizing in their intensity. For a moment, it was as if there was no one else in the room, only the two of them caught up in a brief, mystical moment of time.

Rattled by the strange sensation that had passed between them, Lily looked away and the moment was gone.

When she dared to glance his way again, his smile told her he was just as aware of what had passed between them as was she.

Muttering, "This is just too weird," Lily stood and practically bolted out of the club. Outside, she breathed in the cool night air, practically jumped out of her skin when a deep voice behind her said, "Why did you run away?"

Gathering her composure, Lily turned and came face to face with the guitar player. "Excuse me?"

"Why did you run away?"

"I'm sure I don't know what you mean."

His gaze met and held hers. "I'm sure you do."

With a wave of her hand, Lily said, "Stop it!" And smiled when her power arced between them, driving him back a step.

He stared at her, one brow arched in surprise. And then he chuckled. "Witch woman."

"Vampire man."

His deep, masculine laughter sent a shiver of awareness down her spine.

"Well met, milady," he said, admiration in his voice. "How are you called?"

"That's none of your business," Lily said curtly. "Good night, sir." Turning on her heel, she walked briskly down the street.

If she had hoped to elude the maddening creature, she was sorely mistaken. In an instant, he was beside her, matching her stride for stride, his hands tucked in his pants pockets.

Liliana stopped abruptly. "Why are you following me?"

"Why are you running away again?"

She glared at him. "Because I don't like you. Now leave me alone before I turn you into a newt!"

"A newt?" He threw back his head and laughed.

With an exasperated sigh, Lily began walking again.

And again he fell in beside her. She tried to ignore him, but it was impossible. He was tall and broad-shouldered, with an easy aura of self-confidence that bordered on arrogance.

Not wanting him to follow her home, Lily changed direction and ducked into an occult book store.

Of course, he followed her inside.

Pretending to ignore him, she browsed the shelves, always conscious of the tall, dark stranger behind her. His presence was overwhelming, his scent tantalizing. When she reached the back of the store, she whirled around to face him. "What do you want?"

"Your name."

Lily shook her head. One of the first things she had learned at her great-grandmother's knee was that names had power.

"I will give you mine if you give me yours."

"I don't want it," she said, primly.

His smile was devastating.

Lily's heart began to pound a quick tattoo when he backed her against the wall, his hands flattened on either side of her head, his big body far too close, his breath fanning her cheek. She shivered when she felt his mind brush hers. "Stop that!"

"Why are you afraid of me, Liliana?"

Just as she had feared, he had the power to read her mind. Swallowing hard, she said, "I'm not afraid."

"Yes, you are." He took a deep breath. "I can smell the fear on your skin, hear the rapid beating of your heart." Closing his eyes, he leaned closer. "Smell the blood flowing rich and red in your veins like the finest wine."

Terror rose within her. Frantic, she tried to summon her magic, but fear held her fast in its grip so that all she could do was stare at him, helpless, and more frightened than she had ever been in her life.

"You have nothing to be afraid of," he murmured. "I will not hurt you."

"Why... why should I believe you?"

"Because I said so." He lowered his hands and took a step back. "I am sorry I frightened you. I did not realize you were so young. So innocent." Taking her hand in his, he kissed her palm. "Please accept my apology."

Liliana closed her eyes and took a deep breath, hoping to still the frantic pounding of heart.

When she opened her eyes again, he was gone.

⚜ ⚜ ⚜

Ava looked up and smiled when Lily entered the living room, but her smile quickly faded when she caught the faint scent of vampire. "Where have you been?" she asked, her voice sharper than she intended. "More importantly, who have you been with?"

"I don't know." Sinking down in the easy chair across from the sofa, Lily clasped her hands in her lap.

"What do you mean, you don't know? I can smell him on you. What on earth were you doing with a Transylvanian vampire?"

"I was walking down Bourbon Street when I heard a guitar. Something about the melody drew me inside. The man playing it looked at me and . . . the strangest feeling passed between us. It was weird and a little scary and . . . " She shook her head in wonder. "I've never felt anything like it before. It rattled me and I left. But he followed me."

Ava's eyes widened. "Did he bite you?"

"No! No. Nothing like that. It was like he was looking for someone and thought it might be me. Does that make any sense?"

"Not a bit. What's this guy's name?"

"I don't know."

"Listen to me, young lady," Ava said sternly. "You stay away from the Transylvanian vampires or I'll send you home quicker than you can say abracadabra. Do you understand me?"

Lily nodded.

Ava's gaze moved over her great-granddaughter's face. "Are you sure you're all right?"

"No," Lily murmured. "I'm not sure I'll ever be all right again."

⚜ ⚜ ⚜

Lily tossed and turned all night long. Every time she closed her eyes, the vampire's image rose in her mind. He wasn't handsome in the usual sense of the word, but he was gorgeous nonetheless, his features strong and masculine and compelling. And his eyes—she had never seen eyes like that. Not just that deep, deep shade of blue but the intensity of his gaze. She'd had the feeling that with one glance, he had discovered everything there was to know about her, every hope of her heart, every secret desire.

It had been most disconcerting. Worst of all, she wanted very much to see him again.

About the Author

Amanda Ashley started writing for the fun of it. Her first book, a historical romance written as Madeline Baker, was published in 1985. Since then, she has published numerous historical and paranormal romances and novellas, many of which have appeared on various bestseller lists, including the *New York Times* Bestseller List and *USA Today*.

Amanda makes her home in Southern California, where she and her husband share their house with a Pomeranian named Lady, a cat named Kitty, and a tortoise named Buddy.

For more information on her books, please visit her websites at:

www.amandaashley.net

and

www.madelinebaker.net

Email: darkwritr@aol.com

About the Publisher

This book is published on behalf of the author by the Ethan Ellenberg Literary Agency.

https://ethanellenberg.com

Email: agent@ethanellenberg.com

Facebook: https://www.facebook.com/EthanEllenberg LiteraryAgency/

CPSIA information can be obtained
at www.ICGtesting.com
Printed in the USA
LVHW082304310123
738108LV00014BD/1051

9 781680 683158